1

Jimmy

Jimmy said, 'There was this advert in *The Guardian* . . .' He glanced down at me. 'That's a newspaper.'

I nodded. 'I know what *The Guardian* is, Jimmy.'

He frowned a small frown. 'Yeah . . . well . . . So I rang the number.' He hunched a shoulder. 'And here we all are. How about you?'

'I forget,' I lied. 'Something like that, I guess.'

Jimmy nodded absently. He lifted his eyes clear of the rock and squinted out over the red-muddied waters of the swollen river. 'The bastard's taking his own sweet time about it . . . D'you reckon he knows we're here?'

I said, 'Jimmy, if he knew we were here he'd be headed hotfoot in the other direction!'

His open face cracked in a self-conscious grin. 'Oh, shit! O' course!'

Jimmy would swear like the trooper he used to be. But I was warming to him. His swearing, unconsciously and sometimes impossibly woven into his conversation, had a defensive ring to it. Also, he was a man without serious pretension, and that sat well with me. 'So what were you into before you answered the ad?'

Jimmy shrugged. 'Sod all! Ligging about like a pratt out of water. When are we going to take him?'

I took a look for myself. Thomas Kamerhi was still a good 300 yards short of the river, which put him at least fifty yards long of our effective range. And Jimmy was right; he was not hurrying. Then again he was not exactly taking his time, either. He was being careful. And why shouldn't he be careful? He had everything to be careful about. I lowered myself back behind the rock.

The heat was pitiless. It was hot enough to melt leather. A lack of pity is fundamental in Africa. I said, 'When he reaches that bush like an upside-down steam roller. See it?'

'Yeah,' he said grittily, adding, 'You or me?'

I thought about that. Then I thought about the lost camera, and how it altered the entire perspective of the job. I wondered if Jimmy had added up the numbers. Probably not. Jimmy was not paid to think. I, on the other hand, was paid to do just that. The shot, for several important reasons, should have been

A WARRIOR'S CODE

Treachery and double-cross are the hallmarks of the mercenary soldier. Because who is the real enemy? Is it the man in the cross-hairs, or the friend alongside you? Or is it the man who pays your wages? Martin Palmer knows that a potentially fatal bullet might come from any direction. And yet he must fight, because fighting is all he knows. This deadly challenge will test him to the limits of his endurance. He knows there will always be another paymaster with high aspirations, and enough money to pursue them . . . and money, of course, is the mercenary soldier's creed.

LARRY JOHNS

◆

A WARRIOR'S CODE

Complete and Unabridged

ULVERSCROFT
Leicester

First published in Great Britain in 2011 by
Robert Hale Limited
London

First Large Print Edition
published 2012
by arrangement with
Robert Hale Limited
London

The moral right of the author has been asserted

British Library CIP Data

Johns, Larry.
  A warrior's code.
  1. Mercenary troops- -Fiction.
  2. Suspense fiction.
  3. Large type books.
  I. Title
  823.9′14–dc23

  ISBN 978–1–4448–1283–1

Published by
F. A. Thorpe (Publishing)
Anstey, Leicestershire

Set by Words & Graphics Ltd.
Anstey, Leicestershire
Printed and bound in Great Britain by
T. J. International Ltd., Padstow, Cornwall

This book is printed on acid-free paper

mine. I said, 'Are you good enough?'

Jimmy grunted. 'You're damned friggin' right I'm good enough! You just friggin' watch me!'

Jimmy's vocabulary of swear words was limited; probably a reflection of what was uppermost in his mind. Though 'frigging' would not have been the way he usually couched it. I wondered why he was coding it now. I also made up my mind about the shot. I was on the spot as a backup if it all went wrong. I nodded. 'You, then, and we'll see. One bullet earns you free beers for a week. It takes you two or more, you stand me for a month. Okay?'

Jimmy grinned down at me again; except that this one was open and full of humour. He'd been all grins and swear words since we'd left B-Company compound three days ago. I did not like many people. Myself least of all. But Jimmy was definitely growing on me. He did not seem to have the vicious streak frequently apparent in most mercenaries. That's not to say he did not have one. It could be that I had yet to see it. However, he didn't stand a cat in hell's chance of stopping our man on a permanent basis; not with a single bullet. Not at that range. That kind of accuracy requires a whole lot more than enthusiasm.

Jimmy was not in my platoon, and I had yet to witness him shoot at anything; let alone a living target. And a two-legged one at that. I had selected him for this operation because, as far as I was aware, he had never seen, or even heard of, Thomas Kamerhi. Whereas any one of my own platoon would have recognized the man in a thick fog, at any distance. And Chang, for his own reasons, needed this job to happen without it actually *happening*. Also, Jimmy had not been with the company long enough to have been corrupted beyond his job. At least I hoped both these assumptions were true. But if he was possessed of that degree of shooting skill I would have gotten to hear about it from someone. So I was damned certain he was not going to collect on his beers. In all conscience, I should have quit buggering about and taken the shot myself, taking Kamerhi out cleanly. We were not in the torture business, as Chang was at pains to keep reminding us. But it was too damned hot and I was smitten with lethargy; which vaguely constitutes a reason, certainly not an excuse.

Jimmy said, 'Where d'you want it?' He was studying the approaching man through slitted eyes.

I knew what he meant but felt like being

obtuse. 'Where do I want what?'

'The friggin' bullet!' he grated, frowning down at me. His thick, jet-black eyebrows joining in the middle.

I smiled. 'What is this . . . a side bet?' It was also pleasing that he wasn't calling me sir, or Captain Palmer. Military protocol, even *pseudo*-military protocol, had its place. But this was not the place. I'd asked him to call me Martin, at least for the duration of this affair. But he wasn't actually addressing me as anything. Not that I could remember anyway.

Jimmy shook his head and sweat flew in all directions. 'Nah! I just wanna know where you want the friggin' bullet!'

I couldn't help but chuckle. 'Well, *I* don't want it anywhere . . . but our man needs it just left of his breast pocket. Imagine your bullet is a medal and you're pinning it to his chest. That's where I want it!'

Jimmy looked thoughtful for a moment, as if reconsidering the whole thing. 'Not a head shot?'

'No, Jimmy. No head shot. Slap bang in his heart.' This was the crunch. Would Jimmy figure it out, or would he not. Would he figure out that a misplaced head shot could make identification impossible? As a smokescreen, I added, 'It's the bigger target anyway.' I was treating it as a game, and I shouldn't have been.

Jimmy pulled a slightly confused face. And since he obviously *hadn't* figured it out, he was entitled to his confusion. 'One bullet . . . ' he breathed thoughtfully.

It wasn't a question. I said, 'Well, that's the bet anyway. You want to scrub it?'

Jimmy shook his head and smiled. 'Nope. You're on!' He sat back down, pulled a packet of Marlboro from his pocket and gazed at it wistfully. 'D'you reckon he'd see the smoke?'

I stifled a sigh. 'He'd see . . . '

A bead of sweat ran into the corner of my left eye and it stung like hell. Plus, I was desperate for a crap. We were both out of luck.

'What do they call you, Jimmy?' I asked, filling time again.

He looked at me. 'Eh? Who?'

'Your buddies. What's your nickname?' I don't know how, when or why it had come about, but everyone seemed to have a nickname.

His expression cleared. 'Oh. Well, it was Rancid back in the regiment. Some of the guys here call me Rambo.'

Give me a nickel for every mercenary soldier nicknamed Rambo, and I'd be richer by at least a dollar. I did not ask Jimmy how

6

he had come by either nickname. Instead, I asked, 'How long were you with your regiment?'

He sighed deeply. 'Not long e-friggin'-nuff! Seven friggin' years!'

It was amazing how many expletives he could inject into a two- or three-syllable word. I said, 'Seven years is a long time to make up your mind. Why'd you quit?'

He pulled a rueful face. 'I didn't friggin' quit! I was P-8. Can you believe it? P-friggin'-8!'

P-8? My knowledge of British military terminology was never great, but I had heard somewhere that P-8 was a medical thing. I smiled. 'Clapped up?'

Jimmy shook his head and looked sad. 'Nah, that woulda been a friggin' privilege!' He shook his head again. 'It was me friggin' back. What a sod, eh? A prize friggin' sod!'

Then I had it pinned. Translating *fuck* into *frig* was as far as he could go on my man-to-man suggestion. It was an understandable compromise. I nodded. Then I remembered where we were and why we were here. 'Where is he now?'

Jimmy again removed his forage cap, heaved himself back up to peer out over the rock, head cocked to one side, left eye first. And slowly. He had certainly been trained well enough. 'About thirty yards short of the upside-down steam roller. Christ! He's really taking his time about it! Doesn't he know we've been waiting here for two friggin' hours already!'

I looked up into the searing maw of the sun and wished I hadn't. A movement caught my eye. It was a spider out for a stroll. A damned great hairy thing with a million legs. It paused level with Jimmy's right boot and contemplated the studs as if it were really interested in the technology of military footwear. I gathered up a mouthful of spit. I missed the spider by a mile and it sidled off without a care in its world. What do spiders have to care about? The glob of spit sizzled on the hard-baked dirt.

'Twenty yards,' Jimmy said softly.

I wondered idly what his reaction would have been if I'd told him about the spider. Some people can't stand the things. I wasn't overly keen on them myself.

A wild dog hooted somewhere out on the broiling pan. It sounded lost, but wouldn't be. Desert animals know exactly where they are and what they are doing there. I said, 'Let him come . . . '

Jimmy lowered himself back down to the ground and took up where he had left off. 'Missed the uniform, I suppose.' He shot me a self-conscious grin. 'Vain bastard, am'n't I?' Sad again. 'And the lads, o' course. Friggin' good bunch, they was.'

I recognized his expression as one I'd seen on my own face in mirrors.

' . . . A couple of 'em was right bastards, o' course. Can't odds that, can you? But they was a friggin' good bunch. They 'ad no right . . . ' His voice trailed off and he was silent for a moment, staring blankly at the ground. Then he smiled. 'Wanna hear something funny?'

I felt old. I nodded. It was always nice to hear something funny, and it might just take my mind off the fact that my bowels were on the extreme edge of rebellion.

Jimmy chuckled. 'I thought I was pulling a friggin' good skive. I had this date, see . . . with this chick.'

That in itself was funny. Why, I wondered, had he felt it necessary to confirm the gender? He went on, 'The company was due a bleedin' parade, for some friggin' brass-hat. So I reports sick. Told 'em me bleedin' back was killing me. Friggin' lie, o' course. Anyway, the MO rattles me off for an X-ray, 'n off I trots.' The smile wiped itself clean. ' . . . Guess what . . . ' He shook his head at the injustice of it all.

But we shared a grin. It was a good story.

And it was very probably true. Despite everything Jimmy was, or was not, I didn't think he was the kind to lie about something that was obviously so important to him. Discounting, that was, Medical Officers and double-dated girls.

I said, 'And you never felt it?'

He frowned. 'Felt what?'

'A pain in your back!'

'Oh!' he said, 'Nah. There wasn't none. Not a single friggin' twinge! I only felt it at all when the bleedin' MO pokes his finger where it *shoulda* been hurting!' He shook his head again. 'Must'a done it playing rugby or something.' He glanced down at me, a puzzled look on his face. 'You'd think I'd've felt something before that, though, wouldn't you? Some clue.'

'You'd think.' I agreed. 'But it'll teach you not to skive. Right?'

He nodded glumly. 'Yeah. So the bastards pensioned me off! Twenty-five friggin' quid a week, f'r Christ's sake! Who can live on twenty-five friggin' quid a week. I ask ya! Didn't even keep me in beer!' He sighed hugely. 'Anyway, that's why I'm here. Three-hundred and fifty quid beats the shit out've a lousy twenty-friggin'-five!' He looked suddenly panic-stricken. 'You won't tell no bastard, will ya! About me back, I mean.

10

Curly, nor no one!'

Curly was B-Company's adjutant, and Chang's link to the recruiters. I shook my head. 'Your secret is safe with me, Jimmy.' And it was. Not that it would have mattered one way or the other. I didn't bother to ask him why he hadn't looked for a civilian job. Because I would have had to ask myself that same question. But then, I was on the beach for a matter of days only before my phone rang. My fall from military grace had been well publicized.

An animal of some sort appeared momentarily on the brow of the escarpment above us. Then it was gone. Jimmy also caught the movement. He squinted upwards.

'What was that?'

I said, 'An animal of some sort. Check the gook.'

Jimmy, tiredly, said, 'Oh, shit!' and he raised himself up. He stared out for a moment, then nodded. 'Pass us me friggin' rifle. Bastard's nearly there . . . and not before friggin' time!'

The M-16A4 — the fourth generation of the M16 service rifle — is a good weapon. Not the best, not nowadays, but good. It's not really a sniper's weapon but, fitted with a telescopic sight — and this one was — it's quite good enough. It certainly was when you consider how many ways there are to kill people. Jimmy's gun had 'ANDY' burned into its stock, alongside half a dozen notches. What goes around, comes around.

Andy had been a card, too. In his own way. Kamerhi had tied him to a tree and slit his stomach open with a bayonet. He'd then proceeded to shove handfuls of mud into the gash. I don't like to remember things like that, but, sometimes, the memories just seem to crowd in, one atop the other.

Powerless to do anything about it, I had watched Andy die from a hill overlooking the village. Irvine Patch — self-appointed 'The Admiral' — had commanded that raiding party. Patch, like me, was an American. Not that I have the first clue what that observation means to the price of tuna. Patch hailed from Toledo, Ohio, and several lifetimes ago we had served together under the same flag, in Grenada and other places. Andy came from Tulsa, Oklahoma, and I'm from Minton, Nebraska. So what!

Jimmy was from Portsmouth, England. And Thomas Kamerhi, the guy in imminent danger of being shot anywhere but his heart, came from God alone knew where. And a hundred years from now we're all going to be history, meaningless.

If we weren't meaningless already.

I'm not going to say that Andy wouldn't have hurt a fly; his rifle had six notches on it. But I am going to say that he did not deserve to die like that. No one did, does or ever will do. But such is the coin of mercenary warfare. Which sentiment put me in the wrong business entirely. It's been said that if you can't take a joke, you shouldn't join. Well, I joined. One thing was certain however; if I'd known how to do anything else, I would have been doing it. But I didn't. The world had taught me how to fight, it had not bothered to teach me how *not* to fight! Not that I had ever asked it to.

Jimmy hissed, 'He's going left now. Shall I take him?'

I looked down at my grubby hands. My fingernails were topped with black half-moons of grime. Somehow they, and my legs and my body, seemed detached from my brain. It was as if I was sitting behind the observation window in some huge robot, an automaton. Push a button and a finger moves. It was a very strange feeling.

I lifted my own weapon from the ground and pushed myself up. The sweat ran in rivers down my face. I smelt, and badly. And if I didn't take a crap soon it would be too late anyway. I wouldn't have given a damn.

Kamerhi had started to move downstream,

just short of the upside-down steam roller. He shimmered in the heat haze. *Everything* shimmered in the heat haze! It rose in tangible waves from the suffering earth like steam from a boiling pot. I thumbed off the safety and laid my gun carefully on the rock, which, I noticed for the first time, had a seam of purple ore running diagonally through it. I wondered what it might be.

I calculated the windage and elevation in my mind. But there was no wind, just elevation. For me it would have been a target shoot. And if Kamerhi had not been wearing a flak helmet I could have done the job leaving no more than a neat hole in his forehead. I said, 'If he moves twenty yards closer, you take him.' I added, 'One shot, remember!'

A joke, a seam of ore, an animal or a spider. Normal things, taken at face value. In a place like the DDR — Democratic Republic of Congo — a joke or a bet were as good a motivation for killing a man as any. Seams of ore were better, of course. The animals and spiders were the audience. But we — me and Jimmy — were not doing what we were doing for a joke, or seams of ore; not directly, anyway. We were doing what we were doing because someone of higher rank had told us to do it, and was paying us a bonus

14

for the privilege. End of story. *Almost!* This was Iraq all over again. Or Yugoslavia. Only three things ever changed; language, clothes and weather.

Jimmy squinted along his sights and did not look so sure any more. His face was covered with globules of sweat and I was reminded of a billboard advertisement for melons. He hissed, 'Who is this bastard, anyway?'

I said, 'Just a gook.' This was the need-to-know principle at work. Kamerhi was the target, and that was all Jimmy needed to know. Besides, it was safer, for Jimmy, if he didn't know. I mean *really* didn't know. Unless, of course, I had him pegged all wrong. Not that I knew it all. Nevertheless, what I didn't know I could take a guess at. Kamerhi was here to meet someone. And Chang, for reasons that he had kept to himself, had not wanted that meeting to take place. The guess would be who he was here to meet. But I didn't give a damn about that one way or the other. My hook had been Kamerhi himself. If anyone else were the target I wouldn't have put myself out. Which made it all the stranger that I was disposed to pass the killing shot over to Jimmy. Heat fatigue, I guess. Or pure, bloody-minded sloth.

Jimmy lifted his face from the rifle and

looked at me. 'You call them all 'gooks', don't you.' Pure statement.

I supposed I did. A hang-over from South East Asia, I guessed. But enemies are the same the world over; as is the game we played. Either you're a hero when you kill them, or you're a murderer. I found it very hard to work out the moral distinction. And it was just as well that I didn't think I had to. Generally, in my own experience anyway, the UN took care of the morals issues. And the UN only had morals when it pleased them. Like allowing several hundred Bosnian civilians to be massacred; men, women and children, when I was on the spot with a platoon of thirty well armed men, and could easily have stopped it. And I do mean *easily*. Pull back, they'd said. *It's their fight.*

Jesus! There was no *fight* involved! It was a one-sided feral bloodbath.

Jimmy placed his right cheek back on the M16. 'You been in this line of work a long time?'

A good question. I grunted. 'Since I was three.'

He smiled understandingly. 'Yeah . . . I know what you mean.' He chuckled. 'Gets in your blood, right?'

That, I thought, was either another good question, or a sad but true statement of fact.

When I didn't reply, Jimmy said, 'I don't like killing bastards what don't know it's coming, though . . . not really.'

Was that relevant? I didn't know. I had a feeling that from a victim's point of view it was the better option. Andy had spent some hours knowing he was going to die. So had those poor sods in Bosnia. I shook myself mentally. 'Well, if you don't kill this one, and with one shot, it's costing you beers. You settled and ready?'

'I am that, boss,' Jimmy breathed.

Boss! This was a small improvement.

Jimmy lifted his hand from the trigger and stroked Andy's gun lovingly. To it, he whispered, 'Don't let me down, you little beauty.'

Kamerhi, looking for a shallower spot to cross the river, turned again towards us. His face was nothing more than a dark smudge beneath his helmet, but I knew his features well. The ice-blue eyes and the wide jaw. And that ridiculous hairline moustache. Our paths had crossed several times; usually over gunsights. But here I was merely a spectator. Just looking.

Jimmy took his aim.

Africa, in its current frenzy of slaughter, took its aim.

I looked down at the dirt on the other side

of the rock. There was a horde of ants down there. Red ones. Ants fascinate me. They're always rushing about, carrying stuff. And there are always twin lines of them. One going, one coming. Ants must live very ordered lives. I wondered, though, if they ever paused to pass the time of day with each other. Did they argue? Did they have aspirations? I also wondered how much you would have to pay an ant for it to kill one of its fellows. Or, perhaps closer to the point, how much you would have to pay an ant to turn a blind eye when the killing was going on.

The *Nelson* syndrome.

Heroic.

Except that I saw nothing heroic in General Claude-bloody-Mansfield's version of the Nelson syndrome when we'd returned from that sortie in Bosnia. He'd even smiled! *None of our business, old chap! Just let them get on with it* . . . . The mental images of them *getting on with it* were still eating at me like a cancer. So I hit him. Very hard. Blinding him in his very British left eye.

Fists across the ocean, and all that.

So they'd crucified me.

And you don't get *any* kind of a pension with a Dishonorable Discharge.

CRACK!

The echoes of Jimmy's shot bounced back at us as a diminishing volley. The scrubland on the far side of the river came alive with the yelp and scream of disturbed wildlife. It didn't seem to bother the ants, though. They were either deaf, or in the pay of the UN.

'Shit, shit, shit!' Jimmy spat, back-handing the sweat from his eyes, leaving a dirt-red smear across his face.

I had to concentrate hard to drag my brain back from wherever it had been. His shot had kicked up dirt some yards behind Kamerhi. His line had been fairly good, considering the range. Kamerhi was running; ducking and weaving.

I lifted my gun, ready to take over should Jimmy fail on his second attempt. I said, 'Try again. Catch him on the zig.'

Kamerhi was zigzagging towards a clump of bushes on the river bank, crouched low. The reflection of the sun exploded as one of his feet touched water. Like a firework. And for that instant the river was a beautiful thing. Jimmy sucked in a breath and let it out slowly through pursed lips.

CRACK!

Kamerhi went over in a cloud of dust.

Jimmy straightened and waved the rifle in the air and yelled, 'Friggin' ding dongs! I got the bastard!'

I nodded. Sadly, it didn't seem an important event. I felt none of the satisfaction I had been looking forward to. 'Yeah . . . '

Jimmy said, 'What now?'

His face was the Sioux Falls and this time I was reminded of the 'Happiness is . . . ' series of cartoons. I studied the fallen man. He wasn't even twitching. But that didn't mean too much. Men have lived for some time with a bullet lodged deep in their heart. That was the extreme outside edge of possibility, of course, but it was not *impossible*. I lifted my rifle and put a shot into his hip; his torso was behind a rock. A bluffer can't lie still when he's shot in the hip. Apart from the slight jerk as my bullet hit hip, he still did not move. Silently, I said, *well, that one was for Andy*.

So, part one achieved.

Which was all well and good. But part two was to have been the photograph. The big problem was that Jimmy had lost Chang's camera. I hmm'd a thoughtful hmm.

'Well,' I said tentatively, 'There's the photograph.'

Jimmy looked at me sharply, his eyebrows knitted again. 'I couldn't help that!'

Which was true enough. We were crossing the Tagula River and it was in flood. The pack was ripped from Jimmy's back. I couldn't come over all holier-than-thou because the provisions pack was ripped from my own back in the same way, along with my mobile phone, which had a neat camera facility built into it. The resolution wasn't that hot, but it would have sufficed. Staying alive was prime back at that crossing. As I said, I should really have thought it through. But I hadn't bothered.

However, there *was* an answer.

I wondered whether I ought to do what had to be done in the absence of a camera. Jimmy was keen, to be sure, but I had a feeling that, tainted or not, he was still a human being, down there under the tough-guy facade. Which was probably another reason why I was warming to him.

But then, I reasoned, the camera had been in Jimmy's charge. A pedantic point, I realize, but valid nonetheless. And I was tired right through to my bones; almost too tired to be bothered to take the dump I so desperately needed. I slid my bayonet from its sheath and placed it in Jimmy's free hand. I said, 'Chang needs a photograph. For proof. Remember? Don't come back without it, he said. Chew on that while I take a crap.' We were not in a desperate rush.

Jimmy looked at me, then at the bayonet, its oiled blade glinting in the sunlight, then back at me. I looked at Jimmy, keeping my expression neutral. 'There *has* to be a photograph, Jimmy. The whole damned deal is useless without it . . . ' I reminded him. Proof, it was all about proof. No one took anyone's word on *anything* in our business. I added, 'Or, since we can't give him a photograph . . . ' I let that hang in the suffering air.

Jimmy's face blanched suddenly. 'Oh, Jesus fucking Christ!' he breathed.

'Right.' I agreed. I felt ancient, decrepit, washed out and sick of the whole bloody mess. I was experiencing those kinds of feelings more and more these days. Maybe I ought to take a correspondence course in something or other. Get a new skill.

Jimmy looked terrified. 'But — but . . . ' he spluttered.

I waited to see what he had to say. I really felt for him.

'We just *tell* 'em that we got him. They're bound to believe *you*!'

And pigs, I thought, are aerodynamically blessed. I raised an eyebrow and looked at him.

'I know!' he said briskly, changing tack. 'I'll carry the bastard back. That'll be even better, won't it?!' He was pleading with me.

I did give that some thought. 'You'll carry a dead man back fifty miles. Is that what you're saying? Back over the Tagula rapids? And through that bloody swamp?' I loosened my belt and dragged my trousers down. I couldn't hold it any longer.

Jimmy had his mind on other things. The sight of a ranking officer crapping on the ground would have seemed commonplace to him at that moment. 'I can do it!' he nodded emphatically. 'Jesus Henry, he can't weigh *that* much!'

I crouched there and crapped, and felt instantly better. I did not feel like arguing, but it's amazing how much a dead man can weigh. I nodded down at the river. 'Go ahead, if you reckon you can.' I was wishing that he could, but I knew he couldn't. Even with two of us doing the carrying it would have been a non-starter.

Jimmy offered me the bayonet. He looked decidedly relieved. For our own reasons, we were both relieved. I shook my head. 'Take it with you. You never know.' I smiled up at him and added, 'And mind how you go with your back. Chang doesn't go in for sick parades.'

Jimmy stepped around the rock. I finished my crap then waddled around like R2-D2 looking for handfuls of grass to wipe my arse with. But that was one barren mountain. In the end I didn't bother with sanitation. I doubted I could smell any worse, in any case.

Jimmy did try, I'll give him that. I watched from the rock as he tried to get Kamerhi up onto his shoulder. Five times he tried, and five times he failed. I guessed he was giving away at least twenty pounds. Possibly a whole lot more. I saw the white blob as he glanced up at me over the water. At any other time, under any other circumstances, it might have been hilarious. But it was not hilarious, not even slightly. It did not even rate a smile.

Then Jimmy tried dragging the body. But that was not on either. I looked down at the ants. It may have been my imagination but they seemed to be moving more urgently now; concentrating harder on the task at hand; studiously disregarding the strange happenings around them. Which, I thought, was ironic. That is exactly what I was doing with regard to the bigger picture. Ignoring that thought, I craned forward to get a better look at the ants. Both columns disappeared down, and emerged from, a hole under a big stone. One of them was carrying something at least five times its own size. I was reminded of Jimmy, but did not look back over the river.

I heard Jimmy throwing up.

I looked over my shoulder and saw the spider. It ambled over my way. I said, 'Oh, hi, spider.'

The spider looked me up and down and

24

did not seem impressed, for which judgement I could not fault it. It wandered off again.

I heard Jimmy throwing up again.

I pushed a button inside my head and a hand came up and waved a cheery goodbye to the spider.

2

Curly

Murphy's Café and Bar was neither of those things. It was a brick-built, tin-roofed hut on the slope leading from the compound to the village of Bhami, just over a mile away. The hut had begun life as an air-conditioned off-base ammunition storage unit which hadn't filled the need. The ammo store had been moved into the compound and the hut left empty, until someone — I don't know who — had suggested 'Murphy's'. It was big enough and it had windows and a generator-fed electricity supply. More importantly, for Rest and Relaxation purposes, it was outside the compound. Getting out of the office once in a while has beneficial effects on a person. Good business practice. An effective loss leader.

'Downtown' Bhami was a cluster of mangy buildings and mud-huts that the river should have washed away years ago. The river was the main highway; the road being little more than a dirt track. And for sixty miles in any direction, using the compound as your pivot,

26

there was very little but jungle. A single telephone line constituted the only hard connection to the outside world. It wended its way north from Fariale, was spurred into the compound and the mission, before snaking on up to Mumbgwallo. The latter could rarely be raised because Patch's deep-incursion patrols seemed to use the line for target practice. All very annoying.

On the southern perimeter of the village, snugged in a bend in the river, was a clearing. That was the airfield for any fixed-wing traffic we might have; but it was an airfield only loosely. The runway was a tightly-woven, hard rubber matting laid on the grass. You couldn't actually see it because the grass had won the battle long ago. But it was there. The control tower was a corrugated iron hut that had never seen a paint brush and was, consequently, almost eaten away with rust. There was also a windsock of sorts. A man trying to reach that field from, say, New York, would have a job on his hands. The first 5,000 miles would be easy enough. The last hundred would be nigh-on impossible. He would have to use the river which, approaching from the western hemisphere, would be an against-the-flow trip and would take forever if not longer, or the dirt track which, dependent upon the vagaries of the weather, may or may not be there. Or he would have to use a smallish fixed-wing aircraft, provided he could find a pilot stupid enough to attempt that impossible flight. Or he would have to utilise B-Company's helicopter. He could only use the latter if he had taken Curly's shilling.

Also 'downtown' was a general store and a mission church, and, strangely, a shop where a man would mend your shoes. The rest of the local populace, dirt farmers and Hema tribes-people to a man, were scattered in the hills surrounding the village. The mission church, one of a bare handful of brick-built structures, had been there for a very long time indeed, whilst Murphy's and — I *think* — the store, were only as old as the B-Company compound. I don't know the story of the guy who mended shoes. But we used his services quite a lot.

The man who ran Murphy's was as black as night, and why he called himself Murphy was another mystery. Maybe he didn't. Maybe the name had been someone else's idea. The bar may have been his own, or it may have been some kind of a franchise, subsidized by Chang. I really did not know, and was not desperately interested. It was there to be used when there was nothing scheduled in the compound, and that was it. The man who ran the mission church was an aged German who had a daughter. God alone knew what religion the old German attempted to purvey, or how he — *they* — had ended up out there on the extreme periphery of insignificance. Everyone, with the possible exception of her old man, knew what the daughter was purveying; certainly since the compound had been here. What she did with herself before the sudden influx of some two hundred randy mercenaries didn't bear thinking about.

Murphy said, 'I got whisky. Double malt.' He was squinting at the label as if that was the first time he'd seen it. 'You want it?'

It was all bizarre. Like some movie of a western ghost town. Except that this was in the middle of Africa and the population was mostly Bantu-speaking natives. Murphy, for example, wore threadbare western clothes when he was serving, but reverted to African thobe when he was on his own time. He was always unshaven, but the stubble never seemed to thicken. I think Curly, or, more probably, Chang, had brought him in from some other place when Murphy's had become an entity. The village, such as it was, just happened to be here. Whatever the truth of it all, it had elements of a miniscule, reality-mangled garrison town that, with the possible exception of the church and the few houses around it, would not have existed without the garrison. Certainly it would never have been affected by progress and the changing centuries. There were no communications satellites in the skies over Bhami, or any place near it. It was a dead zone that the outside world seemed happy to ignore.

Chang kept a hefty generator going 24/7. The cables supplying power to the ammo store A/C unit, luckily, had not been removed, and now powered Murphy's refrigerator and a few light bulbs. The actual air-conditioning unit had long since given up the ghost. I doubted that Murphy's Café and Bar was a magnanimous gesture on Chang's part. He was, significantly, an ardent teetotaller, but was astute enough to realize the necessity of keeping his men as cheery as possible, given where we were and why we were there. Morale, in any army, is an important factor. We were not an army, but we were the next best thing. This evening, the only customers, as yet, were Curly and myself. I was drinking beer. Curly, his sharp features accentuated by the harsh shadows thrown by a single bare bulb in the ceiling, was currently empty handed.

Curly said, 'I'll take a shot, Murph. But if you've watered it down I'll cut your balls off!'

Under any other circumstances that would

not have been a joke. If Curly said he would cut your balls off, that's exactly what he would do. But I wondered why he thought a man like Murphy would know anything at all about watering whisky down, let alone *why* someone might do such a thing. There were optics on the wall behind the bar, but Murphy always looked confused when he used them. The till was one of those old fashioned monstrosities that required some button punching and a lever-pull. I had rarely seen Murphy use the damned thing. We all paid for what we drank, but it was probably only a paper exercise. All part of the facade.

It was 6.30 in the evening and, outside, the sky was a canopy of deep pink. The humidity level was, for once, at a fairly comfortable level. It would get worse as the night wore on.

Curly took a swig of the drink and grimaced with pleasure, his cold eyes flashing. He said, 'Wonders will never cease!'

I sighed. 'I think you're wrong.'

Curly frowned minutely, as if wondering what I meant, then his face cleared. 'Oh, here . . . ' He dipped into a pocket of his camouflage fatigue uniform and pulled out a wad of dollar bills. Fifties. He went on, 'Chang was very pleased with your little effort, chum. There's a bonus in here for you.'

Chang was the commanding officer of

B-Company. Chinese, and he liked to run a taut, professional outfit, from the day-to-day administration of a garrison out in the middle of nowhere at all, right down to keeping Murphy's on a business-like basis. To his dubious credit, he certainly managed all that. He rarely ventured outside the compound. I don't know why. He was also the go-between; dealing with Joshua Mtomo — the pretender to the throne of the UPC (Union des Patriotes Congolais), and the rest of The World at large. Mtomo was the man with the money and high aspirations; The World was what he hoped to conquer. In there, too, was a man called Robert Urundi, who liked to think that the country was actually his. Irvine Patch was under contract to Urundi, and had been for some time before I signed with Chang. Chang was under contract to Mtomo. Overall, it was a confusing picture. But that confusion was none of my business, and even less of my concern. I had learned that very hard lesson some time ago.

Status quo.

Africa.

Or wherever.

I said, 'Oh,' and pocketed the wad of notes. Back at the compound I had a tin box full of dollar bills. In terms of cash and collateral, I was a rich man. I did not feel rich. All very strange. I did not think I was the archetypal mercenary — if such an animal actually existed. I once thought I could be one, however, that's for certain.

Curly said, 'How did Jimmy make out?'

In my mind I heard Jimmy throwing up. I said, 'Jimmy took the photograph.'

Curly laughed. 'Yeah! In three-bloody-D! Chang was tickled pink. He says he might have it shrunk and made into an ornament.'

There was no joke intended there, either.

I said nothing. I had known Curly for some two years and had still not really made up my mind about him, one way or the other. Remembering that we were a mercenary unit only loosely attached to the UPC, he seemed just what the job demanded.

He said, 'Chang says Patch is encroaching up north again, digging in someplace, apparently. If that's right, d'you want another crack at him?'

As the company adjutant, that was one of his functions; passing on the day-to-day assignments. I said, 'A job?'

Curly frowned. 'It'll be a mission!'

There was a difference. Missions were required under the terms of employment. *Jobs* were over and above the call of duty, and paid extra. The Kamerhi photograph thing with Jimmy had been a job.

I thought about it. There's no denying that mention of Patch's name did up my pulse rate a bit, as it usually did. But before I could respond the door flew open and a group of company guys clattered in. They looked like the recent intake. 'Cherries', they were called in 'Nam; 'squaddies', if you're British. Untried newcomers who had yet to grow into the new uniforms they wore. A couple of them were already drunk. They pulled their horns in a little when they saw Curly; but not by much. I guessed they were assigned to Jose Santana's platoon; he had the current short straw on training details. And these men would be at a loose end, because Santana was off somewhere on another of Curly's 'jobs'. They sat themselves at one of the two tables and started to sing and generally horse about. Murphy, all smiles that weren't smiles, went over to take their orders. The air of sham was tangible, at least it was for me. A bar in the middle of nowhere that wasn't actually a bar. A barman who wasn't a barman. A garrison town that didn't even know it was one. A local population that was as puzzled as a population could ever be. It was all too ridiculous. On the other hand, it was the only reality we had, and I was part of it.

Curly raised his eyebrows and shook his head. 'Let's grab a bollard outside.' There

34

were a couple of stools out there. One of the men yelled over. 'Hey, Curly, Hanson, here, wants to know if we can borrow the chopper.' Full of false bravado. I cringed inside. They would soon learn the dangers of calling Curly by his nickname. To the company at large he was 'Number Two' or 'Sir', or even Captain Parsons. I think his first name was Hugh, or something like that.

Curly touched my arm and led the way to the door. 'What the hell d'you want the chopper for, Carter?' he said over his shoulder. 'There's no place to go.' Curly let the man down lightly, but would have filed the event away for future brutal exploitation. Curly was very particular about who did and who did not call him by his nickname.

I didn't hear the response because I wasn't listening, but I was mildly impressed that Curly seemed to know the man's name. I had problems in that direction. Faces, I was okay with, but names, aside from the guys in my own platoon and a few others, never seemed to stick. I stepped outside into the stale air. The darkening sky was beautiful, but the beauty ended there. Down here it was seedy and unfinished. The pervading smell was of rotting vegetation and rancid mud.

Curly stepped out behind me and we sat on the stools. 'What about it?' he asked. 'You interested?' He unslung his M16, reached around and propped it against the wall. If he'd seen anyone else do that he would have dropped on them like a ton of bricks. It was standard practice — mandatory, in fact — to keep your weapon actually shoulder-slung at all times, especially outside the compound.

'Sure, if it's a mission.' There was actually a clue in there. He was asking me if I wanted to accept a mission, when missions were there to be carried out whether you wanted them or not. They seemed to be walking lightly around me. As if they didn't want to push me too hard. I should have been giving that observation the weight it deserved. I said, 'What've you done with Baker-Section, Curly? B-spider's empty.' Baker was my section, and B-spider was where they lived.

Curly lifted his hands. 'Don't fret, they're safe.'

I nodded. 'Safe where, Curly?'

Curly looked vaguely uncomfortable. 'I didn't know how long you were going to be out, Marty. And they were sitting around . . . '

I didn't doubt that. Baker-Section was notorious for sitting around when there was nothing specific going down. I said, 'Relax, Curly. I'm just asking where they are.'

'Fariale,' Curly said, an unmistakeably

apologetic edge to his voice. 'An ammo pickup.' With a shrug, he added, 'A walk in the park.'

I wondered why he might think I'd be angry about that. I said, 'Fine. But that's a five-day round-trip.' Fariale was the entry point for ordnance shipped in from various arms dealers around the world. Mtomo himself took care of that aspect.

Curly smiled an uncomfortable smile. 'Yeah. Gives you some time off, though, right?' He dashed on, 'So I'll set it up. Maybe a week, if it all comes together. Oh, and Mtomo's coming up the line tonight. Chang says he wants a parade. First thing. Oh six hundred.'

A parade! Jesus! They were still trying to make out that B-Company was some kind of a real military regiment, when, in truth, we were just a few hundred guys on the make! A mercenary unit. We had UPC uniforms, to be sure, with impressive badges — fancy dress, almost. Probably designed by Mtomo. But most of us preferred to wear standard jungle camouflage fatigues. We also had some fairly efficient weaponry: the helicopter, a dozen or so trucks of various tonnage, jeeps and a couple of half-tracks. Plus some useful electronic stuff. Hard currency can buy almost anything. An exception, in our case, was flak jackets and bullet-proof vests. For some reason these items were not currently available on the world arms market. Boots, also, seemed in short supply. Other than these shortfalls we were fairly well equipped. Even so, we constituted a very dubious regiment!

A-Company was over to the west at Bunia, but they were Hema irregulars supported and outfitted by Rwanda. And C-Company, fostered by Uganda, was stationed way up north in the Great Lakes region, protecting Mumbgwallo airport. C-Company also used mercenaries. But these men were *so-called* Askaris, home-grown black African mercenaries. '*Foreign Volunteers*', the press called them. B-Company, us, was on the books as a paramilitary unit. For paramilitary read mercenary. We also had Askaris on strength. But not many and not often. What no one knew, was whose pen actually wrote in the books! Speak to a Joshua Mtomo supporter and they'd tell you that Robert Urundi was the rebel. Speak to a Robert Urundi supporter and you'd hear the opposite. Speak to a local who was simply trying to live day to day, and he or she wouldn't know what the hell you were talking about. Simple existence was their *only* concern. The African Story.

I said, 'Well, if it makes him happy, give him one.' At the very least, I thought, I would not have to listen to Baker-Section gripe about having to make themselves look presentable for something like that.

Curly stared into his drink. 'Not quite your style, is it, eh?'

I said, 'I don't have a style.' To myself, I added, *not any more*!

Curly went on, 'Tell me about it!' He grimaced. 'But it ain't like Afghanistan, is it?'

I grunted. 'I wasn't in Afghanistan.'

'Oh, yeah,' said Curly in a new tone of voice. 'It was Iraq, right?'

I didn't answer. Curly knew all he needed to know about me, and what he didn't know, he could whistle for. Chang, on the other hand, knew just about all there was to know about me and my history. It was his business to know those things. And it was his business how much of that information he passed around, even to his 2i/c.

The noise from inside the bar swelled suddenly, and there was the sound of breaking glass.

Curly clucked his tongue and raised his eyes to the heavens. 'Bunch of no-hopers!'

I said, 'Your guys hired them, Curly.'

He pulled a face. 'Yeah. But you gotta take what you can get these days.' He drained his glass. 'There aren't many old 'dogs' like yourself to choose from.' He looked at me and shook his head. 'I never figured out why you took my shilling . . . '

Curly used that term a lot, as if he was proud of it. It was a while before I'd had it pegged. He went on, 'You could have hired on with Patch's mob. You could've been up there with them, not going on missions *against* them.'

He wasn't telling me, he was reminding me. All that was stale news. I sipped my beer and said nothing. I had accepted Curly's commission because it was the lesser of several evils, and for no other reason. Even before my discharge from the marines, five years before, it had been common knowledge that this part of the world in general, and the Congo in particular, was the re-emerging Mecca for mercenaries, just as it had been back in the sixties. Hell, the recruiters were hovering at the gates of every military garrison in every corner of the world, and regular army guys were defecting to the money all the time. Patch did just that. So, when circumstance had pushed me onto the market, my antennae had been up and active. When the calls came in, as I guessed they would, I was ready for them. All except one.

Curly went on, 'Now, they've got a *real* organization going for them! Good loot. The best equipment.' He pulled an impressed face at me. 'We've seen some of it, right? And real fucking officers! Not like our chinky friend.'

I said, 'None of it is real, Curly.' I wondered why he was denigrating Chang. He had never hinted at that line of thinking before; certainly not in my hearing. I wondered why he was doing it now. Besides, Chang, a professional soldier to his bootstraps, seemed to be the ideal candidate. I was aware of the warning bells tinkling in the back of my mind. I had heard them before, and ignored them. What everyone else did was their business. But, for sure, someone out there was doing *something*. Kamerhi was supposed to have been meeting someone on our side of the fence. Could that person have been Curly? I discounted that thought the instant it arrived. Had that been the case Curly would surely have gotten some kind of a warning to him.

All the same . . .

There are always problems in units of any size. Barrack room lawyers, and the like. Undercurrents, rumour, gripes. Even plain, common or garden gossip. In regular service I had learned, if not to ignore it, then to accept it with the proverbial grain of salt. In a mercenary unit, however, the ramifications of these things can be far more dangerous. Money talks an entirely different language, provoking wildly diverse bedfellows. I decided to listen to the bells in future. But not today. I needed the mental break.

Curly just looked at me blankly. Then, a shade weakly, he said, 'Maybe not . . . maybe not . . . ' He drained his glass. 'Another?' He indicated my empty glass.

I handed it to him. 'Go on, then.' He disappeared back into the bar and the ruckus dimmed momentarily. I wiped my mind clean of the bells and just sat there, thinking nothing. That was the paramount way to while away secluded moments. Think nothing, calculate nothing, decide nothing. I doubted it was working, of course. But it seemed worth trying. Curly was back inside a minute. He handed me the glass and eased himself onto the stool, carrying on as if the last part of the dialogue had not ended on a negative note.

'Why in the hell did you tie in with us? Really! Why did you choose Chang over The Admiral? I'd like to know.'

I didn't doubt it. I thought, *the bells, the bells*!

It would be a valid point from Curly's perspective, however, if definitely not from mine. Patch had been the first on the scene. He'd resigned his commission in favour of Urundi and his money about a year before my brush with Mansfield, and we had kept some kind of an intermittent dialogue going. The occasional e-mail and such. Plus a couple of meetings when we both happened to be in the same country at the same time. I heard all about his new life and the fortunes he was managing to salt away. On the face of it, it had seemed promising, if not tempting. And I was hard-pressed to fend off his requests for me to join him. But it wasn't for me. I was still trying to impress my father, a career marine all his working life.

But during our last pub crawl — in Berlin, I think it was — Patch seemed to have changed beyond all recognition. As if a switch had been thrown. While we were never close enough to have been called brothers, we could at least share mutual time off with a good degree of fun. Suddenly, it seemed, he was a different person. Edgy, moody and too quick to anger. His eyes, like those of a confirmed drug addict, were never still. It was as if he were constantly on the lookout for danger signs. And with a few drinks inside him he became almost manic; viciously so, picking fights with random guys who dared glance in his direction.

He had promoted himself to admiral, he told me. He had once been a SEAL so the nautical flavour of that rank was not so far

43

out there. What *was* out there, well beyond my comprehension, was that he *chose* any kind of rank at all. There were unmistakable signs of *General* Idi Amin about him. Something had turned him.

His stories, too, were the stuff nightmares are made of. Where we used to swap filthy jokes, now I was listening to stories of unrestricted rape, cruelty for its own sake, and open-season murder. It's well known that power is a corrupting influence. Here in Africa, commanding Urundi's forces, he appeared to have all the power in the world. And he was revelling in it, waving it in front of my face like some kind of a recruiting flag. The power to arbitrarily determine life or death, he bragged, was staggering. Like a drug. And the residue of that drug was there to be seen in his eyes, his movement, his voice. In everything he did. It struck me in Berlin that he was experiencing a kind of withdrawal symptom by not being where his power lay; having to live by rules which were not of his own making. He was the classic fish out of water.

What really sickened me was that he actually seemed to think that that power would impress me. Worse, that it would *interest* me. He was arbitrarily tarring me with his own brush, and that grated more than anything. To say that he was no longer a comfortable man to spend time with would be an understatement. I simply did not know who I was talking to any more. And I was glad to get away.

Then came Bosnia, and my brush with Mansfield.

My father died shortly after my DD, a bitterly disappointed man. I had tried to tell him the way it was, but he was not listening.

And Patch contacted me again. He had heard the news, so why didn't I join him? He would engineer me a commission as his 2i/c. The good times would roll again! Stupidly, I lied through my teeth, and I don't know why. Old time's sake, maybe. He was just too late, I told him. *Dammit*! I had already signed up with another agency. I really should have told him the truth; that nothing could induce me to work alongside the man he had become. It was not hatred, it was revulsion. Just as my father was probably revolted at what he thought *I* had become. My rationalization was that, short of half-blinding a high-ranking British officer in what I considered to be a damned good cause, I had not actually chosen the way my life had turned out. Patch had done just that, and then some! It's a pathetically weak argument, I realize that, but I have no other. But that lie, and incidents that followed, set the seal on the way things eventually turned out.

I did some work for Brierson Global Arms (BGA inc.), in Chile, plus some police work for the Chilean government. That was okay. As were a few stints here in Africa for various mercenary outfits, mostly down south in Zimbabwe; another country that didn't know its arse from its elbow. Then there was some advisory stuff for an off-beat film company in Australia. That bored me witless. When Curly's recruiters eventually appeared at my door I was more than ready to accept another front-line commission. Despite that, or, more probably *because*, Patch was the opposition.

Patch, naturally enough, got to hear about it, and I had one last e-mail from him. *This is going to be a blast*, he said. *Between us we could end up owning the* whole *bloody country!* He had misread me utterly. But the fault was mine. I should have shamed the devil and owned up to the truth.

And so it had begun.

For two years we had played the game out, with Patch thinking that only some unwritten mercenary code — a paganlike oath — was keeping me on the opposite side of the fence.

The most telling incident happened last year.

It was the only time — since Berlin — that

Patch and I had found ourselves within hailing distance of each other. And, unknowingly at first, we had actually exchanged bullets. It was a relatively insignificant skirmish up in Goomi territory.

The important fact was that I found myself out of ammunition at just the wrong moment. I am not so sure that Patch was in the same bulletless boat. But I hope so. We stood there, some fifty yards apart, with the fire fight happening around us. I do not know what was going through Patch's mind, and I'm not even certain what was going on in mine. But I do know that if I'd had a bullet up the spout, I would have used it on him. As far as Patch would have been aware, however, I was still able to fire my weapon. Stupidly, I aimed at his chest and mouthed, '*Bang!*' He obviously took the fact that I didn't actually fire, to have another meaning entirely. We stood there for a few pulsating seconds. Then he shot me a beaming smile and lifted a salute.

Likewise, old buddy. Let's do lunch sometime!

And then it was over. He turned on his heel and was gone.

But my original instincts had been good, I was rock-bottom certain of that now.

For proof, there was Andy. And Clive

Beecher. And Jeff Mack. Baldy. Stiff-lip-Sanderson. Those six gook girls up in the mountains. And, maybe most of all, that mangy old mutt down in Petersville.

Who but Patch could hang a dog with fuse wire?

I realized that Curly was saying something, but had not heard a word of it.

'Eh?'

Curly leant closer to me and lowered his voice. 'I said, they're going to win in the end, y'know.'

I dragged my mind back and inwardly sighed. So he *was* part of it . . . whatever *it* was! Then again, that line of reasoning required a giant leap of faith. If Curly had practical communication with Patch, then why the hell hadn't he warned him that I was taking out his 2i/c? It was a puzzle. As a temporizer, I said, 'It's never over.'

Curly smiled and sat back. 'Until the fat lady etcetera etcetera.' He waved his glass in the air and whisky slopped everywhere. 'But a clever man calculates his options, old buddy . . . '

In drink, Curly would frequently lapse mid-Atlantic. He was British, of course, like Jimmy. From the north of that country, apparently. Britain, I think, has more incongruent accents than America, and that's saying something. Then he surprised me even more by saying, 'I wish to Christ *I* had the chance to change sides.'

I couldn't even begin to fathom where this was headed. I looked at him and was confused. So I stopped looking at him and raised my eyes to the sky, which was darkening by the second. The pink had been replaced by deep crimson whilst, to the east, over the walls of the compound, it was a blue-black nothingness. The humidity level was rising by the moment.

Curly glanced back at the door to check we were not being overheard, and went on, 'But *you* could . . . I happen to know that Patch would still pay a lot for you, chum. He made Chang an offer. Chang turned him down. Told me not to tell you about it.' He chuckled, but the chuckle failed to reach his eyes. He added a conspiratorial 'but I told you, eh?'

Don't delve, I told myself. Take it all at face value and figure it out later. It was certainly not unheard of for one mercenary leader to have contact with his opposite number, and on any level you might care to guess at. Business, as the old saying goes, is business. Up until the moment that actual bullets are exchanged, anything at all is, and always has been possible; deals, double deals, negotiation, even friendship. And strong friendships at that. Just like the friendship Patch thought *we* had going for us! But it all stops when your paymaster yells, '*Fire!*' At that moment you use everything you ever learned about your 'friend' to destroy him. At least, that's the implicit rule. It doesn't always work that way, of course. Sometimes you run out of bullets! I smiled. 'You told me.'

I'm not sure what reaction Curly was expecting from me, but, whatever it may have been, I obviously disappointed him, as I was disappointing myself. He allowed a slight frown to crease his forehead. 'A real fucking army, they've got up there,' he hissed, 'Jesus . . . I can almost taste it!'

He obviously wanted *me* to taste it, and I was having none of it. His frown deepened for a moment. Then he seemed to give up on whatever idea he had been harbouring. He sat back and raised his glass at nothing in particular.

'Here's to Africa, right?'

'A great country,' I said. 'And it'll be a wonderful place when they hammer the last nail in.' Jokes are always good therapy.

Curly said, 'Amen to that!' He didn't see it as a joke at all. We lapsed into an uncomfortable calm, embellished only by the drunken noises from inside the bar.

Up at the compound, the floodlights came to life, creating a magical halo above it. There was the sound of a group of men leaving the gates. They were invisible in the deep shadow below the glow of the floods, but they would be headed here. Time to go.

Curly placed his glass on the ground, grabbed his M16, stood up and stretched. 'So, Jimmy did okay,' he said. His tone indicated that he had given up on his previous train of thought. Which suited me fine.

I nodded. 'Jimmy did great.' I did not tell Curly that Jimmy owed me beers.

Curly said, 'Thank Christ for that. I think I'll bump him up a notch. Echo could use a two-striper. D'you think he'd appreciate a bit of power?'

Echo-Section was Jamie Carlisle's baili-wick. I said, 'Don't ask me, ask Jimmy.' I was becoming a master of the obtuse.

Another of those looks seeped across Curly's taut features. I held up a pacifying hand and nodded. 'Sure, Jimmy'll get a kick out of that.'

3

Nessie

Mtomo did not get his parade.

A couple of hours after Curly and I got back from Murphy's, Chang received a frantic call from Red-Four — Nessie's Able-Section patrol — up in Shagland.

Shagland. It was actually a map reference, but some wag had added names to some of the references on the map; areas of special significance. The names had stuck. Shagland was a section of jungle right up in the Ntebbe hills, some fifty miles north of the compound as the crow flies. There were a few isolated settlements up there, and Patch had been trying to subvert them for a long time. Others had tried similar. First up there, in my time anyway, was a logging company. I don't have a clue what their business plan could have been, but they had actually tried to drive a road through to the place. Essentially, though, subversion had not been on the logging company's agenda, they simply needed the settlements and surrounding countryside to be devoid of inhabitation. In other words, they needed that area all to themselves, and sod the locals. Some four months ago they'd slunk off with their tail between their legs.

The populace up there, for some godforsaken reason, supported Mtomo. This was just as well, because Shagland came under his jurisdiction. They had no time for Robert Urundi, Mtomo's opposite number. I think Patch lusted after that area because he knew something about the logging company's thwarted agenda that we didn't. It was a game of African Monopoly. And I was in jail waiting to throw a double.

Nessie — shortened from the Loch Ness Monster, a nickname without familiarity or even a vague hint of humour — was a Scot, real name Andrew Bridges. He was a pug-ugly brute of a man. Well over six foot tall and big like a mountain. The thing about Nessie was that he spoke several languages, if with a heavy Scots accent. He'd been married to a French girl, living with her and her family for some years. He claimed to actually think in French. And he probably did, because, under pressure, he would revert to that language mechanically. This could have been a problem, because it was usually the pressure moments when orders had to be issued and acted upon very quickly indeed, so if you were in Nessie's platoon, and you didn't speak French, you were pretty much screwed. A compromise was reached. B-Company could boast a few actual Frenchmen, plus a handful of others who spoke the language well enough to be assigned to Nessie's platoon. It was a peculiar situation nonetheless. Right now he was in trouble with one of Patch's deep-incursion patrols and needed bailing out. But that was all we knew.

An ad hoc section was hastily thrown together, seventeen strong, with myself in command. This, simply, because I happened to be in the wrong place at the wrong time when the call came in. Plus, of course, I was a platoon commander temporarily short of a platoon to command. In many ways I was glad. Certainly it was a legitimate reason to ignore the bells and concentrate on what I seemed to do best. The seventeen men were a mixed bunch and I only knew half of them by name. Ron Pearce, my own section 2i/c was amongst them. He had been in the sick bay with dysentery when Curly had commandeered Baker-Section for the ammo run. And I only found that out by accident. Pearce, another ex-marine and a very competent soldier, insisted that he was well enough to come along, and had more or less begged me.

So I had allowed it. I could not, however, have a questionably fit man as second in command for this deal. So I gave him a walkie-talkie and told him to make himself useful where he could. He was happy with that. And I was happy to have him along.

Normally, with a section out in the field, there would be a designated platoon on standby for just such a contingency. This night, for some reason, there wasn't. But there was no time for an inquest. Benson, the South African pilot, was roused from his sleep. We all grabbed weapons and some grenade belts and piled into the helicopter. At just past midnight we were airborne.

Thirty minutes later we were in position by dead-reckoning. The GPS box was useless out here. I stared out the window at the black void beneath but could see no signs of a fire fight. I hit the transmit button of the shortwave radio. 'Red Four! . . . Red Four! . . . Give me a code-two flare. I repeat: Code two!'

Code-two, for this week, denoted a blue flare. Other colours had different numbers. This was to avoid being drawn into an ambush by someone listening in to the transmission. It was standard incursion practice. Not foolproof, but workable. The radio crackled. 'Code-two flare going up . . .'

55

I could hear a crackle of small arms fire as a backdrop to the voice, which carried a very definite edge of something bordering on panic. I did not know whose voice it was, but I knew whose voice it wasn't! Then, a few seconds before the flare burst to life, I saw the flashes on the ground, some way off to our right. Then the flare blossomed. I yelled forward to the pilot. 'See it?'

'Got it!' was the reply, and the deck heeled beneath our feet. I cast a quick eye over the men. They sat there in the feeble glow of the red night-vision bulbs, their eyes glinting like cats' eyes on a freeway. 'Lock and load!' The sound of bolts and safety catches being worked was like a hatful of ball bearings dropped on a tin roof. I smiled to myself and felt a sudden lift in my spirits. This was where it was all at. This was my reality and I was comfortable in it.

I went back to the walkie-talkie. 'Where d'you need us, Red Four?'

The voice came back. 'Right there! Right where you are!' A pause. Then, 'The flare . . . see it? Right on top of it!' I suddenly recognized the voice. It was Raoul Pett, Nessie's comms number. Pett was a French-Moroccan who played poker with naked photos of his girlfriend when he was short of cash. I used to wonder if she knew what he did with them. I guess it was a toss up either way.

The blue flare had floated back to earth but was still smouldering.

Benson's voice came over the intercom. 'I have it . . . going in!'

I slid back the cabin door and the noise of close gunfire burst in with the downdraft of the rotors. The adrenalin began pumping through my veins, as it always would at the prospect of immediate action. Benson put us right down on top of the dying flare and we fell out into the night. As the last of us hit the ground the aircraft, dragging a ribbon of tracer rounds with it, was already clawing its way back into the sky and out of harm's way. Benson would go back to the compound and await our call. In the strobe-like lighting of the gunfire I made out the unmistakable silhouette of The Loch Ness Monster.

'Over there!' he yelled above the cacophony, his arm waving into the night. 'In the wad-die . . . ' Nessie had been something in the desert. Chad, I think. Hence his use of the term 'waddie'. It was a dip in the ground. 'About twenty of the pigs.'

In French, he went on, 'Can you work your way around back of them?'

I was not about to be drawn into a conversation in a foreign language. I could have done it, my French was pretty good. But I didn't feel up to it then. In English, I called, 'Why can't *you?*'

It was meant as a joke. Sort of.

Nessie grunted. 'Because I've got three wounded and two dead already! Don't ask stupid questions!' Then he called me a pig in French. He could make life damned difficult at times.

A mortar shell tore a great chunk out of the sky. It exploded only feet from where the helicopter had put down moments before. Someone screamed out in the darkness. It was bedlam. There seemed to be flashes coming from all around us now.

Nessie rammed his face right up to my ear. 'They got Askaris with them. Can't shoot worth a damn, but they're making a lot of noise. Can you do it?'

I didn't know. If Patch's patrol had Askaris, nothing was going to be easy. I was conscious that my section was grouped around us, kneeling there, waiting for some kind of leadership. I yelled, 'What's the terrain like?'

A string of bullets zapped through the air over our heads, sounding like a horde of angry hornets. Nessie didn't even duck his head. You can be sure that I did! He explained that we were in a large clearing, bordered on one side by a river — which was invisible to me — and on the other by jungle. His 'waddie' was just short of the treeline. Still with his lips hard against my ear, he went on to tell me that there was a track some seventy or so yards back into the trees, and that it was the track where he needed to be. Mainly, I gathered, because that was where his transport was.

He had been on his way to mine a bridge, and he felt the inclination to continue with that operation. The opposition, according to Nessie, was not aware of the track. Ergo, they did not know about the trucks.

I shoved my mouth to his ear. 'Why'd you leave the trucks in the first place?'

He shouted. 'Did you come here to ask bloody fool questions, or to give someone a hand!' That was in English.

It was a crazy, disjointed kind of war, with crazy, disjointed people fighting it. I called, 'I suppose you've already tried to get in back of them.'

Another mortar shell exploded close by, and by the light of the flash I saw that Nessie was grinning. He yelled, 'Bien sûr!'

I guessed there were snipers out on the hidden flanks. I called. 'Well, fuck you!' I didn't often swear.

He laughed. 'Santana would do it for me!'

And he probably would have. I said, 'But

you didn't get Santana . . . you got me! If we take them at all, we take them head on!'

Nessie said shit in French. But he knew me as well as I knew him. He called, 'Bon! I'll take the left flank, you go down on the right. How many men have you got here?'

I said, 'Enough to cover your deficiency, plus seven . . . Khan!' The latter to Ahmed Khan, the two-striper I'd designated 2i/c. One of the dark shapes grouped around us detached itself and came trotting over. 'Yes, sir!'

Khan had been with the company when I arrived. But I had known him before, in Chile and other places. Indian mercenaries were not thick on the ground. The depths of my knowledge of Khan's private life, despite having worked with him before, was that he came from Poona. I didn't even know how old he was. What mattered to me was that he was solid, and not given to panic under fire. As he stood in front of me, waiting for his instructions, I spared a moment to figure whether or not we were doing the right thing, and in the right way.

But there seemed no other way to do what had to be done. As things stood — apart from the snipers — we knew where the enemy was: mostly static, and in a dip in the ground. In the dark, knowledge is a plus. And it was as dark for them as it was for us.

Nessie growled, 'Vite, man, vite!'

I wondered why he was in such a rush.

To Khan, I said, 'Fan out, to the near right. You've got a craterfull of enemy directly ahead, so go in fast and low. Friendlies on the left flank, snipers in the trees over on the right flank some-place, so watch it! We go on my whistle. Okay?'

Khan nodded and started to chivvy the men into some kind of order. Suddenly, for no apparent reason, all the shooting stopped. There was complete silence for several seconds, like someone had pushed a button. We stood there like idiots wondering what the hell was going on. The darkness, without the weird illumination of the gun flashes, was complete and utter. Then it started up again. But most of it was wasted effort, the hornets zipping through the air over our heads. I could see no flashes coming from the far right so, if snipers were there, they would be biding their time. This had a bad side and an even worse side; it meant that someone out there was really using his head.

Nessie called, 'I want their CO alive. Tell your men!'

I sighed inwardly. Hidden agendas will be the death of us all. There was a whole lot of more important stuff to think about before considerations of that sort. I said, 'What the hell d'you need *him* for?' I expected to be told not to ask any more stupid questions.

Instead, Nessie said, 'I want to slit the pig's throat. He's held me up here for two fucking hours!' Only the 'fucking' was in English.

I couldn't think of a suitable reply. So I ignored it. 'We'll need a para-flare. Have you got any?'

Nessie said something in a guttural tone that I didn't catch, and probably wasn't meant to. Then he said, 'You'll get your fucking flare. Now, can we get on with it!'

He was obviously in one of his dangerously fearless moods. I refused to be rushed. 'It goes up ten seconds after the whistle. Okay?'

Again, I didn't catch whatever it was he said. But it seemed an affirmative and there was only so long we could stand there arguing the toss. Either we did it, or we didn't. And the latter was not an option, certainly not in Nessie's book. So I blew the whistle. And in that instant my racing pulse slowed to a tick-over. This was me. This was what I was all about. Reasons didn't matter. The rights and the wrongs of it didn't matter. The stupidity of it all didn't matter. Not even the danger mattered. I was exactly where I needed to be. I was a stateless, worthless mercenary soldier doing what mercenary soldiers do.

This kind of Armageddon was my comfort zone. Everything else was just marking time. Sad, but true.

My first action under hostile fire, however, had been swamped with very different feelings. My whole body had trembled with blind fear and I could easily have voided myself. How I actually had not done that, I do not know. But I remember thinking that I should have stayed home with Mother, if only she had still been alive at that time. I certainly had not wanted to be there, in that place, waiting for either the stray bullet, or the one actually aimed directly at me. It was a horrific feeling. But thankfully it had passed quickly. Like stage fright. I was never to experience those feelings again.

We charged into the strobe-lit night.

Khan was at my right shoulder when he caught a bullet square in his chest, but he eventually reached the waddie and sprayed hell out of the men who were using it as a firing pit. Palmer, a spotty-faced Australian, also caught a chest full and didn't make it two yards. Manfred Haug went down yelling, 'Zeig Heil!' and he didn't get up again. Ron Pearce was another casualty. I don't know when he bought the farm. But buy it, he did. There's a lesson in there if you're clever enough to see it.

The first few seconds of a head-on assault are always the most expensive. You grit your teeth, duck and weave and hope. You don't think. If you thought about the possibilities and the what-ifs, you wouldn't move.

'Salty' Stephens also made it to the waddie, but without so much as a scratch. He and a mortally wounded Khan stood there like rocks, their automatic weapons spitting death and destruction. I don't remember too much about what I did or how I did it but, I too, reached the waddie. I expended at least four full magazines during that brief onslaught. The flare was still in the sky and it was as bright as day.

Someone else — I was told later — whose name I did not know, apparently refused to move. He was the last of our relief section. Nessie, closest to the man, shot him in the head. I did not get a chance to ask Nessie why he had waited back there in the first place. But that, too, like his summary justice, would have been Nessie's style.

Someone over on the far left flank was using grenades, the flashes vivid yellow-red and evil-looking. I hate grenades. They're so damned impersonal. And their effect is unfathomable. Guys have been inches from an exploding grenade and come away without a scratch. Other guys have been many yards away, and had their heads blown off. With grenades you just never know.

Orestes Savas, nickname 'Ori', a Mexican out of Curly's Dove-Section, and a relative newcomer, plus a guy I only knew as 'Chalkie' — last name White, I guess — were yelling like banshees as they went in. They both got through unscathed.

Donald Yelland, another American, got half his face blown away. Strangely, in the chopper, he'd asked me to post a letter for him if he bought it. For reasons now lost in time, I misplaced that letter. Not that I would have posted it in any case. I would have done that for Khan, however. Yelland fought on for a while. God alone knows how he managed to do that. But he did. Then, almost at the last gasp, he simply keeled over and was dead.

Alec 'Maud' Peroni, the only homosexual in the outfit that I was aware of, caught a grenade splinter in his shoulder, but that was all. He was a reasonably good fighter, was our Maud. Oddly, he had brought the nickname with him and seemed to use it proudly. I suppose it was better than wearing an, 'Actually, I'm gay!' badge on his chest. I don't know how he fared for partners, and I wasn't the slightest bit interested.

Al Schwarts, yet another American, was the

medic. He remained where his job dictated he remain; bringing up the rear until needed. He bought it anyway. Someone with a very strong arm lobbed a grenade back there. One of the unknown snipers may have crept around on the far right flank. But it could just as readily have been one of our own. A larger or smaller percentage of casualties could always be laid at the feet of friendly fire. Such was unavoidable, especially at night.

Ying something-or-other, another Chinese merc out of Curly's Dove-Section, also got through it okay. He ran pretty damned quickly, but I don't think he lifted so much as a little finger towards the outcome. I determined to watch him like a hawk in future.

Nessie lost three more of his section.

All in all, it was an abnormally pricey half hour and Curly would be about due to send his men on another trip around the world in search of more unwitting volunteers. I hoped Nessie considered his bridge worth it.

What swayed it in the end, though, was that the remaining Askaris decided to throw in the towel. I guess sight of the chopper had impressed them. They were far too deep in the disputed territories to have the same possibility of reinforcement. Patch's guys, including the snipers who may or may not have occupied the flanks, just melted into the jungle and Nessie never did get to slit any throats. Not then, anyway.

Later, I asked Nessie why he hadn't simply called in the chopper and used it to get the hell out. He just gave me a crooked smile and tapped the side of his nose. This made me think that he had booty of some kind stashed in the trucks. That would also be about his calibre. I did not bother to ask about the field punishment thing. He would, actually, have been well within his rights.

It was pushing dawn when Khan shoved the barrel of his handgun in his mouth and blew the back of his head off. He would have been in tremendous pain, and wasn't going to make it anyway. We knew it and he knew it. We had a dubiously qualified doctor back at the compound, but the man — an aging Pakistani called Ran something or other — was no surgeon. Even the term 'doctor' was pushing it. Cuts, splinters and non-fatal flesh wounds were about his limit. I think he had bought his qualification via the internet. Plus, he was almost constantly plastered out of his mind. The guys referred to the sickbay as, 'The Orlop'. I guess you'd have to look that up someplace to see why the name was relevant. And we certainly had nothing even vaguely resembling an operating theatre. A bullet in a lung requires just that, and nothing less than that.

Mtomo, or maybe it was Chang himself, had decreed that qualified medical support was too much of a luxury in an outfit such as ours. Either everyone lived, or everyone died. A simple logic, taken at its face value.

The nearest hospital with an operating theatre was some four hundred miles away in Shekana. Add to the calculation the fact that, in Shekana, anyone with anything at all to do with Mtomo would have been shot out of hand, and you have an important reason why Khan figured things the way he did. I was sorry to lose him. And I was sorry to lose Ron Pearce. Hindsight is a wonderful, but a depressing thing.

Daylight came and it started to rain.

Nessie took a couple of my men — Ying and Salty Stephens — and went off to do whatever it was he was doing in the first place. Not so much as a thank-you or a kiss-my-arse! I was left with my normal what-was-*that*-all-about kind of feeling. I called Curly and told him the score and could he please send Benson back to get us. Curly asked if it was a critical extraction and I couldn't, in all conscience, say that it was. None of our wounded were anywhere near the brink of death, and the dead were already dead. The upshot being that we would have to wait; Benson, apparently, was *critically* needed someplace else.

So, for something to do to while away the time we collected up all the equipment, theirs and ours, and put it in a pile. Chang would be particularly pleased to get Patch's mortars. They were the one piece of ordnance we were currently short of. The able-bodied prisoners, eleven of them, were pressed into helping, whilst the mortally wounded of them were given the bullet. We made our wounded as comfortable as possible. Maud, using Al's medical supplies, went around dishing out morphine ampoules. Quite unnecessarily in most cases, I thought. But a fix is a fix.

The rest of the guys, including the walking wounded from Nessie's detail, went around relieving the dead of the money and stuff they would no longer need. They also went through the pockets of the prisoners. With that little chore out of the way I had them bury the dead guys they had just robbed. I buried Khan and Pearce myself. Chang's version of mercenary warfare did not rate military cemeteries, trumpet calls and commiserating letters to relatives. Yet another occupational hazard.

The chopper still hadn't come, so the guys fashioned a football out of someone's rolled-up tunic. It was hilarious. I radioed Curly at half time and asked what he wanted doing with the prisoners. I knew what his answer would be. I didn't shoot them; I let them go. None of the men so much as blinked an eye. Askaris were not considered worthy opponents.

Benson finally arrived at around 11.30.

By midday we were back at the compound.

Mtomo had already left. Probably in a huff.

I went to my quarters and had a shave. Then I wrote a quick report on the Shagland incident for Chang; what we did and what it cost us. From my angle, that was. Nessie could sort himself out.

Nessie's trucks rolled into the compound just as I was finishing. A couple of minutes later Nessie opened my door — he never knocked — and stepped in. He sat himself on my bed and lit up a cigar.

I said, 'You're very welcome . . . '

My attempt at cynicism went over his head. He said, 'You want in on something?'

I waved the paper at him. 'Report. You want to put it with yours, or what?'

He looked at the paper and sneered the way only he knew how. 'Fuck the report! Do you want in on something?' he repeated.

I looked at him, feeling a sudden surge of anger rise in my throat. Was I the only guy here trying to do his job? I crumpled the paper into a ball and tossed it in a corner. 'Not, then.' I kicked him off my bed, undressed and climbed in.

He said, 'Beaucoup d'argent!' *Plenty of money*. Inwardly, I groaned. The bells again! First Curly, now Nessie.

I said, 'I've got plenty of money. Close the door on your way out.' It was as if we had just returned from a walk in the park. Bizarre doesn't cover it.

Nessie looked at me and I looked at Nessie. He went on, 'Double you've got already, and I don't care *what* figure that is!'

I sighed. I said, 'I don't want any more money, pal. I just want to close my eyes.'

Nessie looked sad. 'I'd really like you in on it.'

I thought, *You, and the rest of the world!*

I closed my eyes. Nessie closed the door on his way out.

4

Chang

I woke up shortly after midday, but didn't feel rested. I lay there for a while, staring up at the mould lines on the ceiling. My billet was a typical portakabin compartment, twelve feet by twelve. It stank of the mould and it stank of me. This was not because I didn't wash. It was simply that while I had to be there I preferred to keep my own smells in, rather than open the window and exchange them for the sulphurous stench of the rainforest.

It was part of the so-called BOQ — Bachelor Officer's Quarters. But that spider was not just for officers. Most of the administration staff bunked there too. Along with the non-local cooks, cleaners and gofers.

But that twelve-by-twelve was my space. In its tentative favour was that the window faced west and caught the evening sun. You can do a lot with a swathe of evening sunlight if you allow your mind to wander. I had a wardrobe, and a chest of drawers with a mirror screwed to the wall above it, and there was a chair. I no longer had a personal life, so there were no photos or other mementos lying around. Years ago I did have such stuff but it just seemed to get scraped off as I moved through jobs. My Thompson sub-machine gun hung from a hook on the door, and my service revolver and some ammo clips and a carton of cigarettes sat on the drawer unit. I kept the chair by my bed and there were a dozen or so well-thumbed paper-backs piled on it. I read quite a lot. Mostly the same books over and over; because opportunities to buy more were rare. And that was it; that was my life. The total sum of which was kept in a padlocked box in the wardrobe; dollar bills and bank books. The various bits of my mud-spattered uniform lay as and where I'd shed them.

Then I saw the crumpled report on the floor in the corner and it all came flooding back.

Shit!

Out in the corridor a group of Indian workers seemed to be having a heated argument. But it didn't have to be an argument. Our Indian migrants conversed that way normally. They might just as well have been in the room with me. And in one of the other rooms over on the other leg of the spider, someone started to play music. It sounded like some rap song. A quiet lie-in was out of the question.

73

I thought about going to the washroom and having a shave, and maybe a shower. Then I thought about *not* going to the washroom for a shave and a shower. Not won.

I glanced again at the ball of paper and wondered what fresh revelations this day would uncover.

I dragged on some fatigues that were reasonably clean, gathered up the dirty kit, which I'd drop off at the laundry. Yes, the B-Company could boast a laundry. Sort of. I don't know how these guys performed their magic but they did a good job, and your clothes always came back fairly neatly pressed. I slung the Thompson and stepped out. I figured on going to the mess hall for something to eat. The heat outside was oppressive, as it mostly was. But this afternoon the humidity level seemed excessively high. Ten paces and I was drenched in sweat.

I was hoping I wouldn't see anyone who needed to talk, and I didn't.

On the way I stopped to watch Chang giving his pep-talk to a bunch of new boys. Mostly Europeans, they'd been kitted out in jungle fatigues and weapons but still managed to look out of place. Most would be ex-military, but some would not. Chang was on the part about keeping weapons slung at all times, in and out of the compound. '*Your weapon has always been your best friend. Here, in your new situation, your weapon is your lover!*' I scanned their faces; just in case there was anyone there I had known before. There wasn't.

I had heard Chang's speech many times. He hadn't changed so much as a syllable of it. Not in my time. And why should he; it seemed to work. The new boys listened avidly. Luckily for them it had stopped raining. It was a long speech covering every aspect of their new life in a mercenary regiment and how they could more or less forget everything they had ever learned in regular military service. I'll get to Chang later.

The compound was a large fort-type affair. It reminded me of one of those 5th Cavalry forts you see in western movies, except that the twelve-foot walls of this one were constructed of aluminium sections bolted together. Covering a large area, about the size of a football stadium, it had been constructed originally by the British, back in the sixties, when they thought that the Congo was there for the taking. And it needed to be that size. Over two hundred guys lived, drilled, trained, ate, crapped and often died in there.

Over in the opposite corner, beyond the

induction lecture, Echo-Section leader Jamie Carlisle, a British ex-para and our acting CSM (Company Sergeant Major), was drilling yet another group of newcomers. Carter, the guy who'd dared call Curly by his nickname, was one of them. I smiled to myself and wondered which short straw *he* was going to draw. The picture as a whole looked all very efficient, for a mercenary unit. However, you only had to scratch the surface of B-Company for the shortfalls to become apparent.

The 'mess' was just a group of Portakabins sewn together, mobile home style. The company ate in shifts so there was table/bench space for about thirty bodies. There was always someone on duty there to cook simple stuff off the cuff, and for coffee. You could buy cigarettes there, too, and other oddments. Toothpaste and stuff. So it was useful for that. It was, in fact, better than most mercenary messes I'd experienced. There was a section being fed at one of the long tables, whilst down at the other end, near the serving hatch, a couple of guys were having an animated discussion over their coffee. The mumble of voices at the main table seemed somehow subdued. They looked up as I entered and one or two of them leant in and exchanged a few words. I guessed they'd heard about last night's foray up to Shagtown. I could put names to a couple of the faces, but that was all. I returned a few mumbled greetings and stepped on to the hatch. All I wanted was a quiet coffee and a smoke.

I wasn't about to get it.

I had just sat down, dropping the bundle of dirty clothes on a spare chair, when Nessie came in. He came straight down to my table and sat himself opposite me. He leant back over his chair and hissed a quiet, 'Shove off!' to the other two guys. They left without a word or gesture of indignation. Mind you, it would have taken a very brave man to argue with Nessie, even if you weren't aware of his reputation.

When we were more or less alone he sat back and stared meaningfully at me for some moments. Then, without taking his eyes off me, he inclined his head towards the bundle of my dirty clothes.

'Laundry?' he asked.

I was hard pressed not to laugh. I'd been expecting something a damned sight more meaningful than that waste of breath.

I said, 'Nope. Just bought them downtown.'

He ignored that. I guess he figured there had to be an opening line of some kind, and the dirty laundry happened to be there. After shooting a cautious glance about the room he leant towards me. He whispered, 'It's a big deal. Don't you even want to hear about it?'

I wondered if I smelt as bad as he did. I said, 'Not really.'

He clucked his tongue agitatedly and leant even closer, his lips drawn back over his teeth in what could have been a smile, but wasn't. 'You do know what's happening here . . . don't you!' It wasn't a question.

I said, 'No . . . What?' I felt stale again. The atmosphere of betrayal was as tangible as words.

Nessie said, 'I give Chang two weeks at most! The admiral will be sitting at his desk before you can shake a stick at a monkey!' His face creased. 'I *know* it, mon ami. I — ah — I've talked with him . . . man to man!' His voice was barely a hoarse whisper now. He flashed another glance back along the room. 'D'you get it?'

I did. He was not merely in contact with Patch, he was engineering face to face meetings with the man! Whilst I was not exactly stunned out of my skull, it was a surprise. Just as much of a surprise was that he was *telling* me about it. Was he tarred with Curly's brush, or was it the other way round? Was *he* the man Kamerhi was supposed to meet? I said, 'You're pulling out . . . right?'

He shrugged a small shrug. 'If I can drag it all together . . . *you*, mainly.'

I had a feeling where this might be going. 'Me?'

Nessie nodded. 'Patch wants you, mon frére. His 2 i/c has gone missing. He wants you badly.'

I kept my expression bland. But his statement lined things up in some kind of mangled order. Curly knew exactly how Kamerhi had ended his days, and who had ended them. But Nessie, *apparently*, did not. Unless, of course, I had totally misread what he had just said, and the way he had said it. But I did not think so.

But where did that leave me?

If Curly and Nessie were putting their heads together, then it seemed they were not necessarily sharing information. Certainly not all of it. But I could understand that. It would be the smart play. Each was probably waiting until they held what they thought were the right cards before committing to a final course of action.

Another cog seemed to slot into place then. In fact, it was suddenly obvious. Chang — or maybe it was even Mtomo — would have caught some of the bad wind and was trying to stop the rot by taking out Patch's top men whichever way he could. Kamerhi, the guy

Jimmy had 'photographed' would be at the top of that list.

And our 'job' had been secret because it was no secret that at least a half of B-Company had a loyalty which was, at best, questionable, whilst the rest could be bought. Mercenary by name, mercenary by nature. Which was why Mtomo was flashing prodigious amounts of money around. And why Jimmy had gotten his stripes. And why no one sat on my back. Whatever I felt about Chang, I was sure he trusted me. And for reasons that I didn't even understand myself, I was not about to join the rats. Even if the ship *was* sinking.

Chang, certainly, knew how I felt about Patch. Though, perhaps, he didn't know or understand the reasons behind it. He also knew my history. He had a folder on me that was at least as comprehensive as anything held in Pentagon vaults. He — and others, Patch included — knew that if I put my name to something I would bend over backwards to do the job. I had not gone out of my way to cultivate a reputation of any kind, but I had one. At least in the mercenary business. I was comfortable with that. It's trite, I know, but in the end your *word* is all you have. This was something my father had hammered into me. Only one thing survives the body, and that is reputation. A signature on a piece of paper is worthless unless it's backed up by actions. At least that's true in the long haul.

Curly had been right, though: one thing the mercenary business is not, is what it had once been!

Nessie said, 'D'you want to talk about it?'

I said. 'No, old buddy, I don't.'

Nessie exhaled noisily and sat back in his chair. He glared at me and swore. It wasn't 'merde', but it was something like that. He said, 'You're a fool, Palmer! The admiral has this country all sewn up now. Urundi is holding all the cards. Look around you, mon ami. What do you see?'

I said, 'I see a bunch of guys trying to make a living.'

He chuckled a malevolent chuckle. 'What you see is a bunch of *dead* guys trying to make a living!'

There was more than a measure of truth in that. I said nothing. He went on, 'You've done the rounds, Marty. You know what it's all about. And this . . . this shambles!' He stabbed his finger at the tabletop, 'is dead in the water. Mtomo is the east, and Urundi is the west. And where are the oil wells and copper mines, eh?' He added a forceful. 'The bloody west! That's where!'

Shambles? B-Company was no shambles. Many things it may well have been, but shambles was not one of them. Far from it. It was the best it could be with the tools we had available to us, and under the circumstances that prevailed. Strangely, it was as if Nessie had exposed a nerve, some protective instinct that I hadn't realized was there. And the accusation actually needled me. I showed him the palms of my hands. Maybe it was time to add something to the pot. 'You knew all this when you signed up. So did I . . . so did everyone. Live with it!'

I thought he was going to choke. 'I don't *have* to bloody live with it!' With an obvious effort he controlled his anger. 'And neither do you . . . ' Much calmer, he added, 'Just think, Marty, we could have it all. *All* of it!' It was Nessie's mouth moving, but it was Patch's voice I heard. 'The White House talks to Urundi . . . first bloody hand! You know that. You also know that they ain't talking to Mtomo. You're American, for Christ's sake! You know what that means, if anyone does! Besides,' he added, a strange look passing over his face, 'You and Patch are buddies from way back. That makes all the bloody difference!'

He obviously didn't know that that was a one-way street.

I looked at him. 'So you reckon that gives it wings, huh?'

He sat back and smiled. 'You're damned right it does!'

We stared at each other over the table like chess protagonists. Then, evenly, he said, 'How about you just think about it.'

I could see no harm in that. In fact, some actual *thinking* was definitely called for. Mandatory, in fact. I nodded. 'I'll think about it.'

He smiled and stood up. 'That's all I'm asking, a little thought. You'll see it my way,' He spread his hands. 'Because there is no bloody other way!'

He left.

★ ★ ★

Chang must have weighed as much as Nessie, but it came in a neater package. He was a medium sized mountain of rock-hard muscle. He reminded me of Odd-job from the Bond movies. He kept his head shaved and his uniform immaculate. He had begun his military career in the French Foreign Legion, back in its heyday, and he'd ended it running a UN training camp in Belize. I didn't know for certain, but I put his age in the mid fifties. He could just as easily have been forty. He had that kind of face.

I didn't like him as a man but I had to admire him as a mercenary commander. He knew his job as well, if not better, than anyone I had met. He was a mercenary in every sense of the word and — so far, at least — Mtomo knew his price. Chang made no secret of the fact that he was paid three grand a week, plus bonuses. In sterling. The part he kept to himself where possible was that the bonuses included as many young native girls as he could devour. And he had the sexual appetite of a stallion. It would not have surprised me to learn that that appetite had been the cause of his military demise.

His biggest failing, for my money, was a penchant for insentient inhumanity. That part of him — of the business itself, actually — galled me. Unlike Patch and too many others, he was not a cruel man in the generally accepted sense of the word; no more than killing an ox to feed a village would be considered cruel to the ox. Provided, of course, that the ox was killed quickly and as painlessly as possible. Chang would normally strive to do that. But if, in his eyes, a legitimate objective required something else, even seemingly mindless torture, he could string the victim's suffering out for as long as he deemed it necessary. That line of thinking almost exactly mirrored that of the Mafia. *Nothing personal, Legs* . . . . This was not warfare; this was *mercenary* warfare. But the difference is complex. And, that morning, as an addition to his normal lecture, this was the example Chang was attempting to instil in the new recruits.

We didn't take many prisoners. And if, say, Curly had been in charge, we wouldn't take any. But we did have a few in the stockade. Chang had one of these unfortunates tied to a post in the middle of the compound. The new guys were lined up in front of the post. I was standing by the chopper with Benson and one of the Indian mechanics, a middle-aged guy called Rama. Benson had parked his machine here for some maintenance, which included plugging a few bullet holes. And, since I was at a loose end, still minus a platoon, I had been passing the time of day with them.

Rama spat the cigarette butt out of his mouth and threw down the cutters he had been using. 'Oh, good grief!' he hissed, glaring out at the spectacle from under bushy, greying eyebrows. 'We don't have to watch this pantomime again, do we?' His Asian accent was marked but understated, as if he had spent a great deal of time cultivating his English. It seemed to me that most Asians could handle English better than most home-grown Europeans. I did not have a clue what his story was.

Benson, stripped to the waist and covered in oil, nodded. 'Seems that way.' He removed his forage cap and used it to wipe the sweat from his face. He squinted out at the guy tied to the stake, tutted and looked around at the clutter of toolboxes and equipment. I guessed he was looking for his glasses, which he'd left on a toolbox.

I grabbed them and handed them to him. 'Looking for these?'

He nodded and slid them on. 'Ta.' He looked back out at the lecture. 'Ah!' he said, waggling his head. 'This old chestnut!' He smiled. 'D'you reckon the man's a volunteer?' Which was funny.

Rama grunted. 'Either way it gets him out into the fresh air for a while.' Which was even funnier.

Benson stared at him, brows furrowed.

Rama smiled broadly. 'Life of Brian.'

I had made the connection, Benson hadn't. His frown deepened and he aimed a grimy finger at the man at the stake. 'He's called Brian?'

I said, 'Go back to sleep, pilot.'

Rama nodded over at the mess, where crowds were gathering. 'D'you mind if I grab a coffee?'

Benson, still looking puzzled, nodded. 'Fine. Two sugars, please.'

Rama trotted off, chuckling to himself. Benson watched him go then turned to me. 'Brian?'

I said, 'It's a movie.'

Benson's expression cleared. 'Oh,' he said, pulling a dismissive face. 'I don't watch movies. Waste of bloody time!'

I said, 'Couldn't agree more.'

We heard Chang begin his demonstration.

'The true mercenary,' he was saying, in a loud, lecturing type voice 'does not kill for killing's sake . . . ' His eyes swept over the assembled men. 'Who thinks he knows what I mean by this?' His English was immaculate.

No one answered him. Me and Benson exchanged glances. No one ever answered that question. Chang did not often indulge in this *particular* lecture. But it wasn't the first time we had witnessed it. I lit up a cigarette and passed one to Benson. We sat on a wheel apiece to watch. It was something to do. And I was doing anything to avoid thinking about Nessie and his revelations. Over by the admin block a group of older hands were also settling in for the show. Jimmy was one of them.

Chang went on, 'This man is the enemy.' He waved his gleaming bayonet at the unfortunate tied to the stake. The man was quivering with fear, his eyes rolling wildly. He knew he was about to die, so did everyone else. I guess the only thing in the man's mind now was how long Chang was going to drag it out. It was very probable that it had already seemed a lifetime. As for the others, well, I doubted any of them would be ready for this lecture. Even men who had spent several years in the marine corps or the British SAS would blanch at this exhibition. It was a hard one to take.

I looked at the gook and tried to feel some morsel of compassion. But there was nothing. In a fire fight, of course, I would have killed him without blinking; always assuming he'd given me the chance. But this kind of theatre was something different. Nevertheless, I had it in my mind that he could well have been the man who'd cut off Pip Henderson's balls, stuffed them in his mouth, then sewn up his lips with string. Pip, his mouth ripped and bleeding torrents after he had thrown up, pulling apart all of the good work, had taken some time to die. Perhaps the fact that he had been crucified prior to the knitting wool job had speeded things up a little. I don't know, but I hoped so.

I remembered Rama's reference to the film and had to smile. There it is, I thought. Right there. A horrible death and a joke in the same breath. What a life!

No. I felt nothing for the gook. But this was the side of Chang — of the whole damned business — I was uneasy with. Then again, maybe such *was* crucial, *was* valid. Chang, after all, was a product of *someone's* idea of necessity! We all were. In the end, where is the line? Who puts it there, and why? This is not a subject normally discussed over breakfast in yuppie households, but they seem to live with the end products comfortably enough. Stocks and shares. The futures market. Oil. Precious metal. The whole bundle. It's probably a bit like eating a steak. You like what you are eating but purposely disregard the processes that brought it to your plate.

Chang went on, ' . . . And when you are ordered to kill an enemy you will do just that, immediately, and without question or thought. Indeed,' he added conversationally, 'it is for this very reason that you are all here now. But, gentlemen . . . '

Gentlemen!

' . . . you will kill only as need dictates, or as your orders dictate. You do *not* kill for pleasure. Only sadists do that. And you are soldiers, not sadists. Is this clear?'

One or two heads nodded. But no one

spoke. I think they had just realized what the lecture was all about. Chang's mouth tightened slightly at the corners. He bellowed, 'I asked if this was clear!'

Almost as one, they yelled 'Sir! Yes, sir!'

Chang did his steps-back-in-astonishment routine and his face cracked in a wide smile. 'Ah ha!' he said, smoothly now, stepping towards them, lightly tapping the blade in the palm of his other hand, feigning deep interest. 'Film buffs, eh?' He nodded, as if satisfied. 'That's good . . . that's very good.'

Benson leant towards me. He whispered, 'Does someone send these boys the script beforehand, or what?'

I smiled at him. Benson was one of the few guys I actually got along with. His first name was Adam, but everyone, myself included, just called him 'Pilot'. 'Well, *I* didn't get one!'

Chang spun on his heel sharply and waved the bayonet at the victim. 'This man is about to die. But he will be dying for a purpose.' He turned back to the men. 'He will die as an important object lesson to you all.'

He walked slowly up and down the line of grim-faced men. He was studying their eyes. He wanted to know who of them was the more nervous. They all tried to make out that

90

they were big men. Fearless. It's very probable that there would be a few training camp rejects amongst them. Short service guys who, for one reason or another, had not made the grade into a regiment. Though there would be a few of Jimmy's calibre in there too. I wouldn't have had Curly's job for a fortune.

Chang chose his victim. 'You!'

The kid almost jumped a mile as Chang waved the bayonet under his nose. And he *was* a kid. He could've been no more than twenty. Twenty-three max. Fresh faced and awkward looking.

Chang said, 'Where are you from, soldier?'

'England, sir. Bath.'

Chang nodded. 'Bath.' Then, using his conversational tone, he repeated, 'Bath . . . Close to Bristol, is that not so?'

The guy's eyebrows lifted. 'Yes, sir.'

Chang placed the tip of the bayonet carelessly between his lips, as if in thought. 'Yes, Bath, I was there once . . . a pretty place. Very pretty indeed.'

'Thank you, sir.'

Chang hmm'd thoughtfully. 'And what is your name?'

'Munro, sir.' His voice trembled noticeably, probably in relief at not having had the bayonet rammed in his eye.

Chang nodded and smiled. 'Munro,' he repeated meditatively. 'No relation to the singer, are you?'

Munro smiled a nervous smile. 'Who's that, sir?'

Chang put on a face of mock astonishment. 'You haven't heard of Matt Munro?'

Munro shook his head. 'No, sir . . . sorry, sir.'

I let out a sigh. Christ, we were down to using kids who were too young to have heard of Matt Munro!

Chang said, 'My goodness. Am I getting that old? Matt Munro was an Englishman also. A fine, fine singer. You like films; didn't you ever see *From Russia with Love?*'

Munro said, 'No, sir . . . '

Chang raised his eyebrows. 'Astonishing! The first, or was it the second, Bond movie. Matt Munro sang the soundtrack. I want you to kill that enemy with this bayonet. And I want you to do it now, in any way you deem appropriate.'

I personally would have put money on Munro having fainted at that moment. Chang was normally spot on in his choice. The hesitant refusal, or the flabbergasted spluttering, always gave added weight to his object lesson. But this kid didn't flinch. He took the proffered bayonet with a crisp, 'Yes, sir!'

92

He marched straight up to the gook and drove the blade into his heart. The man collapsed on the ropes without so much as a sob. There was a moment of utter silence.

I looked at Chang and knew he was fuming inside; he would have to switch objects in his object lesson. He strode over to Munro and grabbed his shoulder, spinning him around to face the line of men.

'And that, gentlemen,' he growled 'should an officer ever ask you to do so, is how it must be done. Instantly and without question. Well done, mister Munro. You may rejoin your compatriots.'

Benson leant over towards me. 'If that kid doesn't get the most dangerous, pig-swilling jobs for the next couple of weeks, I'll give up smoking!'

It started to rain again. Not rainforest type rain; just misty drizzle.

I left Benson to his work and headed back to my quarters. Jimmy detached himself from the group and intercepted me.

'You got a minute, sir?'

I said, 'Sure thing, Jimmy. What's on your mind?' He had the look of a worried man and I hoped he had not been tarred with Nessie's brush.

He stepped towards me. 'You won't tell any fucker I was sick, will you?'

Which was a relief. I said, 'Now why the hell would I do that?' I tapped the chevrons on his arm. 'How does it feel to be a two-striper?'

He perked up. 'Fucking great! I got an extra fifty-fucking-quid a week on top of it!'

I said, 'Good on you, sport.' We started to walk. I dived my hand into my pocket and brought out the wad of notes Curly had given me. 'Here you go, Jimmy. Add that to your bank account.'

Jimmy looked staggered. 'Shit! What's this for?'

I said, 'What do you think?'

His expression cleared for a moment, then his lips tightened and his eyes seemed to lose focus. I guessed he was remembering what he had done to earn it. I said,

'D'you have a family, Jimmy?'

Jimmy swallowed, probably forcing the images from his mind. He nodded. 'Yeah. Me ma lives in Stockport. Me sister's married to some commercial-fucking-traveller. They got a house up in Preston. I live there sometimes. He's not a bad old sod, I s'pose.'

I did not have the first clue where any of those places were, and it didn't matter. I said, 'Go home, Jimmy. Take what you've got and get the hell out of it.'

Jimmy looked staggered. 'What? Fucking

quit?' His face was a picture. 'Now?'

'Yes . . . now.'

Jimmy stopped in his tracks and looked at me as if I was demented. 'Quit?' he repeated. 'Just like that?'

'Just like that, Jimmy. Go tell Captain Parsons that you want out. It'll be cool; I'll make sure of it.'

Jimmy just stood there and looked at me wide-eyed. 'But . . . ' he spluttered. 'Why?'

I pulled a tired hand over my face. Behind us, the lecture group chorused another 'Sir, yes, sir!', as Chang wound it up for another day.

I said, 'No reason, Jimmy. Just do it.'

Jimmy's smile was not a smile. 'Not fucking likely, *sir*. I'm just beginning to get some serious bread together.' He held up the wad of notes. 'An' I got me stripes. I'm going up in the fuckin' world!'

I sighed and nodded. 'Fine.' It was not much of a protest, but it was something. I'm not even sure why I bothered.

Jimmy looked suddenly serious. 'Why, mate? Why would you say a thing like that?' He was, naturally enough, confused.

I said, 'Forget it. You're happy. I guess that's all that counts in the end.'

Jimmy took the line of least resistance and, I think, forgot it. He smiled, pocketing the money. 'Yeah, I'm happy. I was on the fucking rocks back in Blighty, now I'm something again.'

I forgot it, too. I had invested my two-cents' worth. But if you stack two cents up against an extra fifty pounds sterling a week then there's no real contest. I said, 'What have they got you on now, Jimmy?'

He grunted. 'I gotta take these guys,' he waved out at the lecture group, 'on a route march. See what they're made of.' He pulled himself up an inch. 'They ain't never asked me to do nothing like *that* before!' He was ebullient, bubbling. 'Hey, what did you think of that Munro guy. Fuckin' ace, eh! Was that the greatest, or what!'

I nodded and returned his smile. 'Yes . . . that was ace!' I wondered if Jimmy realized that Munro's action had marked him down for a hard time. I doubted it. When you're young you see what you want to see. Munro would end up everyone's hero but his own. I had a feeling that that was Jimmy's lot, too. He had just witnessed the cold-blooded killing of another human being, and had accepted it, totally, as advertised; as an object lesson. Plus, of course, he had recently decapitated a man he had never seen before. But at the very least he had done his damnedest to avoid that one. Could throwing up be taken as some kind of mitigation? Or was he already beyond redemption? I certainly was, but it had taken me a lifetime to reach that state.

'I think you're wanted.' Jimmy nodded over my shoulder.

I looked. Curly was waving at us from the steps of the administration block. I pointed at myself, and Curly nodded his head emphatically. Jimmy said, 'I'll leave you to it, then, sir.' In and out of military convention like a wisp. He saluted briskly.

I returned the salute. 'Carry on, corporal.'

That pleased him. He turned on his heel and padded off.

In which hidden corner of our minds, I wondered, did acceptance of reality lie?

I glanced around the compound. The sights were the same, the sounds were the same and the activity was the same. But now I had the feeling that I was looking at a parallel layer, one that existed solely at the mercy of the layer beneath it. Like a lava flow with a hardening surface. And if the underlying magma reached a higher temperature . . .

To myself, I said, 'Palmer, you're getting too damned deep in your old age!'

★　★　★

We were in Chang's office. There was just Chang and myself. I could hear a typewriter being hammered in the adjoining office, but that door was closed. Curly, having delivered me, had been dismissed. The A/C unit hummed away to itself under the window and the room was almost cold. I wondered why Chang needed to see me alone. But I didn't wonder that for long. I think Chang was more astute than anyone gave him credit for.

He began, 'First of all, thank you for your efforts on behalf of Red Four. A costly business, I'm afraid, in terms of men. But it did keep Captain Bridges's assignment on schedule. And that was critical.'

I thought, *Critical for whom?* It was entirely possible that we had lost good men just so Nessie could have clandestine meetings with that same enemy. I said, 'It certainly was costly.' An ambiguous answer.

Chang nodded. His eyes narrowed slightly as he looked at me over the desk. I had the feeling that he was about to say something specific, but then he seemed to change direction. He went on.

'Captain Parsons has already told you that Patch is up north again, yes?'

I nodded. 'He told me, yes.'

Chang's office, compared to the other Portakabins and offices of the compound, was plush. Two phones on the desk. One was red. I could not imagine what the red phone was for. A hotline to Mtomo, maybe. There was a drinks cabinet — obviously for thirsty VIPs, a wash basin, short wave communications equipment, a very large filing cabinet and maps on the walls. The room was carpeted, but the high-use area inside the door, was muddy and threadbare. The air smelt of jungle and aftershave lotion. The desk, behind which Chang was seated, was a huge hand-carved mahogany affair, currently littered with papers and folding maps. Out of the window directly behind him, I saw Jimmy marching his detail out through the gate.

'Mtomo wants him badly.' Chang said, adding with a small shrug, 'More so than usual . . . *suddenly*.' The last word was heavy with irony. He offered me one of his perfumed cigarettes. I accepted one, simply to see what they were like. It was not a bad smoke, except that my mouth tasted like the inside of a woman's handbag.

Chang went on, 'I'd like to send you and Santana up there. Sniff out the ground . . . ' He laid his fingers on a map he had obviously been studying, and turned it to face me, aiming a beringed finger at a spot north of Komo village. 'My intelligence puts him in this area. Hill-475. But we do not know what strength he's in, or how long he plans to be there. I need to know what it's all about.'

I was certain that Nessie could have supplied that information, and in some detail; Komo village was no more than an hour's hard drive from Shagtown. I wondered just how much Chang knew of the uncertainties of his command. I also wondered whether it was my place to inform him. In my mind, I pictured the Three Wise Monkeys, and I told myself to leave well alone. Besides, a dose of sour grapes, even a severe dose, did not *necessarily* precede disaster.

Chang's eyes narrowed again and the pause was as pregnant as a pause could be. What, I wondered, does he want me to say? It seemed that everyone and his brother were giving me opportunities to drop some pearl of wisdom in their lap. I didn't have a wise bone in my body. So I voiced the only thought that was in my mind.

'Why Santana . . . particularly?'

Chang lifted a shoulder. If he *had* been waiting for something specific, that obviously wasn't it. He said, 'Santana has mostly black conscripts in his platoon. He says they're loyal to him — and I think they are — and loyalty,' just the slightest of pauses here, 'is at a premium.' He raised an eyebrow, adding,

'Wouldn't you say?'

I would indeed have said just that. But I didn't. Instead, I said, 'I understand Patch was asking after me.'

Chang allowed a ghost of a smile to touch his mouth. He studied the glowing tip of his cigarette. Curly hadn't asked me to keep that information under my hat, so I didn't feel like a snitch.

At last Chang said, 'Patch spoke to me on the radio, it is true. He offered me a great deal if I would let you go.' With his eyes locked on mine, he continued, 'if I would release you from your contract.' He placed the slightest of emphasis on that last word.

I said, 'And you didn't feel like telling me this, Colonel?'

Chang, blandly, said, 'The offer was a personal one. I've no doubt that in his own good time he might find a way to contact you directly.' He ground the cigarette out in the ashtray and studied the black ash on his fingertips. 'If such happens . . . would you consider it?'

Did he really think I would answer such a question? Truthfully, anyway? I said, 'What do you think, sir?'

Chang smiled a crooked smile and he looked up at me. 'I think you would prefer to have *his* head shrunk! Am I right?'

101

I didn't answer that. My personal agenda was no one's business but my own. 'Santana,' I reminded him, pushing the conversation back to its roots.

He seemed to relax. 'Precisely. His blacks could be your close-up lens. I have to know what we will be up against before I commit to anything like a full-scale action. Patch himself is the key; he rarely ventures this far east. Also, just at the moment, and despite his numerical strength, he is on the back foot . . . ' He touched a forefinger to his head in a mini salute. 'Which is yet another operation for which we owe you a debt of thanks.' He did not wait for a response. 'If we *can* take him out of the picture, Robert Urundi's cattle might wander back to their kraals.'

It all made sound strategic sense; sat here either side of a mahogany desk in relative air-conditioned comfort. And it was unremarkable that Chang was referring to Patch from opposing ends of the same spectrum; almost an acquaintance in one sentence, and the sworn enemy in the next. 'So you want a recce.'

He nodded. 'Yes. If I thought I could place implicit trust in Santana I would send him out on his own. But I would not like to put it to the test. Not just at the moment,' he dashed on. 'Dawn tomorrow, then. How many of your own men will you take?' He clucked his tongue in self-admonishment, adding a hurried, 'The ammunition shipment . . . it had slipped my mind.' He lifted a shoulder. 'I hope you don't mind . . . it was expedient, and — '

That pause, I filled. 'Not at all, Colonel. With nothing to occupy their tiny minds they would only have drunk themselves into a stupor. Besides, I don't need men for a recce. I'll just tag along with Santana.'

Chang nodded. 'As you wish.'

I left. It seemed we had agreed several points, whilst mentioning none of them.

5

Santana

Jose Santana was Mexican-American, and he liked to think he was an incarnate Pancho Villa. He wore a moustache like Villa's and carried a holstered handgun on each hip, slung as low as the belts would allow, except that the weapons were Peacemaker Colts, not six-shooters. And he carried his ammunition in bandoleers criss-crossed over his chest. He even liked to be called Pancho, whether or not there was any sarcasm involved. And there frequently was.

But where Pancho Villa was purported to be a big man, Santana was small and wiry. He was a hurry-man, full of nervous energy. If he was ever forced to sit in one place, some part of his body would be constantly on the move. Either a foot would tap, or fingers would drum or he'd be shifting in his seat like a man with haemorrhoids. Sometimes it would all happen at once. I don't think he suffered from haemorrhoids. Briefings were a nightmare. Ten minutes in the same room with Jose Santana and you were yourself a nervous wreck.

What he lacked in stature he made up for in ferocity. He would undertake any seemingly impossible task, and he appeared to do so gratefully. He was a crazy man who had already lived longer than his nature should have allowed.

B-Company had its share of colourful characters.

Santana professed not to like black men.

His hotchpotch platoon was ninety per cent black men.

Nine per cent were white, yellow and brown.

One per cent was the new kid, Munro, who had unwittingly blacked Chang's eye for him. Munro thought he had been assigned to Santana — at least a week before he should have been assigned to frontline duty with *anyone* — because Chang had been pleased with his effort.

Santana said, 'Chang doesn't want me to fight.' It's impossible to write it the way he said it, but he said it the way Pancho Villa might have said it.

We were on the road with the jeep and two trucks because Benson was still doing something structural to his aircraft. Santana was driving the jeep and I was in the passenger seat. We were approaching the outskirts of Shagland from the south. The sun was shining and the birds were singing and, for once, it wasn't that hot and humid.

I said, 'That's right. He wants a recce . . . a quiet, peaceful one.'

We hit a bump in the track and I almost took off.

Santana said, 'But we fight soon, eh? The big one!'

The big one!

There was always a *big one*. If someone ever writes *A concise history of Mercenary Warfare in Africa*, it will be noted that territorial disputes were always decided by The Big One. Everything else, no matter how costly the action, was merely part of a common shuffling for position.

I said, 'It seems that way.'

Over the next ten miles he told me again about his village back in the hills behind Rojo, California. He told me about his mother and his father and his sisters and brothers. He told me about the fighting he'd done in El Salvador and how he had spent a year fighting for the communists.

Santana was omni-directional. Nowhere, all at once. I had a feeling that he was not a mercenary for money, either. But I could not pin his reasons down, no more than I could pin down my own. So, maybe mercenary is the wrong word. Maybe we were both doing this because it was all we knew how to do, full stop.

We passed through the first Shagland village in a cloud of red dust. The only human beings we saw were a few kids playing around a standpipe by the side of the road. The standpipe was new; at least I hadn't seen it the last time I was that way. After that the track got worse. In places it wasn't a track at all. And the terrain was all over the place; up, down and sideways. Then we hit the rain forest in earnest and the sky was blotted from view. Santana had to put the lights on. The stench, mixed now with exhaust fumes, was overpowering. Another seventeen miles brought us to Red River. The natives did not call it Red River. We did. Because it was red. And it was red because of the copper oxide in the water. On the maps it was marked as the 'Hopo River'. Follow Red River a hundred and fifty miles south and west from Shagtown and you would eventually come across a headless corpse. But you would have to be actively looking for it.

We took a break.

Santana and I pissed into the river in stereo. The other guys preferred to piss against tree trunks, leaving us alone. Santana looked sideways at me. 'Why you coming with me, Marty?' There was a broody edge to his voice. I had been wondering whether that particular penny was still in the air. It was not an easy question to answer. Chang should have covered that base when he had briefed him.

Thinking hard on my feet, I said, 'Nothing sinister, old buddy.' I opened my mouth to continue the fabrication. But Santana added:

'Don't lie to me, Marty.'

I looked at him as we shook ourselves off and returned tackle to trousers. I nodded. 'Fair enough.' And it was. I improvised: 'Just at the moment Chang doesn't know where his command ends and his opposition starts. If this had been my mission *you* would be here as the observer. Or Nessie would. Or someone . . . '

He stared at me hard for a few moments. Then his expression cleared and he nodded. He even smiled. 'Yep, I figured something like that. Someone's crapping on someone, right? Situation normal?' He gave a chuckle. 'Fubar, right?'

I doubted I could have put it better myself.

Fucked Up Beyond All Recognition.

'That's about the size of it.'

We turned and headed back to the transport. Santana grabbed my sleeve. 'Do *you* trust me, Marty?'

I gave him the first response to hit my mind. 'It doesn't matter a shining damn who *I* trust! Not here and now, anyway. I guess we've just got to trust ourselves.' On impulse, I went on, 'Look, buddy, we're out here in the country. The birds are singing. The weather's not too bad. The view . . . ' I glanced around us, 'well, *sometimes* it can be bloody picturesque. How about we just forget all that shit and take it as it comes. Okay?'

He gave me a curious sideways look, frowned a puzzled frown. Then a smile picked at his mouth. 'Sounds cool.'

He held up his hand to be hi-fived. So I hi-fived it. I think that took care of it, because he held a quick council of war before we drove off, telling his command that they were to consider my orders, his orders. Which seemed a nice touch.

We skirted the Red River for some ten miles, climbing all the time. River became rapids; rainforest on the right, gorge on the left. Then the track swung away from the river and it was pure rainforest again. The track all but disappeared. Santana was forced to aim his headlights at the less overgrown area and hope it was, or had once been, track. The echoing clamour of the racing engines and snapping branches was mind-numbing.

Suddenly there was sunlight ahead and we

burst out of the forest. The deafening noise was quenched abruptly. And there were the rapids again. But where there had once been a bridge there was now, presumably thanks to Nessie, a pile of tangled wreckage. I did not know why Nessie had blown it up and it didn't matter anyway.

We backed the transports into the undergrowth some way from the track, extracted the equipment and covered the three vehicles with branches and foliage. We all got drenched crossing the rapids but, thankfully, there were no accidents. From then on it was just a hard slog up the slopes. Santana sent three of his men ahead on the point with a couple of radios, set to the lowest power, between them. But the radios were only to be used in the event of actual contact. Otherwise we were observing strict radio silence. It was almost full dark by the time the rest of us eventually reached the foot of Hill-475. The three point men were sitting there waiting for us, playing dice on a groundsheet. I didn't know how everyone else felt, but I was utterly exhausted.

We ate cold K-rations and drank whatever we had put into our water bottles. I mixed some of mine with some of Santana's and we ended up with a fairly acceptable, and a fairly potent, cocktail. We then checked and cleaned the weapons and ammunition. Santana sent a detail up the slope to look for cooking fires; from the upper slopes of 475 you can see for miles in all directions. The rest of us settled in for the night. The detail returned with the sun. No one had seen anything.

We set up the shortwave transceiver and slung an aerial up into the trees. Munro looked at me strangely when I told him to stay there with it. But he perked up when I told him that he should monitor the airwaves in case Patch, if he *was* still up there somewhere, started using *his* radio. I asked Santana to nominate one of his section to remain with Munro as a runner. Then the rest of us hoofed it east.

We hit the eastern stretch of Red River after some two hours of hard march. Santana took the initiative and had his command fan out for the first sweep upstream. He reiterated the radio silence issue. I was impressed with his businesslike attitude. In the past I had not given him that much leeway. The skirmish line must have been over two miles in length, from the river bank to well up into the hills, with the men spaced about two hundred yards apart. At least, that was the way it started out.

By the time we reached the elephant grass of the Kamba foothills, three hours later, some of the men had grouped and were no more than spitting distance from each other. It's not that easy to hold a straight line in the forest. We regrouped and started back on a different tack.

I saw a deer-like animal, a family of spider monkeys, three of Santana's blacks walking together who looked at me sheepishly then separated, a couple of spiders and a snake. The man we had left with Munro was waiting for us back at the starting point. He saluted and handed Santana a slip of paper.

Munro had written: '*Intensive radio traffic. Mostly in some kind of code. I estimate our presence is known.*' He had signed the paper, '*Benjamin Munro.*'

Benjamin. It sounded so young, so naïve. Kids playing at soldiers. Except that this kid had the balls to skewer prisoners without blinking. Something was definitely amiss somewhere.

Santana handed the paper to me. He said, 'The new guy can write.' It was a simple statement of fact. He pointed at Munro's observation and hissed, 'What the hell is this guy, a mind reader?! How the fuck did he get that idea from a load of code?'

I shrugged. 'Who knows. These young guys think on a different level.'

Santana pulled a face. 'Well, I hope to fuck

the smart-arse is wrong!'

If Nessie has had anything to do with it, I thought, then knowledge of our presence was a rock-bottom certainty. As a field operation, it all seemed so bloody futile. Then again, Nessie seemed to use his field operations as his contact opportunities, and since the Shagtown thing he had not been out. I scribbled on the back of the paper; '*Good work. Keep it up. Expect us a.m. tomorrow.*' I handed the paper to the runner and he disappeared back into the jungle.

Santana said, 'Now what?'

I said, 'I guess we keep looking.'

But we didn't have to. One of our outriders came charging into the clearing. He had seen at least a dozen uniformed militia on the southern slopes of 475. That slope meandered clear back to Shagtown. Santana asked him which way they were headed but he couldn't say. The party appeared to be bivouacked, perhaps waiting for something, or someone.

'Any white men with them?' Santana asked.

'No, boss. Just blacks.'

Not desperately promising. But we had to follow it up. We followed the out-runner back into the trees. It rained while we were in there but we didn't feel much of it — the tree canopy of the rain forest is as good as an umbrella. But the ground turned soggier underfoot. The jungle eventually thinned out and the going was easier. Then we were in scrubland. The rain clouds had drifted off and the sky was blue again. The view to the west was the stuff picture postcards are made of. It was possible to see the smoke of the Mang village cooking fires, way off to the east. It all looked very peaceful. And, high in the blue sky, a single con trail of a jet liner neatly dissected the world north to south. We all stood there staring up at it for a few moments. I wondered where it was headed, who was on board and why and where they had come from and where they were going. I also wondered if they knew what was happening way below them. I doubted it. They wouldn't even have been looking. This was a lost world and we were a lost people.

We eventually breasted a hill and the outrider pointed down the far slope. 'Down there, boss,' he told Santana. We looked. There was evidence of recent habitation, certainly; the remains of a fire and some litter, but no people. The outrider shrugged hugely. 'They was there, boss.'

Santana sighed heavily. We were not looking for signs of a temporary incursion.

He picked out one of his men and told him to go down there and look for tracks. The rest of us sat there and watched him. He returned with the news that there were tyre tracks. Heavy stuff. Trucks. There was no way to judge the direction they were travelling, of course, but one headed west, the other headed east; back into the elephant grass we could just make out way off in the far distance. That swathe of grass looked like a vast sand coloured lake, the breezes creating eddies and swirls on its surface.

The tyre tracks could have meant anything. The UN operated in this part of the world. And UNESCO. And several other well-meaning organizations.

Santana said, 'What's over that way, Marty?' He aimed his rifle at the elephant grass.

I checked the map. 'Komo village is over there. About fifteen miles.'

'And beyond that?'

'Tengo . . . Then Patri.'

Santana nodded. 'Okay. Plan-B.'

The handful of blacks he sent on ahead, dressed in the civilian clothes they had been instructed to bring with them, did not seem happy with their lot. They were allowed no weapons, not even bayonets. Just a couple of radios between them. The radios had to stay out of sight unless needed. They were workers hoofing it from Kapula to Lukusu. Innocent migrant workers did not carry arms. This, on the face of it, was a plausible cover story. But these men were not trained infiltrators and I doubted the deception would hold up if a crunch came. UN patrols searched everyone and everything. I knew that and Santana knew that. And they knew that. But they went anyway. There was a strong possibility that as soon as they had a head start on us they would slope off and find something else to do with their lives. And who would blame them. Not me, for sure.

We gave them a good head start anyway. Then we spread out and started off after them.

Santana asked,' How many blacks does Patch have, d'you think?'

I said, 'As many as he wants, I guess. Why?'

Santana shrugged. 'No reason.'

We were deep in the elephant grass when the sky darkened and it started to rain. It came down in buckets and drenched us clear through to the skin. It was not easy going. Then the ground fell away underfoot and the grass sucked itself back into the ground. The rain stopped as we re-entered the tree line of the lower slopes. The airwaves, as far as the range of our walkie-talkies was concerned, remained empty. Santana sent scouts out on our flanks and we trudged on. There were monkeys everywhere.

Nothing happened until the sun went down.

Then it got dark.

Everyone propped their groundsheets up with their rifles and tried to sleep. Santana and I dossed down under the spread of a tree with nuts in it.

Santana said, 'You don't keep blacks, do you.'

I wondered why he seemed locked into that subject. I said, 'In what way?'

'In your platoon.'

'I have blacks.' I went over my section in my mind. It was something to do. I said, 'Six, in fact. Why?'

Santana said, 'I keep them because they don't think too much. Whites think too much.'

I thought, how very true!

Sleeping was not easy because of the monkeys chattering and screeching and generally being bloody annoying. At least the rain held off. At dawn the monkeys started to throw nuts down at us. We pulled ourselves together and set off. Some way short of Komo village we met the 'civilians' coming back. They had talked to some locals, trucks had passed there, but no one seemed to know who the trucks belonged to. It was beginning to look like a thoroughly wasted trip.

But I was enjoying the hell out of it. This was soldiering in its simplest form. We had orders and we were carrying them out to the best of our ability. Sweet relief. Santana took out his cigarettes. But the packet was a soggy mess. He tossed it away. I gave him one of mine and we smoked in silence for a few moments, the rest of the patrol looking on expectantly.

At last he said, 'This ain't working, is it?'

I said, 'Well, you can't win them all.'

He looked at me for a heartbeat. 'It would be nice to win just one!'

I said, 'Picky, huh. So what do you want to do now?'

He said, 'What do *you* think!'

We trudged back to Shagland. Munro looked inordinately pleased to see us. He said, 'All radio traffic ceased last night, sir. I sent you my messenger.' Munro seemed to have the knack for concise, to-the-point reports. He glanced around the small sea of faces. 'Didn't he find you?'

Santana said, 'Sod the black. Let's get the hell back home!'

Munro said, 'You're not going to leave him, are you, sir?'

118

Santana ignored him. Generally, called, 'Load up!'

We arrived back at the compound late the following afternoon. I had managed to sleep some on the last leg, so I felt reasonably fit. As we pulled up the slope past Murphy's, Santana, who'd been uncharacteristically silent for some time, said, 'We're going to cop a bundle, Marty! And from the inside out!'

'Pardon?'

'No birds singing down here, compadre. Just fork-tongued fucking lizards! And they are *fucking* with us.'

You had to think hard to decipher some of Santana's more obscure thoughts. But that statement, simple once I'd got the meaning clear, answered most of my questions about Santana. When you hear the truth, the rest is just words. I said, 'I couldn't agree more! But, later, huh? Right at the moment I need a shower, and I need some food.'

Santana pulled his small convoy to a halt in front of the admin block. The red dust swirled up around us. He said, 'I'll go report in.' He looked at me. 'Anything you want to tell Chang?'

'Bloody right!' I said. 'I'm going to tell him that you could use some driving lessons!'

Santana grinned at me. 'I got us here, didn't I?'

'Only barely. I'm going for a shower . . . then a beer.'

He said, 'See you in the mess then. Or d'you wanna go down Murphy's?'

'The mess. I've had it with walking.'

Santana smiled at me. 'Idle sod!'

★ ★ ★

I had a shower and made the mistake of laying on my bed to dry off. When I woke up the sun was already well below the tree line and the room was in deep shadow. The humidity level was right back up there and I was again drenched in sweat. The remnants of the dying day seeped in the window to cast a pastel-pink glow on the mouldering ceiling, at odds with the stench of my existence. I lay there for a while trying to think nothing about anything. A stupidly hollow prospect, which I abandoned fairly quickly. I was aware, almost for the first time, that there were no more fences worth sitting on. To continue my self-imposed neutrality would border on the dangerously naive. It was time and gone that I woke up.

Twenty minutes later I stepped into the mess and wished I hadn't. Santana was there, still festooned with his usual clutter of ammo belts and grenades, but so were Curly and

Nessie. The three of them were at a table down near the serving hatch. A couple of other guys were at one of the long tables playing cards. I would have stepped back out again, except that the smell of some kind of curry was heavy in the air. The serving hatch was still open and I was starved. Besides, Santana saw me and waved me over.

Nessie opened with, 'We've been talking.' He kicked a chair out from under the table.

I switched on every sensor, and sat down, 'That's for certain sure.'

Santana did not look comfortable. He said, 'Well, I've been doing a lot of listening.'

I indicated their dirty plates on the table. 'What's the curry?'

Curly said, 'Mutton. It ain't bad. Look, matey, this thing's going to implode if we're not careful.'

I held up a hand. 'Food first, then talk.'

But it wasn't going to happen. Nessie, his face set in stone, hissed, 'You've got to choose, Marty. And quickly. Like now!'

Self-enlightened I may have been, but, about to go off half-cocked, I was not. I said, 'Choose what?' I could almost taste the curry I was not about to get.

Curly said, 'Sides.'

I let out a heavy sigh. 'I did that already, Curly. My pay packet says I'm on your side, and that you're on mine.'

Santana ventured an emphatic, 'That's what *I* said.'

Curly ignored that. He clucked his tongue. 'You got to think on your feet in this business, Marty. You know that better'n any of us. Things change. This situation is not the one I signed on for. Plus, I'm damned certain that Chang thinks Mtomo is losing his grip. Nessie, here, has already spoken to the admiral . . . ' He leant towards me, conspirator to conspirator. 'Patch says — '

Nope, I couldn't stomach it. Hunger or not, I stood up and walked out.

Outside, the air was still and heavy with moisture. Apart from the manned towers, the compound seemed deserted. But there were muted sounds coming from everywhere. Mostly music. B-Company was on its own time. Lights burned in most of the Portakabins but the floods were off. I crossed the parade ground and walked to the gate. There was still Murphy's. Maybe he'd have bar snacks or something.

I heard someone running after me in the darkness. It had to be Santana. No one rattled like Santana in full combat gear.

He said, 'Mind if I tag along?'

I said, 'Don't you want to get rid of some of that stuff first? It's only necessary to carry your weapon with you. Belts of grenades are overkill.'

He grunted. 'I like to be ready.'

I said, 'If only I knew what we were supposed to be ready for!'

Santana said, 'Snap!'

6

Benson

It was a day for beaches and ice cream and surfing and picnics. It was not a day for extracting secret people from secret places.

I stared down at the gleaming white sand, and the breakers rolling in from an impossibly blue ocean, and I tried to forget the hammering whine of the helicopter's turbine. I felt oddly at peace with the world. Today, I was taking it all as it came. Studied reaction was now the name of my game. Like the ostrich's brother, I had pulled my head out of the sand. But the deeper stuff could still sort out its own damnation. Today's 'job' was no exception.

This was a Chang special. Written instructions — map references and the like — in a sealed envelope to be opened when airborne. Real cloak and dagger stuff. The method was something of a first for me. But in view of the way things turned out, plus the way things were, it was the best Chang could achieve. All we — me and Benson — had to do was pick someone up from a referenced spot on the coast at a certain time and bring him back to Chang. This person, apparently, was an Mtomo *mole* currently ensconced with Patch's command. I had guessed long ago that such an individual existed, but I never cared enough about it to delve.

This operation was a last-second thing, thrown at us well before dawn that morning. Curly had roused us out of bed and handed over the sealed envelope. I had not looked deeply into his eyes then, but if I had I would have noticed the beginnings of a very different look. It certainly did not dawn on me that Curly was *not* privy to the instructions contained in the envelope. At the time, and despite the ungodly hour, I was just glad to get out of the compound.

Benson, of course, had to be there; he was the only pilot in the command. Mtomo kept a private chopper, a small Schweizer, which he flew himself — and not that badly. But there could well have been other reasons for Benson being there. I was chosen, I guessed, because, in Chang's eyes at least, I was one of the trustees. Beyond that it was an unknown.

I could not see a whole lot of the terrain inland because Benson was flying below the level of the monster sand dunes that fringed that forty-mile stretch of virgin beach. We were so low, in fact, that I was able to see groups of sun-worshipping land crabs scattering as we hammered by. I had the vague thought that it must be nice to be a land crab.

In my headset, Benson said, 'Nice, eh?'

I nodded. 'Nice.'

Benson went on. 'We have beaches like this down south . . . lot of surfing and stuff like that. What a life!'

I couldn't figure out if he meant the life he was currently living, or the one he had left behind. And did it matter? I said, 'How long to the estuary?'

Red River again. That damned river seemed to follow me everywhere. Mtomo's territory boasted two rivers; the Umfolzi and the Red River. The latter coils its way through the territory like some disoriented snake. Strangely, I had never so much as clapped eyes on the Umfolzi. It lay to the north somewhere.

Benson consulted his watch and his panel of dials. 'Not long.'

'Not long . . . ' I repeated, injecting some light-hearted sarcasm in the two words.

Benson smiled and shrugged. 'What's the rush? Enjoy the view . . . I am!'

And he certainly appeared to be doing just that, his gaze more on the ranks of breakers than the way ahead. I said, 'You're a surfer then.'

He nodded enthusiastically. 'Damn right! When I've made my pile I'm going back and open a surfing resort. The west coast is wide open for a real good one. But you need cash, and lots of it, if you're going to do it right.'

Benson was the odd-ball of the outfit. And I don't mean that in its unkind sense. He was the clean-cut type, well spoken and always well turned out. To my mind he stood out like a breath of spring in a sewer. Young, for sure — no more than his early thirties — but experienced. He had flown helicopters for the South African Air Force. And he'd reached a rank equivalent to a marine corps major. His military future had been bright, according to scuttlebutt. Then again, as far as I knew for absolute certain, he could just as easily have been a disgraced serial rapist. I took Benson as he came. I guess he viewed me in the same light.

I'm not sure what made me ask, but I said, 'How do you rate Mtomo?'

Benson pursed his lips and dragged his gaze from the surf. He shot me a quick sideway glance. 'Mtomo is a kaffir. So's Urundi. If they want to have a go at each other, then that's their business. Neither of them will win in the end. They never do.' The look he gave me next was harsher. 'Why? Are you making your plans, too?' He laid stress on the word *your*.

I wondered why I'd broached the subject. Maybe, after my truncated talk with Curly and Nessie the night before, it was my subconscious seeking salvation. 'As well as who?'

He smiled. 'That's whom.'

I returned his smile. 'Okay . . . as well as whom?'

He was silent for a while. Then he did something with his left hand and the aircraft gained height. He was switching his attention from sight-seeing to conversation. 'Fine,' he said flatly. 'I had a long talk with Curly yesterday,' He hunched a shoulder. 'Well, he had a long talk with me.'

That figured. I grunted. 'Join the club.'

He shot me another sideway glance. 'It's all falling apart, isn't it!' Pure statement.

I said, 'From the middle, maybe.' I added, 'What's your position . . . after your long talk with Curly?'

He laughed. 'I don't have a position. Certainly not one dictated by anything *Curly* has to say. If things fall apart, I just climb into my trusty steed and fly off into the blue yonder.'

I said, 'This machine is yours?'

Benson laughed. 'Hell, no! This is a Bell

UH-1D; a model 205, no less. A bloody Black Hawk variant. No change out of five million dollars! Christ knows how Chang got his hands on it! But what would they do if I took it? Ring the Swedish police?'

It was a good point. I said, 'I suppose.'

Benson picked up his thread. 'It'll be sad, for sure, because I'm still wads short of my target. But that's all I have to do.'

I offered. 'You could take it someplace and flog it.'

He chuckled. 'I'm not an arms dealer. And only arms dealers can do that.' He looked over at me, his expression changing. 'I just wondered if you were in on it.'

'In on what?'

He frowned at me. 'Is this deliberate evasion? Or are you really in the dark?'

Which was fair enough comment. But before I could answer one way or the other, he went on, 'You brought the subject up in the first place, remember?' He grunted. 'And I'll bet my seat in this aircraft that you're not in the dark. Not *interested*, maybe. But not in the dark.' He shrugged an elaborate shrug. 'However, if you want to keep your cards close to your chest, I'll ease your burden. Either Mtomo is losing his grip, or Chang is, and the bastards are going to pull the rug out from under pretty damned soon — if they haven't given it a healthy tug already.' He gave me a long, hard stare. 'Does that about cover it?'

I nodded. 'Just about.'

'And?'

'And nothing. I'm sitting in my comfort zone; you're sitting in yours.' I shot him a twisted smile. 'Who knows, maybe it'll all go away.'

'I reckon it's gone too — Hey! Look at that!' He was nodding ahead at a stretch of dark sand. About two hundred yards of it. 'Want some light relief?'

I couldn't think what that was about. I said, 'I could actually use some *heavy* relief.'

Benson laughed and angled his helicopter in over the sand and let us down to within spitting distance. The stretch of dark sand disintegrated in a maelstrom of heaving shells and pincers. Benson played with his controls and pulled us around in a tight circle. My stomach came up into my throat and I very nearly threw up.

The sand was literally alive with crabs. There seemed to be millions of them carpeting that stretch of beach. As Benson eased his aircraft down onto the sand, the suddenly frantic crabs couldn't pull away fast enough and the edge of the crab-free circle built itself into a heaving, five- or six-high circlet of flashing claws and beady eyes. Benson set us down and allowed his rotors to settle into a steady idle. He pushed open his door.

'C'mon!' He was laughing.

The mound of crabs all around us was sinking to sand level, all trying to back away. But there were crabs everywhere and nowhere to back away to. I stayed where I was. Benson smiled, 'Chicken!'

He leaped down and charged deliberately at that ring of menace. The pile-up started all over again as the nearest crabs tried to retreat from his charge. The hairs on the back of my neck stiffened. It was obvious that the crabs were scared out of their wits. But it was a toss-up as to who felt worse about it — the crabs or me.

I relaxed slightly as Benson charged amongst them. He was enjoying himself hugely. It was good to see.

There was one gnarled old specimen on the edge of the circle, on my side. The thing seemed to be staring up at me, its eyes wobbling about on their stalks. Its expression — if crabs can have expressions — seemed accusing. *Bloody kids*, it seemed to be saying. *Why can't they play their games somewhere else!* I slid my window open. 'It's not me,' I yelled at it. 'It's him!'

When Benson climbed back into the helicopter he was flushed red, breathless and smiling broadly. He replaced his headset and switched on the microphone. 'Bloody good fun, that!'

I nodded. 'I'm sure. Don't they bite, or something?'

He shook his head and eased us back into the sky. 'Nah! They're just a bunch of old softies.'

Curiously, I regretted, now, not going out there with him. That kind of mindless diversion could have been just what I'd needed.

We hit the Red River estuary fifteen minutes later.

I'm a cynical old fool, but for a few magical moments the view cowed me, and Africa was part of an alien planet. There was no horizon; the hazy-blue sky simply melted into the distant vista of land and sea. The trees and the surf and the ocean materialized out of nowhere. It was a canvas crafted by a master.

And the estuary itself was huge, stretching way, way into the distance, the water glinting under the sun like a million twinkling lights scattered on a bed of what could have been snow. I think Benson was equally as impressed, because he eased his stick and we just hovered there over the virgin sand.

Then, suddenly, the bed of snow seemed to detach itself from the water, exploding haphazardly, but slowly, into individual flakes. It wasn't snow. They were flamingos. Thousands upon thousands of them. They rose into the air in eddies and swirls. I could hear nothing above the racket of the helicopter, of course, but it was easy to imagine the sound. I had seen many flamingos, but never *that* many, and in one place. I remembered, as a young lad, throwing stones at a flock of them that seemed to be roosting too comfortably. As you do when you are young and stupid. And with that memory, the spell broke.

Africa became Africa again. The river, wending inland to our right, was the Red River. And up there somewhere was a headless corpse.

It was not the country that was at fault. Or any damned country. It was the people. It was us!

Benson eased his stick forward and we drifted closer.

Our spy was nowhere to be seen. Benson put us on the beach just high of the tide line and cut his engine. The rotors took a long time coming to a stop. We climbed out into the heat, the new sensation of silence ringing in my ears. Ten million flamingos resumed their places in the middle of the wide expanse. We wandered over to a dune and sat on the warm sand. Benson took out his cigarettes and we smoked in silence for a while. I looked at my watch. It was close to midday. The spy was over an hour late.

I was fairly gratified to see that there was not a land crab in sight.

Benson said, 'Sod this; I'm going for a dip. Coming?' He didn't wait for an answer. He stripped off and loped the fifty or so yards to the edge of the surf, splashing into deeper water, yelling like a kid. Ten million flamingos again peeled themselves off the estuary like a white blanket, screeching and complaining.

I could think of no reason why not, so I stripped off and joined Benson out in the surf. I expected the water to be as hot as the air. But it wasn't. It was cool and refreshing. So we just fooled around about like teenagers at the seaside. It was absolute bliss. Benson gave me a quick course in body surfing, but I couldn't hack it. I just blundered around splashing and whooping. Eventually we ended up back on the dunes in the threadbare shade of a sand palm, and lay there drying off, chatting about anything but the situation.

It couldn't last, of course.

Benson said, 'Is it right that Patch is

angling after you?'

I said, 'Yeah, I heard that, too.'

Benson gave me an old fashioned sideways look. 'Why don't you go?'

That one had an easy answer. 'I don't *want* to go.'

Benson pulled a sage face. 'I wouldn't either.' He lay his head back on the sand. 'There's something about Patch's set-up that jangles my every nerve. Don't know what it is.' He lifted his head again. 'What do *you* think it is?'

I said, 'I don't like Patch, and I don't like who pays him.'

Benson chuckled. 'Your own people are paying him, for Christ's sake!' He added a belated, 'In the long run.'

I said. 'I don't have any people. I was born in the US, but that was an accident I refuse to be held responsible for.'

Benson looked at me. He gave a slight shake of his head. 'I bet you're a good poker player . . . '

As it happened, I was. But I knew he was not referring to the card game. He went on, 'I know why I'm doing this shit. Why are *you* doing it?'

I told him the truth. 'I don't have the first clue!'

Benson lit a couple of cigarettes and

handed one to me. He said, 'It sure as hell isn't the money, right!'

I said, 'It isn't the money, Pilot.'

He gave me a long, hard stare, before laying his head back on the sand. 'Then I'm buggered if I understand you!'

I said, 'Here's a secret . . . I'm buggered if I understand myself. D'you want a partner in your surf business? I got pots of money . . . '

He looked up at me with a new expression. 'You serious?'

I said, 'Nope.'

He grunted and smiled. 'No, didn't think you were. But, look, if you want a good investment, you have one. If this deal blows apart soon I'll be needing the extra capital.'

I wished I hadn't made the joke, which hadn't really been a joke at all. I said, 'I'm giving all my dollars to Patch.'

Benson looked blank.

I said, 'That's a joke, too.'

But it was no joke. Patch was going to get my dollars. He was going to have a bellyful of the damned things.

Benson sighed, pulled a puzzled face and shook his head. 'You've been out in the sun too long.'

I said, 'I sure as hell have been *somewhere* too long!'

Benson lay back. 'You'll forgive me, old

son, if I stick with reality. And the reality is that pretty damned soon Chang is going to get a bayonet rammed up his backside. And it'll be a toss-up who delivers it. However,' he added, 'And for whatever it's worth to you, me and those bloody birds over there, I don't think Santana has joined the mutiny. Just about everyone else has, but not him. Oh, and maybe Jamie Carlisle.'

I said, 'That's the way I figure it, too.' I closed my eyes. 'So that makes you, me, Jamie and Santana the good guys.'

Benson chuckled. 'The *stupid* guys might just be closer to the truth . . . '

We slept as we lay.

I woke up to the racket of ten million flamingos scrambling noisily into the air. We sat up. I saw what had caused the panic. There was a canoe out there in the middle of the river. But it was a canoe with an outboard motor. I didn't hear it, not straight away, but the flamingos had. Then I heard the phut-phut of its exhaust.

Benson said, 'Only three hours late!'

The canoe with its single occupant angled towards the clearly visible helicopter. We grabbed our weapons and wandered down to the river. We must have looked ridiculous holding damned great guns with not a stitch of clothing on.

It was a girl.

Me and Benson exchanged puzzled glances. She appeared to be Eurasian. About twenty, twenty-five. And as pretty as a picture. She was dressed in blue jeans and Coca-Cola sweatshirt. A forage cap protected her head from the sun, but on her it looked like a bonnet. She nosed the canoe onto the sand and cut the engine. She did not seem at all put out to have two guns aimed at her midriff. Quite the reverse.

'You look silly,' she said in a husky voice. She was not smiling.

Benson, all business, asked, 'You 'Star Sapphire'?'

'Star Sapphire'. Chang's codename.

She said, 'He is my brother. Who are you? Why have you no clothes on?'

Benson said, 'I'm 'Battle'. The identification word, which took care of all the spy clutter.

She nodded. 'Yes.' Then, as if she had been holding it back until that moment, she smiled openly. Her eyes almost made it, but not quite. She said, 'But you do look silly.'

Her English was near perfect, with a trace of what I took to be Afrikaans thrown in. I don't know why, but she averted her eyes while we dressed. The flamingos drifted back in for another mass landing.

Benson said, 'You ready to go?' He seemed to have found another inch in height and was all teeth. And, though he didn't have a single ounce of excess fat on his body, I was certain he was holding his stomach in. Sex was rearing its complicated head.

She said, 'I'm not going with you. I came because my brother could not. I have news, but I must return.' Me and Benson looked at each other. The first hitch. Chang was expecting a face-to-face chat with someone. But that was not our problem. I said,

'Okay. So what have you got for us?'

She said, 'My brother says that the most important news is that Patch has lost his American support. We do not know why or how this happened, but Robert Urundi is now on his own.'

I smiled an inward smile. The playing field had levelled out.

She went on, 'It all threw Patch into a turmoil. He is moving his forward base over to Tengo Junction. He is at full strength at the moment.'

Tengo. So it was a good bet that those tyre tracks belonged to Patch. It was a confirmation of sorts. I'm not a great believer in arbitrary coincidence.

The girl frowned, as if she'd gotten the message back to front. Which, apparently, she had. 'No, that is not so. Robert Urundi is sending him more irregulars. To Tengo. About a hundred, we think. But these men are still at the base at the moment. Bhama tribesmen, and all well armed.'

Benson chuckled. 'Bhamas can't hit the inside of a barn from the inside. They're no problem. Anything else?'

The girl nodded. 'Patch is planning an attack on your compound . . . soon!'

Benson pulled a face. 'Is he? The cheeky swine!'

She shot him a blank look, gave a little shake of her head, and went on, 'Patch has — ' She clucked her tongue. '*Had* — aircraft. My brother thinks they were the property of the United States military. He can no longer utilize them. But he does still have access to Robert Urundi's helicopter and pilot.'

Benson nodded. 'That's Pete Gother. I know the man. Good pilot. But if it's the same aircraft he was flying last year, it's only a six seater. Max! Patch isn't going to move many bodies with that!'

The girl nodded, but I don't think she knew what she was nodding at. She said, 'So that's another big problem he has.' She seemed to be wracking her brain to get the message right. Then her expression cleared.

She said, 'Do you have a cigarette?'

Benson near fell over himself to oblige. I guessed it had been a long time since he'd fallen over himself to oblige a girl. I hadn't fallen over myself to oblige a girl for longer than I cared to remember. There was obviously hope for Benson yet.

There was no hope at all for me. This girl was gorgeous, with a really stunning figure. And I felt nothing at all. Beyond, that was, the fact that I was recognizing beauty for its own sake. I couldn't figure out whether that was good or bad. There had been a time . . .

When the girl was lit she went on, 'Patch had a meeting with one of your . . . ' a slight frown, ' . . . section leaders? Is that right?' It was not merely the terminology she was struggling with. There was something else.

I said, 'That's what we call them.' Benson, his eyebrows falling, glanced at me and was about to make some comment or other. I went on, 'That much we know.'

Benson's face displayed disbelief. He said, 'Do we? Is this a face-to-face meeting we're discussing here?'

I nodded. 'Yes, that kind.'

He frowned. 'You knew about it?'

'I did.'

His frown deepened. 'Who . . . Nessie or Curly?'

'Nessie.'

He looked staggered. 'Well, that's a horse of a wildly different colour!'

I told him the bones of Nessie's revelation.

He whistled softly. 'Jesus! I didn't think it had gone that far!' He said that to himself. It was obvious that though Nessie and Curly had dropped a few choice words in Benson's direction, they had fallen short of fully confiding in him, which, from their angle, would be fair enough.

The girl seemed relieved about something. I couldn't work out what it may have been, but I had a feeling that there was something being deliberately left unsaid. And if Benson had been looking at her eyes instead of her breasts he might have seen it for himself. Anyhow, I figured that if she didn't want to tell us, then she didn't have to.

I said, 'You don't have any *good* news for us, do you?'

She seemed to perk up. Just a shade. She said, 'But this is good news! My brother says that when the news of the Americans came through, Patch had to alter his plans very quickly, and that Tengo Junction is not really the place he wanted to use. He was very angry.'

Benson put in, 'Shame for him.'

The subtleties of the aside were lost on the

girl. And the perk-up went as quickly as it had come. She went on, 'My brother thinks that if you attack Tengo Junction soon — now! — before Patch can . . . ' Again, she searched for a lost word.

'Regroup?' obliged Benson.

The girl frowned a very attractive frown. 'Is that the word?'

I said, 'Probably.'

She said, 'Well, if you can do this, Patch will be caught unawares and unready.'

I said, 'The day Patch can be caught with his trousers down will be the day.'

For my pains, I received one of the looks Benson had been receiving. Then, for no reason that I could discern, the girl's eyes went suddenly moist. She looked from me to Benson, then back again. Her mouth opened a crack as if she were going to say something else. But she didn't. She just stood there like a girl I used to know who cried a lot.

Benson, to his credit, noticed the transformation. He leant in towards her, his hand outstretched. 'What is it? Are you okay?'

She nodded. But she was not okay.

And Benson should have left well enough alone.

My guess was that the girl had barely dented her twenties. But something in the back of her eyes was a million years old, and that part of her, or so it seemed to me, wanted out.

I figured she was pregnant or something. Girls who are pregnant often cry for no reason at all. It's biological, I guess. Either way, I was silently urging Benson to back off. He didn't back off. He craned forward and held her shoulder lightly.

'What's the problem, love?'

Love!

Hellfire and buckets of blood!

She shook her head, her lips trembling.

Look out! I thought, and I turned my attention to the flamingos, who seemed oblivious to it all. And probably were. Except, perhaps, that because of us they were getting a whole lot more exercise than they would any normal working day. And I kept my eyes on the flamingos as the girl let the dam break.

She broke her young heart.

And Benson made it worse by coddling her. When you're feeling sorry for yourself there's no better fuel than to have someone coddle you. A couple of times she tried to stem the flow, and she may have made it if Benson hadn't kept shoving his oar in.

'Don't worry . . . ' he kept insisting.

I think both of us — me and the girl — were puzzled about what it was she *didn't* have to worry about. She calmed down a bit in the end. Except that it was not to be the end. Benson, almost beside himself, said, 'You can't go back there! You're in no condition — '

She bit back a fresh onrush of tears like a trooper. Except that few troopers have onrushes of tears.

She said, 'I — I must. You don't understand . . . '

Benson looked at me. 'Jesus, Marty! A girl like this, in there with Patch and his cut-throats . . . '

In hindsight, that was the one thing he should not have said. And we pretty soon found out why. She began,

'No, really. I'm alright. But I have to go back. Robert Urundi must not be allowed to — '

She broke her heart again and it all came out. I had already guessed the guts of it. They were half-castes, her and her brother. Dutch father, hence the hint of Afrikaans in her accent, and a Matabele mother. Apparently Urundi had shot the father, along with several other whites who had decided to settle in that country. I forget why, now.

What I found significant to the latest outburst was that Patch himself had finished the mother. He'd raped her, then slit her throat. Which was Patch's style when he wasn't hanging dogs with very thin wire.

I actually wished that her story had moved me the way it had Benson. Maybe I'd seen more than Benson. Such stories grow on bushes in Africa. Anyway, at last the girl seemed to catch hold of herself, which I personally found a relief.

Benson said, 'Well, you aren't going back in there. No way!' All stern and commanding.

The girl said, 'I must . . . I *am*!'

So much for stern and commanding.

And there was no arguing with her. She and her brother had jobs to do, and that was very definitely that. But she did look kindly on Benson. Treating him to a smile that would have melted plastic, she said, 'I know you are only doing this for the money.' She reached for his arm. 'But I thank you anyway. And I plead with you . . . with you both . . . '

Thanks very much!

'Be very careful. You have poisonous vipers in your midst.'

I would have been more surprised to learn that the snakes we had in our midst were of the *non*-poisonous variety.

Benson, I guess for something to say, said, 'Well, I sure am doing it for the money. But there's a damned good reason.' And he told her about his surf school dream. Then he

146

said, 'But the banana standing beside me isn't!'

She turned her watery eyes on me. 'You don't do it for the money?'

I said, 'I'm getting paid for it.' I wished Benson had not broached the subject.

The girl studied my face minutely. 'But this is not your only reason?'

I shrugged. 'I can't think of another one.' Which, actually, was no lie.

She smiled in that way women have. 'You are not like Patch's mercenaries. You are . . . *different*.'

I didn't want to know what she meant by that, and I'd had enough of the mush talk. Firmly, I said, 'We're all mercenaries. Is there any other business?'

It did not require a genius to see that Benson would cheerfully have stayed there with her indefinitely. He had the beginnings of a stubborn look on his face, obviously smitten to his core. I raised an eyebrow at him. 'Chang?' I reminded him ironically. 'Mtomo? B-Company? Remember them?'

Without another word the girl leant in to Benson and kissed him lightly on the cheek, nodded me a cursory nod, then turned for her canoe. Benson looked panic-stricken. At any other time, I guessed, and in any other place, that would have been the start of some kind of relationship. But this was not a pleasure beach on some tropical island. The girl knew that. So, actually, did Benson. But he was fighting it. And I couldn't blame him.

As she unbeached her canoe, the girl called, 'If there is a next time, and it is I who meet you, perhaps you ought to remember your swimming costumes.'

7

Baker Section

Dusk that evening.

It rained for an hour, then it stopped.

The sky turned a livid red above the trees over on Pine Ridge Peak. They weren't actually pines over on the peak; they were cedar, or something. But from the compound they looked like pines. The air, for a change, was damp, but fresh. There had not been a lot of rain, but it was enough to soften the baked mud of the compound. Whatever you had on your feet doubled in weight, and size, every step you took. It would dry quickly, I knew that. But it was always a problem until it did. The area in the centre of the compound was laid with the same plastic mesh that had been used on the landing strip down at the airfield. This helped some. But not so's you'd notice.

Chang said, 'Our so-called Loch Ness Monster will be my next object lesson.'

We were in his office. Benson, after we had jointly delivered our report on the meeting with the girl, had been dismissed. It had not yet dawned on me that Curly, who would

149

normally have been part of such a debriefing, was not! Outside the window, the compound floodlights came on, spoiling the effect of the dying day.

I shrugged. Nessie's future was a matter of complete indifference to me. But I had not told Chang that I'd known about his meeting with Patch beforehand. It was my own version of the need-to-know — or was it the need-to-*tell* — principle.

I said, 'What are you going to do about Patch, Colonel?'

Chang rose up from his seat and walked to the window. He stood there for a few moments, gazing out at the evening activity, his hands held loosely behind his back, his fingers toying with the perfumed cigarette. The smoke tasted sickly and I wasn't smoking. He sighed a deep sigh.

'Star Sapphire is correct. If we can give him a thorough mauling now, we could turn the tables completely. One thing is absolutely certain; he will not be allowed the opportunity to trespass any further south than Tengo. And, as for launching an attack *here* . . . .' He let that hang in the air. Then, almost to himself, he added, 'Mtomo will be pleased to hear that the Americans have withdrawn their favour.' He turned. 'I wonder why they did that?'

I took it to be a rhetorical remark, well above my pay grade, and simply lifted a shoulder. I wondered whether or not this might be a good time to mention Curly's transgressions. I decided against it. There would never be a good time for that. Curly was Chang's 2i/c, not mine. And if I had learned anything from my military career — regular and latterly — it was never to volunteer anything — words or service. And it was only then that I became aware of Curly's absence, and what it might mean. I vaguely wondered if something had gone down while we had been out at the coast. But I wasn't about to pursue that subject. I rose up.

I said, 'Well, that about covers it from my angle, Colonel. Anything else?'

Chang pulled a thoughtful face. 'Not for the moment. I'll radio Mtomo straight away. If this is to be a full scale action — and it looks very much as though it will be just that — then he'll need to be here.' His eyebrows fell. 'I'd be obliged if you would keep everyone within hailing distance. If Mtomo decides to fly up, I'll need all officers for a briefing.' There it was again. It was an instruction you would give a 2i/c. So why wasn't his 2i/c here? I wondered if it was a merely a slip, wishful thinking or simply expediency.

'That's Curly's job,' I said, a shade more forcibly that I had meant to. I added, 'But I'll tell him if I see him.'

Chang treated me to a crooked smile that had an evil twist to it. And I wondered if, somehow, he actually knew it all. 'Yes, indeed,' he breathed, the crooked smile still pulling at his mouth. 'Of course you are right. It most certainly *is* Captain Parsons's job . . . '

I let that lay where it fell. Which was a cop-out on my part, of course. The direction Curly took could be everyone's problem. Mine included. But, from the personal angle, I was figuring that forewarned was fore-armed. Right at that moment, however, I wouldn't have had Chang's job as a gift. Curly's loyalty was, at the very least, a question mark to him, or he would have been there at that moment. Even if Chang did not know specifics. I was now certain of that. And Curly was his second in command! How the hell do you run a business when you're not sure who you can pass your instructions through! With that thought came memory of the sealed envelope. I thought, *That's* how! And the ducks started to line up for me. To say that Chang was a man with a lot on his mind, would have been an understatement.

Chang seemed to shake himself mentally.

'Yes, please do that.'

I nodded, hesitated a heartbeat to see if there was any more. There didn't seem to be. So I gave Chang a loose salute, and left. The so-called parade ground was not the only thing that had turned into a quagmire.

The compound appeared to be full of men doing things. I knew that Jamie Carlisle had taken his section, Echo, out on a patrol to scout the track north, but the rest of B-Company was *in situ* and open for business.

Benson was tinkering with his steed over by the helicopter pad. There was someone with him but I could not make out who it was. Rama, I guessed. Santana was berating a detail of his blacks in the middle of the square. Someone else — it looked like Maud Peroni — was drilling the new intake over by the east wall. All six gun towers around the compound were fully manned. Jimmy was up there in one of them.

There was a hullabaloo coming from the mess and tinny rock music coming from somewhere else. Everywhere, someone appeared to be doing something. If Patch had chosen that moment to throw us an air strike — assuming he could put one together — he could have virtually wiped B-Company off the map. I wondered which one of us was Patch's man-on-the-spot. He would have one, that was fairly certain. The way Chang had Star Sapphire. Nessie was the prime suspect, of course. But he was no spy; he was simply a renegade. The problem, of course, would be communication. If we had to take long helicopter trips to get our information, then Patch would have similar difficulties.

A couple of guys were changing a tyre of one of the trucks, and not having an easy time of it on the softened mud, whilst a couple of Bedford three-tonners were being off-loaded over in front of the ammo store. It was a few moments before I realized who was doing the unloading. It was Baker-Section, my section, back from up country. I had a quiet smile to myself, lit up a cigarette and leant back against the wall of Chang's office block to watch.

'Ginger' Wood and 'Smarmy' Patterson had wangled themselves into the overseers' position, whilst Chas MacDevvitt, Ming Kiang, 'Harley' Davidson and my black contingent, which included a couple of the more astute Askaris I had been able to snatch, were doing the donkey work. I was actually glad to see them. Not glad enough, however, to want to go over there and get involved. I needed some time to myself. So I left them to it and wandered in the other direction.

As I passed the chopper Benson called, 'So what's happening?'

Rama was up in the body of the helicopter, hammering at something. I nodded in that direction and pulled a zip across my mouth. Benson stepped out to meet me. Quietly, he said, 'Rama's okay.'

I said, 'So is the Pope. But there's stuff you want to hang out on the line, and stuff you don't. Let's keep the field narrow, huh?'

He nodded. 'Fair play. So, what did he say? Chang.'

I said, 'Nothing positive yet. He's dragging Mtomo up to date. Then I guess we'll see.'

Benson wiped a spot of oil from his nose with his oily rag. His nose turned black. He said, 'Well, I think someone ought to do something. I've got this *naked* feeling . . . ' he grunted, ' . . . again!' I knew that in his mind's eye he would be visualizing the girl. I personally couldn't bring a single one of her characteristics to mind. Which was sad. He went on, 'Something to do with keeping eggs in baskets.' He waved an arm over the busy compound. 'Three well-placed bombs and it's goodnight nurse!'

Goodnight nurse.

Benson's term for anything final.

I nodded. 'Jamie's out keeping an eye on the back door, if that makes you feel any easier.'

He grunted. 'It's the bloody *front* door I'm worrying about!' He added, 'What's Chang going to do about Nessie?'

I shrugged. 'Says he's going to use him for his next lecture.'

Benson smiled. 'Where is he now?'

'Who? Nessie?'

'Yes.'

'I don't have the first clue. Halfway to Bombay, if he's got any sense.'

As if on cue the din over in the mess swelled suddenly. Nessie's raucous guffaw stood out a mile. I said, 'Does that answer your question?'

Benson studied the screwdriver he held in his left hand. 'It's all going to end in tears, y'know.'

'But whose?' I said. 'That's what I'd like to know.'

I walked on.

Santana was yelling, 'C'mon you fucking useless black bastards! Pick your fucking feet up!' Which was no easy task in that sludge.

One of them fell over.

The rest laughed.

Santana heaved the fallen man to his feet. The man was big, as big as Nessie. Santana looked like a midget beside him. I didn't catch what Santana said to him, but the blacks, who'd crowded around, laughed again.

I glanced in the mess door.

They were playing the damned cigarette game again, where two guys, bare right forearms pressed together, dropped a lighted cigarette into the flesh 'V'. The first to pull away was supposed to be the sissy and bought the drinks. At the moment the protagonists were Nessie and some guy I didn't recognize.

B-Company was all drunks and burn-scarred forearms.

Curly was one of the onlookers. He saw me and stepped over, drink in hand.

'What's happening?'

I looked at him and wondered. I said, 'You're the adjutant, Curly. You tell me. Oh, Chang wants to see you.'

Curly laughed a self-conscious laugh and his eyes flashed over the compound to Chang's office. 'Right. Well . . . ' He seemed reluctant. 'I suppose I'd better get over there.'

I said, 'Might be an idea.'

Curly stood there for a few moments, staring hard at me. I could see the questions forming behind his eyes. Curly was a worried man, which would have been something of an about-face. He said, 'How was the trip?' His unconcerned expression was forced. He was fishing.

I shrugged a nonchalant shrug. 'Out and back, no problems.' I smiled. 'Did a bit of surfing.'

'Great,' he said, with a brave attempt at enthusiasm.

Another pause.

Then he said, 'Right.' He swallowed the dregs of his drink, placed the glass on a nearby table, straightened his combat jacket, looked at me, looked again over at Chang's window, then stepped out past me. I watched him plod his way through the mire. I'm not sure what thoughts were going through my mind as he disappeared behind one of the trucks. But sympathy was not one of them.

Nessie won the cigarette game. Everyone applauded and cheered. I didn't wait there to be seen by him. I had nothing to say to Nessie.

Next to the mess was the stockade; the holding area for defaulters and prisoners alike. It was a cussed place to put a stockade, since the inmates, even if they didn't speak a word of English, could hear people having fun less than a spit away. The place stank like an open sewer. I caught a glimpse of a head of blonde hair at one of the barred windows. Then I saw the face beneath it. I did not recognize the man as one of ours. Vaguely interested, I step closer to the window.

'Who are you?' I asked, not unkindly.

The blonde guy shoved his face close to the bars. He spat, 'Piss off!'

I nodded. 'Fine,' and walked on.

Santana was yelling, 'You stupid great hairy black bozo! You do that again, I'm gonna skin you a-fucking-live!'

He must have been taking elocution lessons from Jimmy. One of his blacks had dropped his weapon. Don't ask me why, but the blacks seemed to enjoy working for Santana, and I guess Santana enjoyed working with them. A shrink might call it a love-hate relationship.

Amazing.

By the time I reached the ammo store the unloading was done and everyone except Ginger Wood and Smarmy Patterson had left. These two were sitting on the running board of the truck having a smoke.

Wood stood up and offered me a loose salute. 'Did you miss us, sir?'

I nodded. 'Like a toothache. How'd it go?'

Wood shrugged. 'Piece of piss.'

Patterson dragged himself tiredly to his feet. 'Well, I'm bolloxed, for one!'

I said, 'It's news I'm after, Patterson, not history. You're always bolloxed.'

Wood said, 'What's happening, sir?'

I said, 'Wood, the next man who asks me

that question gets my bayonet rammed up his arse!'

Wood blinked and just looked at me.

I said, 'Where are the rest of the squad?'

Patterson answered. 'Back at the billet, sir. Getting cleaned up.' Smarmy had earned that nickname because he used some kind of oil to keep his hair in place. For my money, if he had to be nicknamed at all, it should have been 'Elvis', because that's who he resembled.

Wood, who looked like a mushroom pizza, his face all spots and blemishes, said, 'Are we going out again?'

Alan 'Ginger' Wood was twenty-something, with the kind of eyes that made it look as if his parents came from Taipan. His hair, naturally, was ginger, and style-wise he plumped for a crew cut. Like Khan, Wood was solid and dependable. He was British and had served with a parachute regiment. I don't know why he quit. A simple matter of money, I think.

On the edge of my vision I saw Curly step out of Chang's office and plod over the parade ground in the direction of Maud and his gathering of recruits. At the very least he, Curly, was still at the vertical. I wondered what had transpired in Chang's office.

To Wood, I said, 'Maybe.'

160

He said, 'The big one?'

I looked at him. 'Do we ever get any small ones, Wood?'

He frowned. 'Yes, but — '

I cut in, 'You probably know more than I do. What does the scuttlebutt say?'

He and Smarmy exchanged knowing glances. They had been doing what soldiers do. They had been talking, and they had been listening. I wondered if they had actually *heard*. If they had, and they asked me about it, I would not have had a helpful response for them. So I changed the subject. 'Incidentally, Wood, you're 2i/c now.'

Wood, my only other two-striper, nodded. 'I guessed that, sir.' He pulled a face. 'It's a pure-bred sod about Ron, though. How'd it happen?'

I told them.

They stood there looking glum for a few moments. Then Smarmy said, 'That'll larn 'im!'

Wood ventured, 'Any more loot in it for me, sir?'

I said, 'It's nice to see you've got your priorities stacked up right.'

I used to wonder why the bulk of Curly's conscripts were British, until I remembered that Curly was British. I said, 'You'll get more bucks if you do a good job.'

Wood nodded. 'Fair enough, sir.'

I said, 'And you can start by keeping the section in some kind of order.' I added, 'For a change.'

Wood smiled. 'For a change.'

I said, 'Right, cut along. Do a weapons check straight away. Keep all the guys together and I'll be there myself in thirty minutes.'

I walked on.

Maud came running over. He slithered to a stop and threw me a salute. 'Curly says your section gets half the cherries, sir. Where d'you want me to throw them?'

I glanced out over the floodlit square in time to see Curly disappearing into the mess again. No doubt he and Nessie would be putting their heads together with a vengeance now.

Maud went on without waiting for a reply. 'I'm sorry about Pearce, sir. He was a good man.'

I nodded. 'Luck of the draw, Peroni. Anything promising in the new batch?'

Maud pulled a face. 'A couple of them are young enough to've attracted my personal attention. But, mostly, they're okay. Not a civvie amongst them, which is something. Two Yanks, if you're interested.' He added a quick, 'Which I know you're not! They'll fight, sir.'

Peroni did not come over like a fairy. Because he wasn't one. He was homosexual. But in my experience of him he was a very private homosexual, and aside from wondering why he seemed to revel in his nickname, you might never have known his sexual preferences. He had served with some regiment of the medical corps. In uniform he looked like a lady-killer.

I said, 'Run them over to B-spider and pass them to Wood. He's my 2i/c now.'

Maud saluted and trotted off.

Santana yelled, '*That's* how I want you to fucking do it, you great useless dumbos! Now let's try it again!'

Outside the walls of the compound a dog was barking.

8

Mtomo

Unlike most African hopefuls I had worked for, Mtomo did not wear a uniform. He dressed the way you'd expect to see a Wall Street financier dressed. He certainly lived that part. His house, on the shore of Lake Ngomo, was a small palace. Only politicians and the super-rich lived up there. He wore a black, pin-stripe suit, grey silk tie and white shirt. His well-tailored jacket was not buttoned, but I suspected that was so we could catch glimpses of the red suspenders. He had squeaky new shoes on his feet and wasn't too comfortable with them yet. They were caked in mud. The flower in his buttonhole — a Devil's Thorn, I seem to remember — screamed ambiguous overkill. He was an effect that didn't come off. But I did not hold that against him. Rather him the way he was than resplendent in some bemedalled general's uniform to which he had absolutely no right. I put his age at somewhere around fifty-five, but he could have been anywhere within — or *without*

— ten years of that. I figured he had a gut but was holding it at bay with a stomach band of some sort.

But he was a big man, about six-six, and broad shouldered. He looked very powerful and probably was. His voice was the voice of a man who expected to be listened to. Though I had been in the same space with him several times, we had never exchanged more than a few words. I wondered vaguely whether Chang had brought him *fully* up to speed. I actually doubted it. Problems like that, whatever the cause or circumstance, could be construed as failing leadership.

'We may never have a better opportunity to deal our so-called Admiral Patch a major blow,' he said.

There were seven of us in Chang's office. Mtomo, Chang, Curly, looking as sullen as a teenager who'd been grounded, Nessie, who merely looked thoughtful, Santana, Jamie Carlisle, and myself. Except for Mtomo, we were all in full combat fatigues, ready to go. All we needed was a plan.

Mtomo was standing because he chose to stand.

Santana was standing because Chang's office boy had been unable to rustle up enough seats.

Mtomo moved over to the map on the wall.

'Let's see,' he began. 'Tengo Junction. That's ... ' his sausage-like forefinger hovered over the map.

Santana said, 'Up a bit.' Then he added, 'Sir.'

The finger moved up the map. 'Ah, yes. There.' He tapped the spot. 'Hilly terrain, as I recall. Mountainous in places.' His English had a trace of the States in it. I could never make out whether he laid that on or not. His fingers did a tap-dance on the map, then he turned to Chang.

'Am I correct in assuming that he has never ventured this deep into our territory before?'

Chang nodded. 'Not *this* deep.'

Mtomo hmm'd and turned back to the map, treating the area to another finger dance. It was something of an act, of course, I understood that. He and Chang had had at least an hour together before we were summoned. I couldn't think what *else* they would have discussed in that time.

Mtomo waggled his head, as if in deep thought. Then he seemed to come to a decision. 'Dependent upon what we decide here, Colonel, how long would you need to get there?'

Chang said, 'Three, four hours in the trucks, if we push hard. Less than thirty minutes by air.'

Mtomo nodded sagely.

That, he put on. There was nothing sage about Joshua Mtomo. He turned to us. 'Well, the quicker we arrive at some degree of accord, the better. Colonel Chang assures me that, for the moment, we hold the element of surprise. With that . . . ' he smiled broadly, ' . . . and swift, decisive action, we will carry the day.' The smile vanished as he went on. 'This will have to be a full-scale operation, gentlemen. Command versus command. Anything piecemeal would be doomed to eventual failure.' The smile reappeared momentarily. 'A clash of the titans, eh! A glorious grand finale!' He looked at each of us, his eyebrows raised to the question. He was expecting some kind of a reaction. He received none. A look of slight annoyance crossed his face. Then he went on, 'I have some fifty or so, ah, volunteers, coming up by road. Askaris. Not *fully* trained yet, but useful, no?'

Barely trained militia were about as useful as corns. These would be men of Mtomo's ever-expanding personal bodyguard. Chang, for his own reasons, nodded. 'In this case, I think, yes. If it is to be a full-scale assault we will need every gun we can lay our hands on.'

Mtomo nodded. He seemed happy about that. 'They should arrive before midnight.

Gentlemen,' he went on, 'I do not need to tell you just how important this mission could be. Rout Patch now, and we win the war. No question!' He glared around the room. 'A single throw of the dice.'

Again, he paused for effect and received nothing for his pains. I was beginning to feel a shade embarrassed for him.

He tried again. 'I repeat, gentlemen, hit Patch hard now and you could finish him. Colonel Chang believes a strike is possible without too heavy losses. And I am prepared to accept his judgement. If you succeed . . . ' a pause and a slightly apologetic smile, ' . . . *when*, you succeed, you will find yourselves very rich people indeed. This I personally guarantee.'

Not even a flicker of a smile from anyone. That tired carrot had been used far too often. Generally preceding a request for some kind of a suicide mission.

Jamie Carlisle said, 'I suppose our intelligence is sound, sir?'

Jamie was ex-British navy. But that was just about all I knew about him, despite having known him for some considerable time. That was strange. But it was simply that, short of day-to-day work, our paths had never seemed to cross on a social level. I guess that happens sometimes. He certainly had the look and the bearing of a man I could have shared beers with. But it had never happened.

Nessie's eyes flickered for a moment and I guessed he was asking himself that same question. He would no doubt have been thinking that only *his* intelligence was sound. He had, after all, been in direct contact with Patch a few days before. And I was fairly certain that Chang would not have brought Curly up to date on the news we had brought back from the girl. So they would both, Nessie and Curly, be wondering what the hell had happened to warrant this sudden flurry of activity.

Mtomo — looking even more peeved that his sweetener had not been accepted with greater enthusiasm — with *any* enthusiasm, passed Jamie's point over to Chang with an incline of his pumpkin head.

Chang said, 'Undoubtedly,' and left it at that.

Jamie did not look convinced. With the possible exceptions of Curly and Nessie, whose minds would be travelling their own routes, I don't think any of us was convinced. We would be committing the entire command on the second-hand maybe of one girl. Certainly she had convinced me, back on the beach, that she believed what she was telling us. But, in hindsight, who was to say that she

169

had not been purposely fed the news as a clever piece of disinformation? Hindsight is wonderful, if only it could be summoned *before* the event!

Mtomo said, 'Before I leave you to thrash out tactics, are there any further questions?'

No one spoke.

He nodded. 'Very well.' He turned to Chang. 'I will wait in your quarters, if this is agreeable to you.'

Chang nodded. 'Of course.'

Mtomo clumped out of the room, probably thinking what an unimaginative bunch of mercenary soldiers we all were.

So we got down to cases.

And after an hour or so we had a semblance of a plan together. It was full of ifs and maybes, but it was the best we could do. At the very least it brought everyone to the right spot on the map at the right moment in time. It was not a battle-plan, it was more a simple itinerary. Battle plans would be down to seat-of-the-pants decisions taken on the spot when we knew the disposition of Patch's command. If, indeed he was there at all! But it involved everyone able to carry a weapon. Chang himself would command the airborne segment, whilst I had the ground assault. This was fine with me. I'm not sure it was fine with Nessie or Curly, who refrained from advancing any ideas at all. They both just sat there and listened.

The few wounded we had in the compound would be Mtomo's responsibility. He would have to relinquish sole rights on his helicopter for a few trips to God knows where. The compound, for at least twenty-four hours, promised to be empty of everything but the lizards, cooks and cleaners. At the end of it all Chang caught my eye and tacitly told me to be the last out the door. It was not a hard message to pick up since I'd been expecting it.

Chang, when we were alone, said, 'About our problem . . . '

I said, 'Yes?'

He said, 'It is unfortunate that I need every trained man I can lay my hands on. I certainly cannot afford to rob a section of its leader at this late stage.'

I nodded. 'Sure.' He seemed to be apologizing to me and I wondered why.

He went on, 'If we had more time . . . ' He let that hang in the air. Then he pulled a face. 'I simply do not know what Parsons and Bridges are planning.'

His use of both their given names, as opposed to adding their rank, was significant to something. But I didn't know what. I put in, 'D'you think they have a plan? A specific one?'

Chang looked at me, sucked in a breath and let it out slowly. 'I only know that there remains the possibility that we could be walking into a trap.' Which statement, I thought, was a refreshing piece of reality.

I said, 'Yep. That certainly is a possibility. I guess it depends upon how much you trust your mole.'

'Star Sapphire?' said Chang, looking slightly puzzled. 'Oh, I have implicit trust in *him*! No, captain, my problem is that I have been unable to discover the identity of Patch's eyes and ears here.' Chang tapped his forefinger on the desk. 'In *this* command!' He grunted. 'And I discount the two aforementioned entirely in this respect. They are the devil I *know*! It is the *unknown* conspirator that concerns me more.'

I said, 'Yep. That would scare the shit out of me too! But what do you do about it, Colonel? Call off the strike?'

Chang sucked his lip. 'By God, I would like to! But this opportunity is just too promising to miss. No, I have to grab the chance, and carry it through. And quickly!'

I had never doubted that. I said, 'So lock them both in the stockade for the duration.'

He said, 'And who runs their sections?'

I said, 'Promote someone else.'

He sucked in another long breath. 'Would you, Captain? Would you do that, at this late moment, as things are, if you were me?'

I was getting slightly angry. Suddenly it was all being heaped onto my shoulders. I said, 'I'm not you, Colonel. I'm me! I'm not in charge. You are! Curly is *your* damned adjutant!' But I knew exactly where Chang was at.

More mildly than I had been expecting, considering my outburst, he said, 'I made a mistake with Parsons. I freely admit to it. Everyone makes mistakes from time to time. That man was one of mine.'

I did not actually think that was entirely true. Curly was good at the job he had been hired to do. His fall from grace had come later, and dictated by circumstances. Chang should have seen it coming and done something about it. But it was all water under the bridge now.

I said, 'So what are you going to do, Colonel?'

Chang said, 'I am going to watch Parsons as the hawk watches its prey. And I am asking you to do the same with Bridges.'

I smiled. 'That was *always* my plan, Colonel.' I did not yet have a clue how I was going to achieve a result as far as Nessie went, but I did know, with certainty, how it was going to end. And it would end before we even reached Tengo. It *had* to.

Chang walked over to the map, looked at it for a moment, then turned back to me. 'There is one other thing.'

'And that is?'

Chang paused for a moment, then lowered his eyebrows and said, 'Whichever way the engagement goes, Patch — ' Here, he seemed to switch his direction. 'I want Patch alive!'

I looked at him. 'You want Patch alive.' I repeated. I was reminded of Nessie's instruction up country.

Chang nodded. 'Alive.'

I said, 'Win or lose.'

Chang nodded again. 'It is imperative.'

I let loose a sigh of my own. I said, 'Well, Colonel, I want him as dead as dead people come. In fact, people don't *come* any deader than I want Patch. You *know* it!' I added, 'So where does *that* leave us?'

Chang smiled a very thin smile. 'This coming battle, as you well realize, and if the worst comes to the worst, could be the end of B-Company.'

I grunted. I doubted that such an occurrence would rate a page-five mention in *The Minton Sentinel*. I come from Minton. And *The Minton Sentinel* only runs to four pages. I nodded. 'It could well be just that, Colonel.'

Chang continued, 'Yet it could also remain simply another battle in Mtomo's war. Without Patch, Robert Urundi will be nothing. He would have to begin the business over again. More or less from the start. Mtomo could still pull something from the fire.'

I did not get what he was saying. I said, 'I see that. But I still want Patch dead. In fact I'm going to kill him myself. That can't make the slightest difference to Mtomo's future plans. Patch out of the picture, is Patch out of the picture. Alive, or dead. Right, Colonel?'

Chang sighed heavily and looked down at the floor. At last he said, 'If only it were that simple . . . ' He held a just-a-moment finger in the air, picked up one of his telephones and asked Mtomo to step in. Less than a minute later Mtomo came in the room.

He said, 'Well?' He was looking at Chang.

I had the feeling that Mtomo knew exactly what subject had been under discussion.

Chang said, 'Perhaps *you* would care to explain matters, Joshua.'

Mtomo pulled a face of tetchy annoyance and he shot me a single glance. 'It is simple, surely! I want Patch alive, whether the engagement is successful or otherwise.' He was saying it to Chang as if I was not in the room.

Chang said nothing. He sat himself down behind his desk and lit up a cigarette with, I thought, vaguely exaggerated movements, as if to let Mtomo know that he was disowning the problem. Mtomo, a non-smoker, crinkled up his nose even further and, with apparent reluctance, turned to me. He said, 'You have some objection?' It was obvious that he knew damned-well I had an objection.

I wondered why he wasn't asking about the plans we may have come up with. Of the two subjects I figured that would have been the more important. But he didn't seem at all interested in that. Fine. I said, 'Sir, win or lose, I'm going to slit Patch's guts for him. If I get half a chance.'

Mtomo sighed an exasperated sigh. 'And if you are *ordered* to bring him in alive? What then?'

I thought, that's the last 'Sir' you're going to get from me! I said, 'If we win, you won't need him, because we will have won. If we lose, I don't see where it'll make a lot of difference. We got ifs crawling all over us. By dawn tomorrow we won't need any more ifs. And it is simple: if I get Patch in my sights, I'm going to pull the trigger. Then I'm going to slit his guts. I'm not going to be overly concerned with ifs. Because, if we get that far we will have used up all the good ifs . . . '

I was surprised at how readily I was warming to the subject.

I went on, 'And here's another thing; I could say whatever you want me to say . . . here and now. That would be easy. But I've only got to come out of the bad side of a bad if, and it'll mean nothing in any case. Besides which — *forgive me* — there is no way on God's suffering planet you can instruct seventy-odd men, plus a load of trigger-happy irregulars, to be careful where they place their bullets. If it looks like we're coming out on top, B-Company is going to be seeing nothing but red . . . blood!' I felt my mouth curl into a snarl. 'I wouldn't put it past them to start killing *each other*, once they get the taste in their mouths! And if it looks like we've blown it, the result will be the same. They'll go down screaming blue-bloody-murder, killing until they don't have the strength, or the active red cells, to kill any more! I'll take one of those, Colonel, if I may.'

I suddenly needed a smoke, perfumed or otherwise. Chang's mouth gave a twitch, I thought of amusement. But I could have been wrong. He actually lit one up and handed it to me. I sucked at it greedily, then fired my final salvo at Mtomo.

'This is not going to be a Sunday picnic, *mister* Mtomo! It's going to be a bloodbath. Start to finish. No prisoners. No quarter. Get it?'

Mtomo, his face set in stone, looked at Chang. Chang looked back at Mtomo. Then he began to study the ash on his cigarette.

Silence reigned supreme.

Mtomo let out the breath he had been holding. Then, quietly, but with an edge of menace to his voice, he said to Chang, 'Must I accept that?'

Chang continued his study of the ash for a few moments. Then, without raising his eyes, he said calmly, 'The assurance you ask is one that I could not give myself, with the best will in the world. Even if we both — Captain Palmer and myself — agreed to what you ask, there could be no guarantee at all that Patch would not suffer a fatal bullet from any one of a hundred directions.'

Mtomo clucked his tongue. 'I do not ask for guarantees. I only ask that, if it is at all *possible,* you will bring Patch to me . . . alive.' He turned to me then. 'If we are unfortunate enough to lose the coming action my cause would still stand a chance, *if* I were to have Patch . . . alive and well.'

I said, 'Not that it would alter my plans

any. I'd be interested to hear why, and how . . . '

Here, he and Chang exchanged glances. Mtomo took a step towards me and he lowered his voice. 'Certain, ah, certain powers have indicated to me that if I can present Patch to them — *alive* — they would be prepared to, ah, assist me further.'

I wondered why he had lowered his voice.

'I gather,' he went on, 'that Patch could be useful to these people. In what way, I do not know. Nor do I care. I assume they would hold him up as some kind of a western puppet. A show-trial, or some such.'

That, actually, could figure. I said, 'The commies.'

Mtomo shrugged an exaggerated shrug. 'A struggle is a struggle. Help must be enlisted from any quarter that shows promise.' He waved an arm vaguely in the air. 'You, Colonel Chang here and the rest of this command, are here on a temporary basis only. For the duration, so to speak. Whilst I have more, um, long-term roots to contend with.' He hunched a shoulder. 'I do the best I can.'

Mtomo did not wait for a response from me, but turned back to Chang. 'So, would you agree that, if it seems *possible* to do so, you will deliver Patch to me?' He rushed on,

'If we succeed tomorrow — and I pray that this will be so — then I concede that Patch can be disposed of, as is seen fit. However, if you do not succeed . . . '

Neat, I thought. On the matter of defeat, it was 'you', whereas when success was the object, it was 'we'. I had to hand it to him.

Chang filled the pause. 'For myself,' he said, 'I will do my utmost to comply.' He did not glance at me.

But Mtomo did. 'And yourself?'

I ground the stub of the perfumed cigarette out in Chang's ashtray. I said, 'With no apology at all . . . I had Patch in my sights one time only. I didn't pull the trigger then, for a million reasons. The very least of which was my personal survival. Believe that! Believe also that I have remained a part of B-Company with — I *think* — only one thought in my mind: Getting him in my sights again. I could have gone over to Urundi and done a Jesse James job on Patch. In the back, without him even knowing who'd killed him, or why. But Patch is one mercenary I am not going to lie to. For preference, I want to look in his eyes when I kill him, and I want him to be looking into mine. No subterfuge, no play-acting.

'If that doesn't turn out to be possible,

then I'll have to settle for just killing him, whether he knows it's me or not. I won't lie to him, and I won't lie to you. If I get the chance, Patch does not walk away again!'

Mtomo looked at me long and hard. Then he said, 'And if we win and, somehow, Patch manages to escape? What then?'

That was a good point. But I couldn't see where it might be headed. I said, 'Then you can still count me in as a staunch member of B-Company. Business as usual. I'm not trying to be deliberately cussed here; I'm simply going to finish Patch if I see the chance. No frills. No time-lapses, no show trial, no third chances.'

I had a thought. One that, perhaps, I should have kept to myself. But I did not keep it to myself. 'But I guess there is still that other 'if'. The one that *could* make you a happy man.'

Mtomo lowered his eyebrows. 'Oh?'

I nodded. 'That's the, 'if I buy it before I even clap eyes on the man'. That if!'

Mtomo's eyes remained dull for a moment, then light seemed to dawn in them. His eyebrows came up and he glanced over at Chang. I thought, Palmer, you're a bloody fool! But I no longer cared.

Mtomo came back to me, a studiously blank expression on his face. He nodded briefly. 'Very well. I must accept all you say. That's all.'

And I was dismissed.

As I crossed the bustling square I wondered if Chang would agree to put a bullet in my back at the appropriate moment.

Sure he would.

No question.

9

The Road to Tengo

So Mtomo did get his parade after all.

At midnight.

Under the 8,000-watt glare of the compound floods, around which the flying insect nightlife swarmed in great suicidal snowstorms.

Against normal odds, it hadn't rained. The moon was a sharply defined silver disc high in the matt-black sky, so big you could see the mountain ranges on that peaceful planet. You could look up there and forget everything, and for a few moments I was back in the plush seat of a planetarium I had once visited. But moments like that don't last very long in the middle of a stinking jungle where the smell of gun oil was, for once, stronger than the stench of the rotting scenery.

All five sections of B-Company, plus a rank of the newly-arrived Askaris, who would be spread amongst us, were drawn up — neatly for a change — on three sides of the square. Each man wore tiger stripe camouflage battle dress, plus Kevlar helmet, plus all the other

183

equipment necessary for an incursion. The trucks and jeeps, facing outwards at the gate, constituted the fourth side of the square. Benson's helicopter was slap in the middle, whilst Mtomo's machine was parked over by the stockade.

I'm not sure what thoughts were in everyone's mind, but I think it was generally accepted that this could be the last time the compound would witness anything vaguely resembling a fighting force. No one had said as much, at least not in my hearing. There was just this strange air of finality. Or maybe it was just my own slant on the situation: I had very probably organized my own assassination. The thing was I didn't much care. Well, I *thought* I didn't!

The air was as still as death itself as Mtomo walked up and down the ranks of men, trying to look important. A word of encouragement here, an empty quip there. It was a valiant attempt at playing at real soldiers. At the end of it he shook Jamie Carlisle's hand and told him he had done a damned fine job. And, in terms of Jamie being our RSM, he had. I was mightily impressed with Jamie's work that night.

Chang could not think of what to do with the prisoners in the stockade. So he indulged in another of his personal object lessons. He knelt them down in front of the helicopter. Six of them.

'This man is the enemy.'

He gave them each a bullet to the back of the head. Including the blonde guy, who went out with another curse on his lips. I never did find out who he was or what he had done. These executions defied all the usual rules of war, of course, but they were another of Chang's solid motivational lectures, aimed, I think, at the Askaris. Do what you're told or you know what you can expect.

The so-called admin staff, including Chang's staff, Murphy, Rama and the other local guys, stood in a disconsolate group by the gate. With them were the half-dozen Askaris Chang was leaving behind to guard the compound. God alone knows what thoughts were going through *their* minds. I had no idea what they had been told, if they had been told anything at all! They could well be scratching around for a living before too long. Mtomo had a few private words with Chang then climbed into his helicopter. We all stood there at attention as he lifted off in a cloud of dust.

Able-Section.
Baker-Section.
Charlie-Section.
Dove-Section.

Echo-Section.

B-Company was about to determine its fate.

I, like a fool, had probably already determined mine!

★ ★ ★

Able, Baker and Charlie sections, augmented to a greater or lesser degree by the Askaris, piled into the trucks in a clatter of rattling equipment. Dove and Echo would follow in the chopper. Benson would have to make two trips. Maybe three if he couldn't find space for the reserve ammo. He was to put them down a few miles south of Tengo Junction, near an abandoned railway siding which had once served the copper mine.

By which time Able, Baker and Charlie sections should be close to their final positions for the assault. It was a simple plan with plenty of scope for improvisation when we knew the full score, but getting it to work would be far from simple.

I did not know what part Chang was going to take in the actual assault, and was not too bothered. He would no doubt slide himself in where and when he thought fit. All I knew for certain about his plans was that he was going to be within striking distance of Curly. He would then want to get within striking distance of *me*! And I don't know why I wasn't more concerned about that. Maybe it was some kind of subconscious denial of the truth. God knows I excelled at that recently.

I'd had a word with Jamie and seconded both Jimmy and Maud Peroni to the ground assault. I wanted Peroni with us for several reasons, not least of which was that we would more than likely require a medic before anyone else. Another reason was that I felt I could trust him. I had chosen Jimmy for that reason too. I placed Jimmy under Santana's command. Tonight, I would need people around me, or close to hand, that I could trust. With the obvious exception.

Wood drove the jeep. I sat alongside him, with a map. Nessie solved one of my problems by insisting upon riding with us in the space behind the seats. He may well have been thinking the same as me; keep the target in sight at all times. But it actually didn't matter to me *what* he was thinking. His fate was already sealed. So, probably, was my own.

The jeep was first out the gates. Santana was in the cab of the first truck behind us. Behind him, Peroni was at the wheel of another jeep. Everyone else was strung out in convoy behind.

Murphy's Café and Bar was in darkness, of course. But it already looked like something that had been deserted years ago. I didn't give it a second glance.

And so it began.

The planetarium disappeared as we ploughed into the trees.

Wood said, 'Dark down here, innit?' and kicked the lights to full beam. Behind us, Nessie was trying to light a cigarette. His lighter kept getting blown out. Since I had the windscreen in front of me I lit a couple up and passed one back. Wood did not smoke.

Above the rattle and the clatter, I said, 'So what have you got planned, pal?'

Nessie grunted. '*Rien!*'

Wood threw me a glance. His face was invisible in the blackness, but I guessed he was looking puzzled. He did not comment.

I leant back towards Nessie. 'Nothing, eh?'

'That's right.'

It was a meaningless word game.

We bumped on through the night.

In some ways the clear night was a blessing, in others it was a curse. For tactical reasons I hoped it would cloud over soon. A lot can be achieved in total darkness, rain and a high wind. But it would be what it would be.

The first Shagland village was just a

collection of darker shadows with silver angles for roofs. Wood, his voice shaking with the rutted track, said, 'I had three of them here once, y'know, sir. All at the same time. Sisters, they were, I think. Cost me a bundle, did that!'

Behind me, Nessie laughed. 'Trois? La même temps? Merde!'

To Wood, I said, 'Good for you.'

Then we hit the hills proper. The jeep bounced, skidded and lurched. I had to keep shifting position because my money belt was cutting into my waist. Apart from the contents of a few deposit boxes in various places, everything I owned in the world was in that belt.

Wood kept pulling too far ahead of the trucks and I had to keep telling him to ease off. A little later the truck behind flashed its lights. I said, 'There you go, Wood. You've pissed them off!' He pulled up.

But it wasn't that at all. It was only Santana wanting to relieve himself.

Everyone piled out and did the same.

Nessie, probably fed up trying to light his constant cigarettes in the slipstream, decided to change places with the guy who had been riding shotgun in the Charlie truck. It was a guy called Gituku Ammas, a Nigerian out of Nessie's Able-Section. I only knew his name because he had once been on my defaulters list. Though I could not remember why. He had ammo belts strung around his body to an impossible degree. Plus grenades and his M16 and all the other bags, pouches and trappings that went with an incursion. He had difficulty fitting himself into the space Nessie had vacated. He mumbled some kind of a greeting, and me and Wood nodded back at him.

Then we got underway again.

Then it rained and we all got wet.

Halfway to Tengo Junction.

The suffering miles dropped behind us. I did try to use the time to get the situation straight in my mind, to organize my thoughts. But clear thinking was impossible on that roller coaster ride through the black jungle. So I stopped bothering.

Later, Ammas started to sing. Softly, mournfully, his voice also shuddering with the crazy gyrations of the jeep. Some gook song or other.

Wood, thankfully keeping his eyes on the barely seen track ahead, inclined his head back. 'What's your name, sport?' He had to shout to be heard above the din.

Ammas leant forward. 'Ammas, sir.'

Wood was simply passing time. He said, 'Where do you come from, Ammas?'

The man said, 'Port Harcourt, Nigeria, sir.'

Wood said, 'You love Joshua Mtomo?'

The man laughed. 'I love arse!'

We all laughed.

Later, we had to pull over and wait for the trucks to catch up again.

I knew where we were, but not, *exactly*, how we got to where we needed to be. I got the map out and studied it under a shaded flashlamp.

Wood said, 'We follow the telegraph poles, sir.'

I said, 'Eh? What telegraph poles?'

Wood, a chuckle in his voice, said, '*Those* telegraph poles!'

He relieved me of the torch and aimed it into the trees. He was right. I had missed them completely. He handed me back the torch. 'These poles go on up to Tengo.'

I had it pegged now. But since I had missed the poles, I allowed Wood his moment of glory. He went on, 'They don't follow this track, not all the way up to Komo territory. They slide off up ahead someplace. That's where we want to be.'

The trucks hove into view and stopped behind us.

Moments later Santana appeared at my shoulder. 'What's up, boss?'

I sighed. 'Nothing's up. Just checking.'

Santana waved an arm up ahead. He said, 'Another ten miles. There's an intersection.'

Wood said heavily. 'Yes, sir, I've got it pinned.'

So we all had another piss.

We ploughed on into the night.

Then we came to the intersection, where the poles shot off at a tangent. Wood followed the poles. The track here was barely a garden path. Again we had to wait for the trucks to catch up.

Some thirty minutes later we passed a broken-down hut which looked like there'd been a time when it hadn't been broken-down. Then the headlights picked out the railway lines running alongside the track. I told Wood to pull over and douse the lights. I looked at my watch. We were on time with a few minutes to spare.

Santana had the lights of his truck doused even before it appeared around the corner behind us. The other trucks pulled in behind him and switched off. For a few moments we all sat there, the engines ticking as they cooled, the darkness closing in around us, no one saying a word. It was an unspoken reference point of some kind. The real beginning, maybe. I sucked in a breath, held it a second, then let it out slowly.

Wood, softly, said, 'Over to you, mister starter!'

Okay, I thought, let's get to it.

I sent Santana on ahead with some of his section to check out the lie of the land. I also posted half a dozen men out in the trees. It was too dark to see who I was pointing at, so I just pointed at a shape and told it what I wanted. The rest of us checked the equipment. Nessie kept himself to himself, and I wasn't about to grumble about that. The rain came down as a fine drizzle and there was the beginnings of a breeze in the air. I was hoping that the breeze would strengthen into something that would mask noise, but was not about to rely on it. But seventy men, festooned with ammo belts and grenades, no matter how careful you were, rattled and clattered like a skeleton on the proverbial tin roof. There was not a lot to the clouds. Every so often the moon would show itself to be still up there, and the countryside would be lit almost as bright as day.

Fit to be called clandestine, we were not.

Jimmy appeared at my elbow. I said, 'What the hell are you doing here, Jimmy? You're supposed to be with Echo!'

He grunted. 'Search me, sir. They shifted me.'

I said, 'Who's *they*?'

He said, 'Curly, just before we pulled out.'

I said, 'To which section?'

He said, 'I'm with Able now.' He added a quiet, 'Nessie . . . '

I was thinking about that as Nessie stepped up. He told Jimmy to go finish the weapons check then he stood there looking at me. I said, 'What?'

He lifted a shoulder.

Maud Peroni appeared out of the murk. He said, 'One of the new intake has just spewed his ring up, sir. He's scared witless.'

Nessie grated, 'If the pig cops out on us I'll blow his useless brains out.'

I said, 'Tonight, old buddy, you don't shoot anyone but enemy.'

He mumbled something I didn't catch and slunk off. And it dawned on me that Nessie might just be considering us the enemy now. Either way, I knew exactly how I was going to deal with him. However, one thing at a time.

To Maud, I said, 'Nervous stomach, maybe.'

Maud chuckled. 'Yeah . . . let's say that. I just thought you'd like to know. In fact,' he added, 'I'm not so sure about any of the, ah, the newcomers.'

'Obviously,' I said, 'Neither are they. Just keep me posted.'

Later, Santana came back in.

The track was clear up to the fork that led off to the mine, about a mile ahead. Santana figured that if Patch had perimeter dug-outs, they would be on the slopes of the hill overlooking the junction itself which, according to the map, was some five miles to the east of where we were at that moment. We — Santana, Nessie, and myself — had a quick council of war in the back of Santana's truck. This was all spur of the moment stuff so there was not a lot of detail to discuss.

Nessie said, 'If we're going to make this work, I'm going to need to use the radio.'

I thought, I bet you bloody well are! I said, 'No radio traffic yet. You know that!' I had three sets of walkie-talkies in my pack; one set was US — able to receive but not transmit. This set, I would give to Nessie when the time came.

Nessie scoffed. 'It can't make that much difference now! We're almost on top of them!'

I said, 'No radios. I'll hand them out later. We use runners until I say otherwise.'

Santana said, 'Ah! The old runner chestnut!'

But Nessie was not convinced. 'And what if the shit hits the fan before we want it to hit the fan? What then? We'll have to organize on the spot!' His tone softened to a winge. 'Organization, Marty . . . you're always bleating on about it. How can we organize when we can't talk to each other!'

Under normal circumstances, of course, he would have had a valid point.

I had not told him that he and Curly were the very last people in the world who would be given radios that night. Certainly not working ones. Neither had I attempted to cover up the fact. I could have told him, there and then, however, that when the shit hit the fan he was not going to be around to see it happen.

Suddenly, seemingly out of nowhere, the rain thundered down. It was about the time when Benson should have been loading up for the first trip up. I did not believe in omens, but it was a good sign.

10

Arne Benst

Maud said, 'Thanks, but you can stop now if you like.' He was talking to the rain.

The rain, and with it quite a strong wind, had stayed with us all the way to the sidings and beyond, forcing us to don ground-sheets. Groundsheets were not designed for personal comfort; they were a catch-all for keeping equipment functioning. But the conditions had blanketed any sounds we made more effectively than some demented rock drummer at a midnight mass. I had tried to catch some sound of the chopper coming in but, if it had come in — and it *should* have done — then I heard nothing of it.

Wood was still back at the siding. He had my flashlight with him. That single flashlight was all I could allow Benson by way of a flare path. Anything stronger would have reflected on the low clouds and be seen from miles away.

Santana and Charlie-Section had gone on, minus Jimmy, who I had swapped for one of Mtomo's gooks. Santana had asked no questions about that, though I'm certain he had already guessed that I was about to pull a stroke.

I said, 'Okay, Peroni, get the section into position and wait for Wood.'

Maud disappeared into the night.

Jimmy, who had also asked no questions, said, 'What do you want me to do, sir?'

I said, 'Step into my office, Jimmy,' and I led him off the track and into the trees. Jimmy must have wondered what the hell I was doing. But he said nothing.

I said, 'You know Arne Benst. Right?' I had seen them drinking together several times.

Arne Benst was Nessie's 2i/c.

Jimmy said, 'I do.'

I said, 'How would you rate him?'

Jimmy thought for a moment. Then he said, 'Bent as a fiddler's elbow!'

'Does he get along with Nessie?'

Jimmy thought some more. 'Not 'specially, I don't think. Why, sir?'

I said, 'I want you to get him.' Nessie was preparing his Able-Section to move out to its allotted position.

Jimmy said, 'Get him?'

I said, 'Yes. I want you to bring him here to me. Right here, Jimmy. Not out there on the track. Here! And I want you to do it on the QT. D'you follow?'

198

Jimmy said, 'The QT, eh.' Pure statement.

I said, 'That's it. Just like the other thing. No one knows about it . . . '

Jimmy said, 'What's up, sir?'

I said, 'Nothing's up. Are you going to do it?'

Jimmy, as I expected he would, said, 'O' course! Now?'

'Yes, now.'

Without another word Jimmy disappeared into the sodden, rain-lashed darkness.

Chang's safety measure had been to disable one of the radio sets. But on the trip down I had thought of a better way of achieving the same end. But a lot depended upon Arne Benst.

That Nessie was going to try a stroke of his own, I had no doubts, nest feathering was one of his specialities. Chang had figured that he would somehow try to radio Patch that we were on our way. The US comm set would have taken care of that, but not its follow-on. Nessie could have walked straight into Patch's camp, taking his chances with the outposts.

I was going to take no such chance. Not if I could help it.

Jimmy came back with Benst four minutes later.

Benst, suspiciously, said, 'What you want?'

Benst was a Swede. He was also the shiftiest character I had ever laid eyes on. He trusted no one, and no one — least of all Nessie — would have trusted him. But there was always the possibility that Nessie might have taken him part way into his confidence. It always takes one to know one. Nessie, after all, had chosen Benst as his 2i/c.

The rain was still hammering down but, where we were, in a small clearing, we were sheltered a little by the overhang of branches. But it was near pitch black and I could see Jimmy and Benst as nothing more than blacker shapes. Neither of them could see the silenced Webley I had in my hand, aimed at the middle of the shape that was Benst.

I said, 'For your information, Benst, I have a gun aimed at your belly. It's loaded, cocked and off safety. Do you understand that?'

Benst said, 'Eh?'

Jimmy said nothing.

I said, 'I have just the one question. How much is Nessie paying you?'

Benst said, 'Paying me?'

'Right. Over and above your 2i/c salary.'

Benst said, 'Eh?' again.

I laid a heavy sigh on him. 'Benst. You've got a further fifteen seconds to cough up. After those fifteen seconds I'm going to blow you all to hell and back! The time starts now!'

In the back of my mind I heard the studio orchestra begin its countdown music. A harp had the lead line. Plink! Plunk! Plink! Almost in time with the rain cascading off the leaves.

Benst said, 'I think I know what you say about. But Nessie pay me nothing. He ask me. But I do not accept.'

Taken at its face value, that told me quite a lot. With an unkind stab at his use of the English language, I said, 'What I say about?'

Benst grunted. I saw his eyes flash in the darkness as the moon poked its nose out of a gap in the rain-filled clouds. He said, 'You say about Patch . . . is right?'

I said, 'Is right. Are you telling me that you didn't go along with him?'

Benst said, 'Is true.'

I said, 'Why?'

Benst gave a short, humourless snort. 'Is easy. I di'nt go along with it because Patch is gonna cut our throats — no different what he say.'

Which would be about right. 'Has Nessie approached anyone else in your section?'

I saw the shape of his shoulders rise and fall in a shrug. Then the moon nipped back behind the clouds. He said, 'I dunno . . . is possible.'

'So what was the proposition?'

Benst said, 'Nessie say we could earn lotta

201

extra bread, from Patch, if we put a rat on B-Company.' He was silent for a moment. Then he went on, 'I tell you now, Captain, Nessie mean to kill you. Maybe soon, maybe later. I di'n say nothing before because . . . ' I sensed another shrug. ' . . . because is not my business.'

That had a ring of truth to it.

Jimmy breathed, 'Jesus fucking Christ!'

To Benst, I said, 'Well, it's your business now, Benst. How would you feel about taking Able-Section in?'

With a new tone to his voice, he said, 'Without Nessie?'

'Without Nessie.'

Benst chuckled. 'I feel fine about it. Nessie is an arsehole!'

I said, 'Then you have the job.'

Benst gave a throaty growl. 'I want more money!'

His reaction had been spur-of-the-moment, and so was my reply. I said, 'How much money d'you reckon Nessie has on him, right at this moment?'

Benst only had to give that a moment's thought. If anyone's money belt was bulging, it would have been Nessie's. He said, 'Is mine?'

I said, 'You fetch Nessie here, without blowing anything to the section, and it's yours.'

Benst, enthusiastically, said, 'I go.'

I said, 'Fine . . . but Jimmy goes with you.'

Jimmy had that wobble back in his voice as he said, 'You ain't coming, boss?' The poor sod had been dropped into the deep end of something he hadn't seen coming, and I felt for him. But it had to be this way. Nessie had to be dealt with in private, and I was covering as many bases as I could.

I said, 'If Nessie sees me he'll smell it out. Just act natural. You'll be okay. And, Benst?'

Benst said, 'Ya?'

'Just tell Nessie that you want to talk to him, alone. Make it look like you've changed your mind about his deal. Got it?'

He said, 'I got it. But is better Jimmy don' go.'

I said, 'Jimmy goes with you! In fact . . . ' I was making it up as we went along, and I wish now that I'd put more thought into the scheme. I found Jimmy's hand in the darkness and thrust the silenced Webley into it, making no pretence at concealment. 'Take this, Jimmy. If he tries anything cute, use it.' To Benst, who may or may not have been aware of what had changed hands, I said, 'Jimmy now has the gun, Benst. Just play it cool and relaxed and we'll all get through this thing. You have five minutes. I'll be right here.'

Jimmy muttered a shaky, 'Jesus!' But he went with Benst.

I slipped my bayonet from its sheath.

At least with Nessie out of the way I could put my mind to the strike. I wondered vaguely how Chang was faring with Curly. Maybe he had arrived at a similar solution. Then again, maybe not. Curly did not bother with a regular 2i/c. His section was a lash-up from top to bottom. Then again, Chang could take it over himself. He could get his uniform dirty for a change.

The rain eased slightly as I waited but, for what I had to do, I did not know whether that was good news or bad news. All that mattered was that I ended it here and now. I stepped to the side of the track and pushed back into the undergrowth, and it was that simple action that saved me.

The sheer bulk of the first black shape to enter the clearing told me that it was Nessie. I was slightly to the left of the track Benst and Jimmy had taken. And I was there so I could deliver an unobstructed, single thrust. I had not planned on ceremony. Kill Nessie, and that would be it.

As I drew my arm back, the clearing was suddenly lit by two almost simultaneous flashes. But the only sounds were that of the rain, the phut-phut of a silenced gun, and

Nessie's explosion of breath.

I had been looking at Nessie's shape. But, out of the corner of my eye and in the strobe-like effect of the twin flashes, I saw that it was Benst doing the shooting. And I knew, in that instant, that Benst was another man I had dangerously underestimated.

Though none of B-Company dared mention the fact to each other, it was accepted that each man would carry his money with him. Mostly in belts as I had. Some of the guys managed to get theirs to a bank. But not many. And no one was going to chance leaving his hard earned cash behind at the compound. Certainly not on strikes such as this one. Money, after all, was the root of everyone's presence.

Benst had obviously figured that if he was going to get Nessie's money, why not take mine, too? I had never made a secret of the fact that I had plenty of the stuff. It would be the way Benst's brain would work. He'd probably made up his mind the moment I mentioned Nessie's money.

I had an eyeblink to curse myself for a fool before the gun flashed again. Three times. Directly over Nessie's collapsing body. But I was no longer where Benst had thought I would be; where his bullets were going. I was standing almost at his right shoulder.

He saw me, of course, but only as he was firing his third shot into the empty clearing. By which time I had gotten over my surprise. I hardly had to alter the direction of my thrust at all, because Benst had stepped forward onto the spot Nessie had occupied only a second before. And as my arm whipped through its short arc I wondered what the hell had happened to Jimmy.

The gun fired once more, as Benst tried to pull it around in my direction. It went off just below the bayonet, the bullet zipping under my arm. Then, in the next millisecond, the bayonet wasn't there anymore; it was buried in Benst's armpit.

He stood there for a second, as if he were gargling, and I held his weight on the bayonet, turning it like a skewer to inflict maximum damage. The shape of his head was close to my mouth, and I remember saying something pithy to him. But I don't remember what it was. Then, gently, but certainly not kindly, I allowed him to crumple down to join Nessie on the saturated, evil-smelling ground.

'You unholy bastard,' I breathed down at him. But it was simply a reaction. He had done exactly what I *should* have been expecting him to do. The fault was mine, and mine alone.

I turned him over with the toe of my boot and heaved the bayonet from his armpit, then felt around for the gun. I knew it would be mine, because no one carried a silencer by default. Not in that outfit. It was not hard to find, and it was my Webley. So where was Jimmy?

The night was suddenly ripped apart by a blinding flash of lightning, the anvil-crash of the thunder arriving almost instantly. The rain stopped as if a tap had been turned. I stood there for a moment, gathering my shattered wits. Then I went looking for Jimmy.

And I fell over him not fifteen yards along the track.

Strangely enough, I felt even worse about Jimmy than I had about Khan.

This was no way to begin a strike against a man like Patch!

11

Hill 806

I took Nessie's section forward to its position, because there was no one else to do it.

I had sent a runner out to Wood, telling him to take over Baker-Section and carry on without me. He had sent a note back. The chopper had arrived on time with Dove-Section, plus Chang. Dove was Curly's section, so Chang was in the right place. I hoped he was thinking a damn sight clearer than I had been with Benst. But that was all water under my bridge now. Chang, apparently, was organizing Benson's second trip up with Jamie's section. So nothing much would be happening there for an hour or so.

Apart from three already dead, things were pretty much on schedule. But then, it hadn't been much of a schedule in the first place. Even so, what I had done with Nessie and Benst was to bite back at me in the hours ahead.

Tengo Junction lay — still lies, in fact — in a valley. It is the centre point of a loose triangle of two hills — 806 and 19 — and a mountain. The mountain is to the north of the railway line, and is totally covered with nigh-on impenetrable forest. The largest things to exist on that mountain, called Tengalla, are monkeys.

Chang once sent a patrol up Tengalla. It reported progress of less than fifty yards. Tengalla is an impossible mountain.

South-west of the railway, as far as our maps were concerned, was Hill-806. It is called other things on other maps. The mine and the sidings are on the south slope of 806. The railway spur, which fed the sidings, separated 806 from Hill-19. At the base of Hill-19 — north and west — was the ubiquitous Red River. Or one of its main tributaries.

You could not escape Red River in Mtomo territory.

Red River separates Hill-19 from the main railway line and the spur. And there is no bridge, certainly not within striking distance.

The junction itself is a collection of old ICSRC — the Indinga Copper Steam Railway Company — huts. I never knew who, or what, Indinga was. And, in its heyday, Tengo Junction could boast two trains a month. But those trains had a lot of fun at Tengo, because the points of the spur would invariably be rusted solid. The ICSRC was never much of a railway company.

The plan, as it stood, was clear. If sketchy.

Able-Section, mine now, at least for a while, was to head directly over Hill-806, between its twin peaks, making for the one nasty part of that hill — a sheer face of rock overlooking the junction. This bit could only be roped down. The fifty-calibre HMG crews, however, would not need to climb down initially, because atop that rock face was to be their position. I didn't spend a lot of time explaining the sudden change of leadership, or the lack of a 2i/c, because we did not *have* a lot of time. I simply told them the way things were and left the rest to their imagination.

Baker-section, with either Wood, or now — if he felt so inclined — Chang at the helm, was to work its way west of 806 and approach Tengo along the rail line. It was strange, but up to that moment I had completely forgotten about Chang and the new danger. I can only put that down to the fact that, despite everything, I was enjoying myself. By going in with Able-Section instead of my own I had very probably queered any plans he may have made towards putting a bullet in my back. I could not think of any one of Baker-Section who'd be willing to shoot me in the back, but with the right numbers, just about anyone can be bought. Either way, they'd have to pull some pretty fancy footwork out of the bag to get at me now. That, alone, was worth a smile.

Charlie-Section, under Santana, had the M224 mortars and was to skirt the east slope of 806, keeping the spur at its right hand, moving to a position above, and to the south of, the junction, from where those weapons could be used to best advantage, before moving in to engage.

Dove-Section had the inflatables and was to use Red River as its way in. A lot here depended upon how Chang handled Curly. But that no longer concerned me. That was all in the lap of the unkind gods.

Echo-Section, under Jamie, would be choppered in by Benson at the critical moment.

Critical moment!

I doubted there were going to be any *non*-critical moments!

By the time I had Able-Section ready to move it had stopped raining completely and the moon cast a fitful glow through the high clouds. Hill-806 reared above us, a black impossibility against a dark-grey background. It was too dark to make out ground detail; you simply put one foot in front of the other and hoped there would be something there to take your weight. With this in mind I ordered everyone to remove magazines from their weapons and make certain there were no shells in the chamber. One accidental shot would put paid to everything.

★　★　★

A voice said, 'Where the hell are we?'

It was way too dark yet to make out faces. And I didn't recognize the voice, or the accent. He could have been British. Then again he could have been an Aussie or something like that.

At the voice, I said,' Who are you?'

The voice said, 'Who are *you*?'

Great!

I said, 'Keep moving. Straight on up!'

The voice said, 'Oh, it's you, sir.'

He must have recognized my voice. I wished to hell I could recognize his. This could be dangerous. A command of 'Hey, you! Go forward!' could end in disaster. This was one of the reasons why, where possible, you man your section with people you know. But this, and with a vengeance, was not my section. And there on that slope, after all that had gone down, my brain just didn't want to pull the threads together. I was soaked clear through to skin, freezing cold, and the eighty kilos of equipment I had strapped to my body seemed to have doubled in weight. I should have thought of this problem before we hit the slopes, but I hadn't. I was going to have to sort something out.

As we pushed on up into the trees I racked my brain to see if I knew any member of Nessie's section well enough to ease my load. Then, at last, I thought of someone.

At the nearest black shape, I said, 'Where's Pett?'

A muffled voice somewhere out to my left said, 'Here.'

I said, 'Get over here.'

Curses, clatters and more curses. Then the man was at my side. I said, 'Give me a rundown on the section.'

As we paused there, more black shapes slithered and cursed up the slope past us.

Pett said, 'What d'you mean?'

'A rundown,' I hissed harshly, angry at myself rather than him. This should not have been happening. 'What d'you think I mean! Who's in it?'

A shape to my right slipped and fell amidst a clatter of equipment.

Someone over there hissed, 'For Christ's sake!'

Pett said, 'I still don't get you. You wanna know names?'

Hallelujah! 'Yes, names! And who belongs to them.' I was explaining it all wrong, I knew that. But I simply could not hit clarity.

Up ahead, someone else hissed, 'Fucking great hole here! Watch it!'

Pett, to his credit, put his numbers together and came up with the right answer. He said, 'That's Grant.' His French roots were evident in his heavy accent, but his use of the English language was text book, with quirks thrown in.

I sighed, 'That's the idea.'

Pett went on, 'I don't have the first clue about the Askaris. Nessie put them on the spare ammo detail, but they're just getting in the bloody way!'

I remembered that Nessie had accepted a good number of them into Able-Section. I had only taken a couple into Baker.

On a whim, I put a feeler in Pett's direction. 'What are your feelings about Nessie?'

Pett said, 'He was a bastard! What really happened back there?'

I said, 'You don't know?'

He said, 'Just that you blew him away.' Then he grated. 'Had it coming, if you ask me. There was talk he was selling us out to Patch. That true?'

I said, 'It's true.' Just to keep the air clear, I

added, 'Benst was tarred with the same brush.'

Pett said nothing. Which could have meant that he believed me, or, in equal measure, that he didn't. I didn't push it.

We started again up the slope.

Suddenly there was the hole directly in front of us. It opened up as just an ebony-black mass against a matt-black background. It could have been merely inches deep, or a cavern. We skirted around it. Pett turned and hissed,

'Hole here! Watch it!'

One of the men behind us stumbled, cursed, and stumbled again. A voice said, 'I can't see a bloody thing!'

Someone else cursed in a language I did not recognize. But Pett had it pegged. He said, 'That's Grierson. He's a buddy of Benst. I'd watch that one . . . ' He added, 'If I were you.' So he really did understand my problem and was prepared to ease it.

I said, 'I intend to watch everyone!' To myself, I added, *Including you*! From here on I was not about to take *anyone* at face value.

Pett said, 'I tried to transfer to your section a while back. Nessie wouldn't have it.'

I said, 'You should've asked me. Anyone else in the section close to Nessie or Benst?'

Pett said, 'We got a black who used to

drink with them a lot. I guess he was in the syndicate.'

'Syndicate?'

'Yeah. A loot syndicate. Nessie's got a whole wagonload of stuff stashed away in some village up in Shagland. Dunno where, exactly. The bastards are always looting and stashing it away.'

No surprises there. I said, 'So's everyone.'

Pett grunted. 'I suppose so. But with Nessie and Benst and the others it was big business.'

We plodded on in silence for a while, sometimes upright, sometimes sprawled on the muddy ground. But ever upwards.

When I felt I had the breath to spare for it, I asked, 'What do you know about Curly?'

Pett gave a half-chuckle. 'Curly? Nothing much. He's the fixer, right?'

'Yep. Did he fix you?'

'Yes. In Tunis. Me and a few others.'

I was not going to volunteer anything about Curly's part in the doublecross, so I let it drop.

A voice from up ahead hissed, 'The ridge!'

At-bloody-last!

To Pett, I said, 'Do me a favour.'

'Sure.'

I said, 'Watch my back.' And I stepped on up through the darkness.

We were atop the cradle formed by 806's twin peaks. Over to the east the sky was becoming a tint less muddy. I checked my watch; we had about two hours before full dawn, which gave us no more than an hour's workable darkness. In that time we had to deal with any piquets Patch might have positioned on that slope of 806, and on to the head of the rock face.

The men of Able-Section were sinking, panting, to the ground around me. When movement up the hill ceased, I said, 'Okay. Before we start down, does anyone have any questions?'

A voice said, 'Yeah. Where's Benst? The voice had a sullen edge to it.

I said, 'I told you down there, Benst has been relieved of his post. I'm in charge now. Any other questions?'

Another voice said, 'This is all a fucking larrups!'

I had not heard that word before, but its meaning was obvious. I said, 'Then let's try and un-larrups it! Start by checking your weapons. But,' I added forcibly, 'still nothing up the spout! You don't shove your magazines in until I tell you! You all got that?'

The sullen voice said, 'I wanna know what's happening. Where's Benst?'

This one was obviously not a listener. I

said, 'What's your name?'

Hesitation. Then, 'Grierson.'

I said, 'Okay, Grierson, and anyone else who hasn't got it yet. Benst has been relieved of his post, and so has Captain Bridges. From here on in you only have me. But, make no mistake, if you don't move when I tell you to move, you get the same treatment you would have gotten from Nessie. A bullet in the skull. Is that plain enough for you?'

Someone else said, 'Aw, shit, let's get on with it!'

Grierson said nothing.

I said, 'Okay. I want the HMG crews front and centre.'

A number of shadows detached themselves and crowded around me. The clink and scrape of metal on metal seemed deafening.

I said, 'Pett?'

Pett's voice sounded from a few yards back down the slope. 'I'm here.'

I said, 'Right. Everyone, Pett is your new 2i/c. Bear that in mind.' In Pett's direction, I said, 'You okay with that Pett?'

He said, 'If everyone else is.'

I said, 'They don't have the choice! You do. Is that okay, or not.'

He said, 'It's cool.'

Then, to the body of men around me, I said, 'HMG crews, move your stuff over to the left. Give us fifteen minutes' head start, then follow on down. Be ready to set up at any time.'

The shadows clanked away.

To the rest, I said, 'Askaris!'

A number of shadows rose up amid a mumble of acknowledgements. I could not make out how many there were. A dozen or so, it seemed. 'Who speaks English?'

A guttural voice said, 'I do, boss!'

'What's your name, soldier?'

'Sim, boss.'

'You got any rank, Sim?'

'I got two stripes, boss.'

There were a few groans from the guys still on the ground. Askaris rarely earned rank, they just seemed to come by it. I said, 'Okay, *Corporal* Sim. Gather your flock together. You're the rear guard. You wait until the HMG crews have gone, then you count to a thousand, and follow on down with the ammo. Got that?'

Someone hissed, 'The day a bloody Askari can count to a thousand, will be the day!'

I ignored that. 'The rest of you . . . who thinks he's good with a bayonet?'

Without hesitation a voice said, 'You got a volunteer.' It was a young voice.

I said, 'Who's that?'

The voice said, 'Graham.'

I said, 'Graham something, or something Graham?'

Another voice chuckled. '*Sweeney* fucking Graham. Need I say more?'

Graham's voice said, 'Just Graham.' Definitely a young voice. Too young for the knife? I wondered.

'Are you good enough?' I was reminded of Jimmy, who never did come across with the beers he owed me.

He said, 'Try me.'

I said, 'Okay, I will. Give the rest of your load to someone else. Including your rifle. If we can't do this with knives, and quietly, we won't need to do it at all.'

I waited while the transplant took place. Then Graham moved over to stand beside me. I smelt pot on his breath, despite the stench of the countryside. I let it pass. Besides, given the chance, I would have relished a joint myself at that moment.

The wind up on that hill was quite pronounced, and cold. I guess we were all shivering. I certainly was. But I knew that once over the rise and on the north slope the wind would die. The cloud cover directly overhead was about nine-tenths. But north of Tengalla there was a great swathe of stars visible, and the swathe was edging southward. If we were lucky the clear patch would miss the moon. If we were not so lucky, it wouldn't.

They were just two of a hundred 'Ifs'.

I said, 'I want absolute silence on the way down. No lights, no cigarettes, no nothing. I can't tell you how we're going to play this because I don't know . . . yet. If we make it to the valley undetected, the game's on. Provided Patch is down there. If we don't . . . well, it'll be because there's piquets out. And if there's piquets out — '

A voice said, 'It'll mean Patch is there!'

I said, 'Right. It's all seat-of-the pants stuff. Live with that! Just stay on the ball and do what you do best. Pett!'

'Sir!'

I stripped myself of weapons and the rest and handed it all to him. 'Find a mule for this lot! Then give us ten minutes before you move out. HMG crews! You have twenty-five minutes before you move from here. Check your ordnance. In fact, everyone! Do it now. Let's have no misfires!' Generally, I said, 'Who has the ropes?'

A voice said, 'Here!'

I said, 'Who's *here*?'

The voice said, 'Anders.'

'Okay, Anders, you're carrying our only way down the last fifty feet. Don't, for Christ's sake, lose it! Graham!'

'I'm still here!'

I said, 'Right!' There was no reason to wait any longer. 'Let's you and me go see if there's anything to find.'

12

'Sweeney' Graham

I'd been right about the wind.

Fifty yards down the threadbare north slope of the cradle it died to nothing. In daylight, or even semi-daylight, we could have romped down that slope with barely a sound. There were no trees to get in the way that high up and it was mostly grass underfoot. The rocks, some of them knee-high, were well spread apart. The problem was that we couldn't see them. It was as if we were stepping into a black abyss. Each step was a complete mystery.

But it was much, much warmer.

On the very odd occasions when the moon did appear for a second or two we were able to plan a route ahead to a distance of about twenty feet. But there was always that rogue boulder that we hadn't seen, or had simply forgotten about. And we could afford no trips, no stumbles. Patch could have set up an outpost anywhere on that slope and it would be totally invisible to us until we actually stepped into it. So it was a case of a few steps, then listen, a few more steps, then listen again. A brief spurt of speed here, with a mental, moonlit picture of the terrain ahead fresh in our minds, then back to the slow grope ahead, bent low, feeling for the next obstacle.

The effect on back- and calf muscles was torturous.

We were twenty minutes on that section of the slope, then we hit the trees. Small, bush-like at first, but growing as we moved forward and down.

It rained intermittently, but heavily. Sometimes thunderously. Brief moments of sound-swallowing respite. Yet still that great gash in the clouds moved steadily closer. The only thing in Able-Section's favour was that the route down was fairly obvious. Me and Graham just kept going down, almost straight down, in what could have been a water course. We might have missed an outpost by twenty feet, and the outpost — if one did exist — might have missed us. With luck the same would apply for the rest of the section, following us down.

I began thinking about a whole new set of 'Ifs'.

I thought the clouds had suddenly thickened above us, but it was the beginning trees of the slope two- or three-hundred feet short of the rock face. We halted our descent and listened. When the rain was not coming down there was no sound at all. We gave it a full minute, standing there motionless, then moved on down. We might as well have had our eyes closed as we stepped into that tangle of trunks and branches. And the only thing to indicate direction was the slope. We simply kept headed downwards.

My face was being flayed raw by the branches, and going forward at a crouch was worse. I'd feel a thick tree trunk ahead of me with my fingertips, I'd step aside, and, crack! I'd headbutt another one.

It might have been raining at that time. Then again, it might just have been the leaves dropping the accumulated moisture. Either way, I was not getting any drier.

Graham was moving down about ten feet off my right shoulder. We seemed to be making enough noise to wake the dead.

Then, suddenly, there were no more trees, and I saw a light ahead and below me. And a light out there in the middle of nowhere could only mean one thing: Star Sapphire had been correct. It was just a pinprick of light, deep in this black nothingness, but it had to be the junction; the direction was right. I peered at it, trying to judge distance. But that was impossible. That light could have been a torch at five hundred yards, or a lighted cigarette at two feet!

But it *was* a light!

Then Graham was there beside me. His hand came up and his fingers sought my mouth. When they'd found it they pressed hard on my lips. I nodded my head and the fingers went away. Graham pulled me close to him and pressed his lips to my ear.

'On the right,' he whispered, barely audibly, more sibilance than words.

I looked to the right but could see nothing. I strained my ears. Then I heard it. A low voice. Then there was a tinkle, like a metal cup hitting rock.

A breeze sucked at the trees behind us. It was a mere breath, but it covered the sound of the voice. Forty feet, at most.

I looked up.

The area of stars had spread. It was almost directly overhead now. But it was going to miss the moon by a hair's breadth. Nevertheless there would be overspill of light. Enough.

Enough for us, and enough for the owner of the voice.

But there had to be at least two of them. Unless the man, and it was a man's voice, was talking to himself, or a radio.

I felt Graham pull away from me. The nebulous black shape of his body sunk downwards. I did the same, feeling for obstacles with my fingertips. We were on what appeared to be solid rock.

But how far from the drop?

I transferred the bayonet to my left hand and crept forward gingerly on my knees. Graham's shape had disappeared.

I thought, you can rain now, if you like!

And why not blow, too, while you're at it.

It did neither.

But there was sound. I had not heard it before, or I had just gotten used to it being there. It was the steady drip, drip of the rain off the trees, ten or so yards behind us. And there was the merest gurgle of a small rivulet cascading down over the rock. It was precious little, but it was something.

There were two men over there.

It was now possible to distinguish the two tones. They seemed to be talking incessantly, and I thanked them silently for that as I edged forward on the rock.

I'd gone about five yards when my fingertips felt a sudden dip. It might well have been simply a hole in the rock, but it could just as easily have been the drop. Everything below my eye line was black. I did not bother with an attempt to find out. I angled to the right and started forward again, using the voices as my guide. Graham, I assumed, was well above me on the slope.

For each foot of forward progress the voices gained a decibel in volume. I could now make out some of the words.

' . . . Down the road . . . bent . . . barely moving . . . I for . . . '

'Ha, ha! She . . . seen it and . . . went over to . . . '

For three long seconds the wind swelled out of nowhere and the trees above groaned and scraped and the water pattered down from the leaves. When the almost absolute silence returned I was a precious three feet closer to the voices.

Then I saw the glow. A shaded torch, or something, low down, seemingly piercing out from rock. I altered my angle of approach a shade.

' . . . Tard didn't move. He . . . round the . . . bent double. Ha . . . '

Clink! Clink!

' . . . Get round this . . . ood . . . '

Then, like magic, a black rug appeared to be moving away from the peak of Tengalla, way off to the right, leaving behind the mountain itself. Or, rather, the black rug was where the moonlight was *not*. Some of that glow transferred itself over to 806. Definite shapes became evident.

I eased forward, foot by interminable foot,

hardly breathing, my fingers brushing the rock, the toes of my boots lifted clear, my back and calf muscles screaming for respite. My kneecaps — which were taking all my weight — were knots of fire.

Fifteen feet.

Twelve.

Ten . . .

'Freddy didn't move . . . threw us all to hell, but . . . and back . . . '

'Yeah. I had a . . . self . . . see a damned thing, but . . . '

'Ha, ha!'

Clink.

I could make out their faces now. They were settled in a hollow in the rock, sipping at mugs. Two white men. I could see the barrel of one of their weapons protruding above the hollow.

Knee forward. Down. The fire burned its way into my muscles.

Hand forward . . . down.

Other knee up . . . forward.

I gritted my teeth against the pain of it and had to force my lungs to suck air slowly, deeply, soundlessly.

Left hand, with the bayonet, forward. Ease it down on raw knuckles. Breath out . . . slowly, slowly, slowly! Hand forward, millimetre by millimetre.

' . . . Doesn't know 'is arse from 'is elbow!'

'Not a bad old sod, though. 'E'd do anything for ya.'

'Yeah, but you never know 'ow 'e's gonna be from one bleedin' minute to the next!'

Five feet. Almost on top of them, but not quite close enough. Why the hell aren't they seeing me! Hell, they're as plain as —

A sudden flurry of movement above me. Both faces turn at the same instant. Then Graham burst into view, at full stretch, diving into the hollow, bayonet glinting in the oblique glow of the moon.

I put everything I had left into my leap forward.

And it was all over in seconds.

One of the men lay half out of the hollow, his throat sliced through. Graham's work. The other lay sprawled in the 'V' of the hollow, my bayonet in his neck. He was not yet dead, but he was on his way out. I withdrew the bayonet and put it in again somewhere else. The man went limp.

They had the torch propped on a ledge, its reflector half covered by a cigarette packet. Their thermos flask lay shattered. And there was a walkie-talkie hissing softly on 'receive'.

Graham hissed, 'Any more, d'you think?'

I wondered why he assumed I might know the answer to that. I said, 'Don't have a clue.'

230

I looked at my watch. There was no time now to go looking. Pretty soon the rest of Able would come blundering out of the trees.

I added, 'Have to take that chance. But there's no doubt now.'

Graham said, 'That Patch is definitely in residence?'

'Yeah.'

I glanced over at the light I had seen before. But it wasn't there any more. The moonlit swathe was now on the junction itself, and moving steadily south over the basin. And the sky over to the east, over Hill-19, was definitely lightening.

Graham picked up a still lighted cigarette that one of the men had been smoking and took a deep drag at it. Then he passed it over to me. 'It's good shit!' he said tightly, on the slow exhale.

I took it, looked at it, thought about it, then ground it out.

Graham sighed. 'Great!'

I said, 'Yeah, but that's your lot! Cut back and guide the section in. Oh!'

He hesitated.

I said, 'You did well.'

'Yeah,' he said grittily, 'Sweeney Graham, that's me!'

Then he was gone.

13

A Surprise That Should Have Been No Surprise

We did not need Anders and his ropes.

The two guys of the outpost already had a rope ladder fixed up, which figured. I left the section on the ridge and felt my way down the ladder for a quick look around.

The valley floor was a uniform sea of black gloom. There was no shape to anything. Just a black nothingness. The moon, if it was still up there, was now hidden behind Hill-806. I couldn't make out whether there were any clouds above us or not. I stood at the base of the rock face and squinted around me. But for all I could see I might have had my head stuck up an overflow pipe. For safety, I kept my hand on the rope ladder.

One thing. There was a wind down there. Not a gale, but a gentle wind, and blowing east to west, down the valley from the junction. This, at the very least, was better than it blowing towards the junction, carrying sound with it. But there were no sounds to be heard on that breeze. I stood there motionless for a full five minutes, straining to hear something other than the sigh of the breeze through nearby leaves. But there was nothing. Against all the odds we seemed to have made it, undetected, to where we had to be.

I tried to put myself in Patch's shoes. It was possible that he knew we were here, or at least that we *planned* to be here. But only vaguely possible. I didn't think that Nessie had had time to pass any specific information through to him since we had put our final plan together. Chang's plan of attack assumed that Patch did *not* know. And that was a fair bet. But, if I were Patch, and I was this deep inside *his* territory, I'd take nothing for granted. I'd litter the area with piquets and machine gun nests and grenade traps until I made the final move against the compound. And I would do that even if we were only pausing for a brew up, let alone using the area as a staging ground. And the valley was an open door, especially this side of the valley. The eastern side had the river to guard it; the elongated north perimeter had the ridge as reasonable defence and the west side was thick jungle.

One of my problems was that I could not picture the topography in my mind. I had been through Tengo on a couple of occasions, headed elsewhere, but had never had reason to pause there. And you can only glean so much from studying a map.

However, we were here, and we appeared to be undetected. That much was a definite plus.

I made up my mind and climbed back up the ladder.

Pett said, 'How does it look?'

I said, 'We'll go on down. Are the fifty-calibre crews in yet?'

Someone said, 'Here!'

Everyone was crowded around the gully in the rock.

I said, 'Grab your ammo and set up your pieces along this ridge, but back in the trees. Your job will be to cover our advance over the valley when it happens. They're almost certain to have a couple of machine gun nests somewhere out there. And if they do I'll need them taken out first. If and when they're spotted I'll radio the co-ordinates.' Which thought led me to a pertinent subject: 'I need a comms number?'

No one spoke. I did not expect a volunteer so I wasn't disappointed when I didn't get one. I broke out the radios, slung one around my shoulder and thrust the other at the nearest man. 'What's your name, soldier?'

'Ammas, sir.' I recognized the voice. It was the guy in the jeep.

I said, 'Okay, Ammas, you're Johnnie-on-the-spot! Keep it on receive but transmit nothing. But if you hear someone — *anyone!* — transmit the word 'Springtime'. You'll know it's hitting the fan, and you can yell as loud as you like! Got it?'

Ammas said a dubious, 'Springtime, sir?'

There was enough doubt in his tone to make me wonder if I ought to give the job to someone else. 'Yes . . . springtime. It's the codeword. And your call sign is Able Two. Got that?'

Star Sapphire. Springtime. For a hard man, Chang chose soft code words.

Ammas, still with a dubious tone to his voice, said, 'Able Two. Right, sir.' Then, an even more dubious, 'I wait until I hear the codeword.'

I sighed an inward sigh. I could have pulled the rug from under him and designated someone else, but he would have ended up a laughing stock. I did not feel like doing that. I said, 'Just stay on the ball, soldier. You'll be okay.'

'What d'you want to do with this?' It was Sweeney Graham's voice. I could not see what he had in his hand but I knew what he was talking about. It was the radio the two men had been using.

I said, 'Keep it with you. Patch'll be on the

other end of it. It could give us an edge. When we're all down the ladder, stay close to me.'

Generally, I said, 'Everyone, pass the word. When we get down there no one talks above a whisper. And unless it's pretty bloody important, don't say anything at all! Just get down there, stay together, and wait. Go!'

The HMG crews detached themselves and disappeared into the murk. The remaining men, hissing curses and grunts, started to grope their way down the ladder. The Askaris, laden down with all the ammo boxes, had a hard time of it. But we were well ahead of schedule. Full dawn was still at least a half hour away, but the sky was lightening now, even as you looked at it.

Pett was at my side. 'What if they had a check-in schedule going?'

I had thought about that. 'If Patch doesn't get a call when he should have gotten a call, and he can't raise them, I guess he might send someone to check it out. But we'll deal with that as and when. I don't think he's going to push the panic button just because he can't raise one of his outposts. Equipment doesn't need a reason to go US in this bloody country.' I had another thought. 'Which four men d'you think you can trust?' I added, 'And you can forget about the Askaris.'

Pett gave a soft chuckle. 'Well, there's four I know I *can't* trust.'

I said, 'Which four is that?' I knew what was coming.

Pett didn't let me down. 'Any four you like.'

I smiled. 'Jokes later. When it's light enough down there to see your boots, but not the ground, I want you to take four men and make your way up along the rock face. I wish I could give you Graham; he's good at sniffing out foxholes, but I need him with me. Go up about fifty yards . . . a hundred or more if you think you can do it quietly, then spread out. But keep your heads down until the balloon goes up.'

It was now possible to make out fairly distinctive shapes on the valley floor below the ridge. That angular lump of blackness, about eight hundred yards out, left of centre, would be the old ICSRC signal box, beyond which was the rail line. Over beyond that would be the spot Baker-Section was making for; if they weren't already there.

I swung my gaze to the right.

There were trees almost directly ahead. Only they wouldn't be trees, they would be big bushes. Even as I looked they were taking some kind of shape. Way beyond them, something like half a mile away, were the huts of the junction. That light I had seen before was still there. But it wasn't coming from the huts. It was off to one side, close to where I figured the points would be. But I still could not judge the distance. And it seemed, now, to be higher up. A tower, maybe.

The stars were all but gone now, and there was a definite hint of blue in the sky. Tengalla mountain stood out like a reclining black bear. I could not see Hill-19, but it wouldn't have gone far.

'Right,' I said to Pett, 'Let's do what we came here to do.' I swung myself out over the rock and climbed down to the valley floor.

Marty Saltman. Now there'd been a guy. Quiet, inoffensive and good at his job. He had been my communications number in Iraq. He was always talking electronics. He could make anything do anything if there was a socket to plug it into. He hailed from California, some hick town. He really knew electronics.

I don't know why I thought of Marty. Pett, who climbed down the ladder after me, was not even vaguely like him. Not in looks or manner.

I took a last look up at the rock face. It was beginning to look like a rock face now. The fifty-calibre HMG crews would be well placed up there, as Patch had obviously realized. He was going to wish he had put a couple of less-talkative people up there.

The men of Able-Section crowded around me. I could not quite make out expressions yet, but tension was definitely in the air. Some, I knew, would be wondering what the hell had possessed them to become mercenary soldiers in the first place. Others would be looking forward to the coming action. It takes all types. For myself, I felt strangely calm and in touch. While I was not exactly looking forward to what we had to do, I was in no way afraid of it either. And that was always a handy state of mind to carry with you.

Pett grabbed his choice of men and led them back to the base of the rock face. Then he trotted back to me. 'We'll shoot off, then.'

I looked down. He was about right. I could just see my boots. I said, 'You got plenty of ammo?'

He said, 'Sure. I've got Grierson, too.'

I did not realize it at the time, but he had taken Grierson along with him so he couldn't pull any stunts, him having been buddies with Nessie and Benst.

I said, 'Right. Cut along. Luck, huh!'

He said, 'Sure,' and he moved away.

I wished, later, that I'd thanked him for taking Grierson off my back unasked. Some things you don't get a second chance at.

Mostly, I become aware that I have a conscience when I'm trying to sleep and not managing it. I don't often put my head on the pillow and go straight out.

The sky was now a deep-blue silk streaked with silver-gold threads and the valley was spread out in front of us.

Tengalla was no longer a black bear; it was a mountain.

The rock face behind me was just that.

And the bushes out in the valley had some hint of colour to them.

But still, apart from the breeze sighing through the bushes, there was no movement at all. The valley looked, and felt, deserted.

The men were looking at me, waiting for leadership. Graham was at my elbow, the radio pressed to his ear.

Then, as I opened my mouth to speak, there was an explosion. Over beyond the signal box, the flash coming slightly before the CRUMP! It was so utterly unexpected that it stunned us all. Heads turned and someone spat an incredulous, 'Bugger!' The sharp crash of the explosion ricocheted around the valley as a diminishing echo.

'Cover!' I yelled.

Everyone found a bush and dived behind it. I stayed where I was. Graham stayed with me.

Baker-Section had either made premature contact, or one of them had tripped a grenade trap. I figured it was the latter, because nothing happened for a good ten seconds after the explosion.

The Red Chinese, in particular, are hellishly good at laying traps. They use grenades sometimes, but mostly they simply use whatever is to hand. Bamboo, for instance.

Bamboo, sharpened to a needle-point and dipped in human excreta, then placed right where a man is going to walk, will suit their cause better than a bullet. Out in the jungle, a man walking into a bamboo trap is rarely killed outright. He might just as well be, from his own point of view, because he's going to die anyway.

But he doesn't die.

Not then.

He becomes a load to be carried and cared for and thought about, when there are a hundred other things to be carried and cared for and thought about. These casualties would normally hold up proceeding for a day or so, then they'd die. But by then there would be someone else who hadn't watched where he was walking.

The bamboo trap is not merely a killer weapon, and one that needed no maintenance, it is also an assault on the mind. Men

241

dreamed about bamboo. Or, they had nightmares about it. You could have a perfectly innocuous stretch of open ground. Yet, at times, you would not find a single man willing to walk over it.

Bamboo grows prodigiously in the Far East.

Bamboo does not grow prodigiously in Africa.

Graham had the walkie-talkie still jammed hard to his ear. His expression was a picture of confusion. 'I heard nothing! There's nothing!' We both stared out over the valley. But there was nothing to be seen. No movement, no running figures, nothing.

Chang was certain to have heard that explosion. Anyone within two miles of Tengo would have heard it! So where was the codeword! Whatever the cause of that explosion, the time was *now*! I lifted my radio and pressed the transmit button.

'Able . . . Able . . . Ready to go!'

I flicked to receive. There was an empty hiss for a moment, then I heard Santana's voice, loud and clear.

'Charlie! This is Charlie! Shall we commence firing?'

That meant that the mortars were in position and ready to go. I wondered what Santana could see worth lobbing shells at!

None of which debates answered my question.

The radio spluttered again. 'Echo! Echo! What the hell's happening?' That was Benson's voice. The tuning slightly off. He was using the helicopter's radio.

Where

was

Chang?

The radio again.

'Dove! This is Dove! I'm not there yet! Have we started?'

Curly's voice. That was one of my questions answered, and several more posed. Chang was with Curly's section, or should have been. What the hell had happened! Certainly Chang must have failed in whatever it was he was planning.

I switched to transmit. 'Baker! Come in Baker!'

To receive.

Static.

Then, 'Baker here! Grenade trap! Grenade trap! One dead, two out of it. No contact yet. Shall we go on?' That was Wood's voice.

Curly's voice again, 'Dove! I am not in position. Repeat! I am not in position!' He sounded frantic. It was surreal. His was the last voice I had been expecting to hear.

Santana's voice, 'Is this Springtime?'

243

Come on Chang!

'B-Company! Attention B-Company!'

I looked at the handset. That last voice was definitely coming through a loudspeaker, but it was not the speaker of the handset. It sounded as if it was coming from everywhere, echoing metallically backwards and forwards off the surrounding high ground. From the air itself.

'B-Company! This is Patch! We know you are out there. Now, listen! There is someone here who wants to say a few words.'

There was a clatter that sounded like the hills were coming apart, so loud was the amplification. And there was a second of brain-piercing feedback. There must have been a whole nest of speakers out there by the junction.

A new voice said, 'B-Company. This is . . .'

My brain pounded suddenly. There was no mistaking that voice.

' . . . your commanding officer. The situation has changed. We are no longer at war. I repeat, the situation has changed. Walk in to the junction. Walk in to the junction. You will be received cordially. I repeat again, this is Colonel Chang, your commanding officer. The situation has changed. Do not open the assault. Walk in now. There will be no hostilities!'

The echoes died away into the hills.

Then there was silence.

I swallowed hard.

Chang had made some last-minute deal with Patch.

My Patch!

My

bastard

Patch!

I don't know how long I stood there, the walkie-talkie still hissing in my ear. Seconds, maybe. Or it might have been minutes. None of the men close to me said so much as a single word. They crouched there, behind their bushes, their eyes turned towards me. It was like a screenshot from some damned shoot-'em-up computer game.

Then the hidden speaker boomed its message again. I barely heard it.

Chang, the ultimate mercenary, was following the dictates of his chosen profession. He'd struck a better deal with Patch. While us poor saps were crawling around mountains!

The seconds ticked by.

Dawn came up like floodlights and it was all there in front of me. The valley floor, bush- and scrub-covered for about a mile, over which I could see the pitched roof of the signal box and, beyond that, the rusting corrugated iron roofs of the small ghost town that was — or had once been — Tengo Junction.

I woke up at last. Sod this for a game of soldiers! I thought. I pressed the radio to transmit. What I completely failed to realize was that if I spoke over the air I would be picking up the fallen reins. But I was not thinking, I was reacting, when I should have been *really* thinking!

'Baker-Section! Are you there, Wood?'

The reply was immediate. 'I'm here, sir.'

I said, 'Stand by.' Then, 'Benson?'

Click!

'Here! Dove-Section all ready to go. I think Jamie wants to do just that.' Benson's voice sounded far-away, listless almost.

'Stand by. Charlie-Section?'

'Here, my captain!' Santana. Bright, full of joy. Expectant.

I said, 'Stand by. Echo! You there?'

A breathless Curly. 'Yeah . . . but I'm not in position yet. Five minutes, at least!'

I smiled a crooked smile. I could not help but wonder where Curly's mind was now, and what stroke Chang had pulled so he could leave that section and do his thing. At the radio, I said, 'Everyone! You all heard what Chang had to say?'

They all reported that they had. Curly added, again, that he was not yet in position.

I said, 'Pass it to your sections. Anyone who wants to walk in must do it now. They have two minutes.' Then, over my shoulder, I called, 'HMG crews! You hear all that?'

Ammas's voice came floating down from the rock face. 'We heard!'

I called again. 'Pett!'

'Yo!' Far off.

But they would not have heard my instruction over the radio. So I called,

'Anyone who wants to walk in can do it now. But if you're still here in two minutes, you stay!'

I heard the sound of running footsteps, from over where Pett's voice had come from. I could not see the owner of the legs because of the undergrowth, but I did not have to guess who it might be.

Behind me, the Askaris were bunched together and seemed to be in deep and animated discussion. Sim was at the centre of it. I was reminded of a scene in the film *Zulu* where the Askaris took the first opportunity to slope off out of it. I did not blame them in the film, and I would not have blamed these guys in reality.

I waited the full two minutes.

Then I called, 'Are all you layabouts certain of this? You got one last chance to walk in.'

Someone said, 'Stuff Patch! And stuff the fucking chink!'

Someone else said, 'Fucking right! Bastard!'

The Askaris were still debating the issue.

I glanced at Graham, who simply shrugged at me. But his expression said, *why not?* He waggled Patch's radio at me. 'I'd say that this is about null and void now, right? They're bound to have realized we have it.'

He was right, of course. I said, 'Maybe. Then again, maybe not. Hang on to it anyway. The way things are going we need all the breaks we can get.'

Graham grinned. 'And then some!'

I went back to the radio.

'This is Able. Is all business transacted?'

Someone, it sounded like Benson's voice on the radio, said, 'Are you with Able-Section now?' Matter-of-fact, as if we were passing the time of day.

I pressed the button. 'On temporary loan. Everyone, let's have your reports!'

Wood, sounding peeved. 'I told you. One down, two out of it.'

There was the thin, staccato crack of a pistol shot which could have come from anywhere. There was barely any echo.

Santana's voice. 'I shot my bastard!'

Benson, sounding bored. 'No change here.'

Then, bringing another smile to my lips, Curly's voice, sounding frantic. 'We couldn't fucking walk in if we wanted to! We're still out on this fucking river! Two minutes!'

The speaker screeched again. 'This is your commanding officer! You are *ordered* to walk in! You will not be harmed. We have a new deal. You will all have new contracts.' Strange, for Chang, there was a note of desperation in his voice. And, I think, it was that note of desperation that sealed events. This was certainly true for me.

At the radio, I said, 'Benson! What time of year is it?'

But it was Santana who came back at me. He said, 'It's fucking Springtime . . . what else! And my three babies are sat here waiting to go to work!'

I hesitated, trying to pull it all together. The rights, the wrongs, the goods and the bads. But there was no clear picture in my mind. We were out there in the valley, and they were sat there in their concealed positions waiting for us. And that was it. Any sensible commander — and by picking up the reins, that's exactly what I had promoted myself to — would have pulled back to regroup and replan. But common sense, it seemed, was not in the air. And it was all getting away from me.

Then the radio spluttered and Curly came in. 'In position at fucking last! And I like that time of year, too.'

I thought, Well, hell, Curly, if you of all people like it, then who am I to disagree! I pressed the transmit button.

'All mortars. For effect. Open fire! Fire! Fire!'

14

Radio Tengo

A mortar does not go off with an explosive crack.

The tube sort of spits the shell out. The sound is a hollow, metallic Pteeewwww. And if you're quick you can actually see the projectile zipping high up into the air, slowing almost to a stop at the top of its curving trajectory, then disappearing as it regains speed on its way down.

And that, discounting the grenade trap, was how the battle for Tengo Junction opened.

Six mortars spat their projectiles in a ragged volley. Three from Santana's position on the eastern slopes of 806, two from Baker-Section, over beyond the signal box and one from over at the base of Hill-19, Curly's contribution.

I didn't actually have to wonder why Curly had not gone for a walk. He would have gotten as much change from Patch as I would from Chang if I'd gone in. As with many things in this life, it would be the lesser of two evils. On the other hand there was nothing to have stopped him from simply walking back to the trucks and disappearing into the jungle.

The same, I guess, applied to everyone.

Most of the Askaris did just that, except that they didn't bother with the trucks. Later, all that could be found of them was a small mountain of ammunition cases.

Also, I never saw Grierson again. Dead or alive. So the probability was that the minute we moved forward he slipped away from Pett and hightailed it back to that village in Shagland to pick up Nessie's stash of loot. The runner I had heard had to be someone else.

Before the first mortar shell landed I yelled for Able-Section to move. We went forward at the run, crouched low, weaving through the bushes. As charges go, that one was about as iffy as any charge could possibly have been. Hindsight is a wonderful thing. I did not have the first clue as to where Patch's men were holed up, what weapons they had or how many there were of them. The only certainty was that there would be weapons in high places. The tower and the signal box, and maybe some scattered in the hills somewhere.

This, stupidly, was not an action; It was a re-action.

Then Santana's HMGs opened up, so I

assumed they had acquired a target somewhere.

The valley burst into a thunder of bangs,
rattles and echoes. I thought I heard the
'speaker blasting its message again. But I
couldn't be certain.

The first hundred yards were a doddle.

Then there was a sound of a million bees
swarming around my head. Someone over to
my left let out a yell. We were in amongst
shoulder-high bushes then. But bushes do not
stop bullets. I could just see the upper half of
the signal box. The sun was lifting directly
behind it so my side of it was in deep shadow.
Even at the squint I could barely make out
the windows so couldn't see the men in there.
But I could see the flashes of their weapons.
Brens, I figured, from the rate of fire.

Normally, I like the Bren gun. It's my
weapon of choice, in fact, if the choice is
there. An oldie but a goodie. It fires a .303
round and there's barely any kick at all. That,
of course, is true only if the butt is snugged
into *your* shoulder. If you are at the business
end of a Bren it's a different gun altogether.

Graham was running alongside me, the
radio clasped in one hand, his Thompson in
the other.

The bees moved down from the air over my
head and started to kick swathes of leaves

from the branches.

I yelled, 'Down!'

The few men in my line of sight threw themselves to the ground amongst the bushes. Graham, beside me, landed heavily and his gear spilled everywhere. I lifted the radio.

'Able Two! Able Two! Take out that bloody signal box!'

Those Brens had to be silenced. Up ahead some fifty yards the bushes thinned out almost to nothing. Beyond that we had a fair stretch of open ground to cover before we had more bushes to cloud the issue. We'd be cut to pieces.

The bees again.

Except that the bees had wasps amongst them now.

At least one of our HMGs had seen the fire from the box and was already responding.

The bees went away and there were only the wasps.

I yelled, 'Forward!'

We charged on.

Then, the bushes weren't there any more, there was just a hundred yards of dirt. I still could not see any of the other buildings of the junction; they were over beyond another clump of bushes. I stepped back into the dubious cover of the bushes figuring that what they couldn't see they wouldn't fire at.

The sun was above the distant hills now, blasting a dazzling glare right down the valley. This was good for Santana. And good for Curly. And a very definite plus for Benson. Wood, with Baker-Section, would not be too bad off either, because that side of the valley still had some shadow over it, stretching almost out to the signal box. But it was not so good for us. The signal box was all but swallowed in the glare.

Graham yelled, 'What the hell's all that about?'

It looked as if one of our HMGs was pasting nothing but a patch of dirt, over on the far side of the open ground. Great puffs of earth were flying into the air, as if someone was detonating a series of underground charges.

A voice over to my right called. 'It's a foxhole!'

The man was right. The flying debris cleared for an instant and I saw what appeared to be a large wooden door, set in the ground. It had probably been covered with dirt before the HMGs zoned in on it. Then a couple of the 50-calibre shells hit the wood itself, sending great chunks of it flying up to join the dirt cloud. The value of placing the HMGs up on the ridge was confirmed at a stroke.

There was a hollow boom over on our right flank. It sounded like a grenade. Pett had either found another foxhole or they'd run into another grenade trap.

'Echo! Echo!'

It was the radio. Jamie's voice now. And it dawned on me in a flash of something bordering on horror that I had yet to tell anyone to advance. Except, that was, my own section. I went to transmit. 'Where are you, Jamie?'

Jamie came back. 'Still here, for Christ's sake! What do you want us to do?'

It was a valid question. And I had no answer to it. I said, 'Sit tight there! Just keep up the covering fire. I won't know what the score is until we close the junction.'

Another explosion. Off to the left this time.

Then another.

Grenades again.

I risked a peep around the bush. It looked as if the signal box was smoking. But I couldn't be sure; the sun was still almost obliterating it. To Graham, I said, 'Pocket that radio and take this one. I need my hands free!'

He glared at me. 'So do I, f'r Christ's sake!'

I said, 'Who's in charge, Sweeney!'

He mumbled something I didn't catch, but he did take it.

I said, 'Right, tell Baker to get over to the

base of Tengalla and move in from there. Remind Wood to cut the telegraph wires. Then find out what the rest of Charlie's up to.'

Graham gave me an incredulous stare. 'Anything else while I'm at it!'

I ignored that.

The assault on the foxhole came to an end and the dust began to settle. The tracers of the HMGs moved further towards the junction, stopped, then concentrated on another position I couldn't see. Another foxhole, I guessed.

Three men were charging up the other side of the open ground, right to left, from over where Pett would have been. I yelled,

'Covering fire on the foxhole!'

There'd been no sign of movement since the HMGs had moved on. But a well dug-in foxhole is a fairly secure place, despite fifty-calibre machine guns. That's if you had the nerve to keep your head down as the world collapses around you.

From the bushes on this side of the open space came a fusillade of machine gun fire, some to my left, some to my right. The air around that foxhole was alive again with flying dust and debris.

One of the running figures suddenly threw his arms in the air and collapsed. The two others ran on. I could see one of them fumbling with a grenade.

So who had gotten the other guy?

I quickly scanned both sides of the open space. I could see nothing. That bullet must have come from a firing slit on the far side of the foxhole cover. I flicked my M16 to full auto, pressed the trigger and held it. My bullets stitched a line of exploding dirt over to the foxhole. Then I held it there, waving the barrel slightly from side to side. Debris flew everywhere. Then Graham, behind me, was firing too. The end of his barrel was inches from my right elbow. The noise was deafening, mind numbing.

The two running men dropped to their knees. An arm went back, then arced forward. I vaguely saw the grenade falling on the quickly disintegrating wooden cover. But before it had even landed the two men had dived sideways behind a bush. I stopped firing and so did Graham.

CRUMP!

A mass of earth and wood splinters mushroomed up.

I yelled, 'Cease firing!' The fire from Able-Section had been continuous. Despite everything I was aware that our ammunition was finite. And we had barely made any real contact.

I yelled, 'Forward!'

We broke out of the bushes and tore out over the open ground. Further ahead, over at the junction, I could see smoke and the occasional flash of a detonation. I still had no clue what we were up against, and that knowledge was paramount.

There had been two men in that foxhole.

It would have taken God Almighty to make them look like men again.

We hit the bushes on the other side of the open space and charged on, dodging bushes and rocks. Graham, alongside me, was wheezing like an old steam kettle. He had one of the radios jammed to an ear.

Then the bushes ran out and, there, about a quarter of a mile directly ahead, were the huts and detritus of the junction. It looked like a small Wild West ghost town. I yelled for a halt and ducked behind a great outcrop of granite. Graham collapsed beside me. We both sat there grabbing for breath. If it was possible, I was wetter from sweat, then, than I had been from the rain all night long.

Graham, the radio still to his ear, wheezed, 'Charlie's got half a dozen men forward to the base of 806.'

I said, 'Tell them to hold.'

At the radio, Graham said, 'Hold that position! D'you read?'

A tinny voice said, 'Holding. Mortars still engaging.'

I could see that for myself.

BLAM!

BLAM!

BLAM!

Three explosions, coming one after the other, tore the ground apart off to my left. They had started to use their own mortars. But this was one area where we held a slight advantage. Provided, of course, that you weren't unlucky enough to be directly beneath the fall of shot. Mortars are great for taking out fixed positions, but not so great when your target is moving. They were dug in; we were on the move. At least for now.

Graham, who seemed to have gotten his breath back, said, 'From Dove.' This was Curly. ' . . . A hundred yards short of the spur. One dead.'

I said, 'Ask him if he can hold.'

I gave Curly a moment's thought.

Why hadn't he pulled out? It was not like Curly to risk his neck. Not the Curly I thought I knew. Perhaps I had never known him at all. He was inept, devious, seemingly totally untrustworthy, even in the mercenary sense of the word. Yet he had stayed. Was *staying*. Was, in fact, fighting!

Graham said, 'They've got a strong position.'

I nodded.

BLAM!

BLAM!

Those shells were falling on empty ground, and I suddenly realized why.

In Chang's plan, Able-Section was to have taken out any possible opposition in the signal box, then move on in up the rail line. That, because the rail line at that point was sunken to a small extent. And that was where the mortar rounds were falling.

Which led me to another thought. 'Get Baker on the line!'

Graham nodded. 'Baker! Baker! Come back!'

From the radio, 'Baker here.'

I said, 'Tell them to hold. Now!'

Graham said, 'Baker! Hold that position. Hold that position!'

The radio squawked. 'No opposition here. We can make another two hundred yards easy!'

I grabbed the radio from Graham and pressed to transmit. 'Wood! Is that you?'

'Yes, sir. We've got a clear — '

BLAM!

BLAM!

BLAM!

I said, 'Wood! Stay put. Stay put. Don't bloody argue, just stay where you are!'

I had barely gotten the words out when the mortars spoke again, only this time the explosions came from over in the lap of Tengalla. I yelled at the radio,

'Wood! Scatter! Scatter! You are pinpointed! Scatter! Do you read?'

Nothing.

I cursed myself. Of bloody course! Chang knew the original plan better than I did. He'd be directing Patch's fire for him!

Wood's voice: 'Hell, that was close.' Then, more from the radio than the air, 'Blam . . . blam . . . blam . . . '

I could see the smoke billowing up over there.

Wood again, 'Pulling back! Pulling back!'

Blam, blam, blam . . .

Other shells were falling elsewhere now. Over by the bend in Red River, where it turned right along the main line. Curly's position.

And over at the base of 806. Santana.

Graham was looking at me all peeved. I guessed that was because I'd taken his job away from him. To the radio, I said, 'Benson! Are you there?'

Jamie's voice. 'Echo here. We're under fire. We're under fire. Heavy!'

Of course they were coming under fire. The helicopter was one of the first things Patch would want taken out. I pressed to transmit. 'Pull out of there immediately! Don't wait, and don't tell me where you go or where you end up. You got that! We're being monitored. Do you read?'

I heard the tinny sound of the helicopter's engine winding up just before Jamie came back on the air. 'Moving out. Standby.'

I went over to transmit. 'All sections! All sections! Shift positions. Just pull back and stand by. Do you read?'

One by one they all acknowledged.

To continue the action from our current positions would have been pure suicide, not that it had been desperately far short of that in the first place. Patch would know exactly where to place his strongest elements.

Then the loud speaker boomed. 'B-Company. This is Colonel Chang.'

He didn't sound happy, or gloating. Maybe he was the opposite of these things. 'Your position is hopeless. You cannot regroup without radio contact, and we have all channels monitored. It is not too late to walk in. I have Admiral Patch's assurance that you will be treated fairly. Walk in now. Walk in now!'

The air had suddenly gone still and silent,

except for the soft crackle of flames over in the signal box.

Chang was right, of course.

To do anything like an effective job would have necessitated use of the radios. And Patch would be able to hear every word of it. I was still smarting from my own stupidity at not realizing this at the start, and was on the verge of offering the choice to the men . . . again!

Santana changed my mind.

'Able! Able! This is Charlie. Watch this — '

Pteeewwww.

Pteeewwww.

Pteeewwww.

For fifteen long seconds the mortars continued to fire. The explosions of the shot-fall merged together as one long blast.

Santana must have pin-pointed the speaker truck from his position on the first slope of 806. For, in the middle of the crashing explosions, a single burst of high-pitched feedback screamed out above the thunder.

When the explosions ceased there was utter silence.

Then the radio clicked on.

Santana again.

'Radio Tengo has closed down for the day!'

15

A Brief 'Lawrence'

And so we pulled back.

Tengo Junction was left to lick whatever wounds we had inflicted in that first brief action.

I took Able-Section back about a mile to the cut in the rail line where 806 joined the south-eastern fingers of Tengalla. This was the only spot along its entire length where the engineers who built the line had found it necessary to blast a path out the living rock. That cutting, at its deepest about fifteen feet, provided some kind of cover for us to lick *our* wounds.

Most of the Askaris had disappeared. And I didn't blame them one little bit. They may have found their way over to the junction, but the better bet was that they had simply melted away.

Pett, I found out later, had been one of three men killed by the grenade trap we had heard go off on our side of the valley. I'm not sure how many other men we lost, and for the simple reason that I only had a vague idea of how many we had started with.

Unforgivable, actually, despite the impossible circumstances. I was not feeling too proud of myself.

One thing now in our favour — if there was anything at all — was that Patch, with Chang at his elbow, had been all set up to receive us before. When, *if*, we went back in again he'd be dealing with question marks. On the other hand, so would we. Still!

Benson called up:

'Able! Able! Echo repositioned. We need to talk, Marty!'

My heart sank a little. I figured that Benson, being Benson, was going to tell me, face to face, that he was pulling out. He would not simply have left. I went to transmit.

'This is Able. Pick me up.' I looked at my map and gave him a reference. Chang would have his map, too, and was very probably listening. But we were well out of reach of anything they could throw at us now.

Benson said, 'Got it. A few minutes. Out!'

I looked around my command. Most were asleep where they'd thrown themselves. Sweeney Graham, picking up Pett's baton without being asked to do so, had organized a piquet. Everyone, it seemed, was thinking ahead and doing stuff for me without being

266

asked. I wondered when I was going to start thinking ahead and doing stuff for *them*! The right stuff! So far I had displayed nothing but stupid, and highly expensive, bravado. I had placed myself in command without thinking it through, and it had cost us. I wondered what might have been if I had waited for someone else, Jamie maybe, to respond to Chang's sudden appearance on the other side of the tracks. But he hadn't, *I* had. The ball was in my court. Leadership by default.

Graham was sat now on a rock, his weapon cradled in his lap, looking at me. There was nothing in his expression. He was just looking. Patch's radio, still hissing gently, lay on the ground beside him.

The men were scattered about haphazardly, some smoking, some dressing their own shrapnel wounds, some just laying there. About thirty men in all. I gave that some thought. *About* was not good enough, and never should have been.

To Graham, I said, 'We need a head count, Graham.'

His exposed skin was filthy with grime. I supposed mine was too. He nodded a tired nod. 'Of course we do.'

I went on, 'We also need to get someone out there — '

He cut in, well ahead of me. 'Casualties . . .

I'm on it. Well,' he added, 'I will be.'

'Do we have any medics?'

He pulled a dubious face. 'Well, we've got Benjy.'

'Is that good, or bad?'

He grunted. 'If you're fit, it's good. If you need a medic, it isn't so good.' Then he gave a tired chuckle. 'Nah, Benjy's okay for the small stuff. I'll fix it.'

I nodded. All this uncertainty was because I had dealt with Nessie in the way I had. I had robbed this section of its leader and its 2i/c at a stroke. It did not help that at the time my own options had been limited. A finger would have to be pulled out. But this was not the time for an inquest.

I said, 'I'll be back as soon as I know the score.'

Graham sucked in a breath, opened his mouth to say something, then seemed to change his mind. In the end, he said, 'Bring me back an ice cream.'

I said, 'Get your own bloody ice cream!'

I ran back through the cut, two sleepers at a time. I saw the helicopter swinging round 806 as I approached the open space beyond. Benson did not put down. He hovered there, two feet off the ground as I climbed aboard. Then he wound on more revs and we shot up. I slipped on the headset.

Benson did not say what I thought he was going to say. 'We have a major problem!'

I smiled a secret smile. His use of the continuing tense was heartening.

I used the sardonic reply. 'Tell me about it!'

He shook his head. 'No . . . you don't know about this one! Patch has an Oerlikon down there.'

I said, 'Eh?'

An Oerlikon has a sound all of its own. And it has a range all of its own. It's a 20 millimetre monster that can fire 450 shells a minute 2,000 metres, straight up if necessary. I said, 'I didn't see an Oerlikon!' Nor had I heard one. There's no mistaking the bark of a weapon that size. And there's certainly no mistaking the kind of damage it can inflict.

Benson grunted. 'You wouldn't have. They have some rolling stock on the line just east of the junction. Jamie spotted it first, as we were pulling away from the sidings. They had it covered with scrub at first. Two flat-tops. There's a truck on one of them, and a half-track on the other. They piggy-backed a goddamned Oerlikon on the half-track. It wasn't fully set up before, but I reckon it is now! I'll show you in a minute.'

He was swinging back south and east of 806. He pointed down. 'Echo is down there, right below us.'

I glanced down, but my mind was grappling with the possible ramifications of an Oerlikon.

I saw Echo-Section grouped on the slope just below the cradle of the twin peaks, just above the tree-line, within yards of the spot where Able-Section had been earlier. One of the figures waved. I waved back.

Benson said, 'Am I right in thinking that Nessie is out of the picture?'

I said, 'Benst, too.'

He shot me a glance. 'I won't ask.'

I said, 'You'd be wise not to.'

He shrugged. 'Fair enough. I hope you have good eyesight. Five seconds is all you get. And if they've got that bloody shooter loaded already you won't even get that!'

We sank down to just above treetop level.

There were the sidings. And I could see the bonnet of one of the trucks. I still couldn't see Tengo.

Benson said, 'Set?'

I said, 'Go for it.'

They must have been following the helicopter's progress by sound. Benson pulled back on his stick and fed some more gas to the turbine and we shot up above the east slope of 806 like a rocket, and the tracers arced up to meet us from several places.

Benson spat, 'Shit!' and went into a

manoeuvre that had my stomach up in my chest cavity. The tracers sunk soundlessly beneath us. Then Hill-19 got in the way. I was glad it was there.

Benson said, 'That blows the sight-seeing trip out the window! You'll just have to take my word for it.' He went on, 'I guess we *almost* caught them on the hop. They must've commandeered those flat-tops and railed themselves in. The Oerlikon would be to blast hell out of the compound, going by what Star Sapphire had to say.'

I said, 'Star Sapphire didn't damn well tell us about the Oerlikon!'

Benson shrugged. 'What do women know about guns.'

I looked at him. I had not been referring to the girl, who'd merely been the messenger. I said, 'A Freudian slip, was that?'

He shot me a glance, a puzzled expression on his face. Then his expression cleared. He hunched a shoulder and, for a moment, looked sheepish. 'Well . . . you know what I mean!'

There were far more important fish to fry. We were east of Hill-19 then, and swinging north to meet the other end of Tengalla. The rail line glinted momentarily below us, right alongside Red River. I caught a brief glimpse of the junction, way off to the west, between

19 and Tengalla, then it was gone.

I said, 'I'd like to know when Chang went over.'

Benson said, 'That's easy. He was on his own after I brought Echo in. He was using the RCA transceiver. He probably called Patch on Single Side Band. That would have been safe. None of the handsets can get SSB.' He added, 'Chang's a bastard!'

That, I thought, depends upon your point of view. I said, 'Chang just knows what's good for him. But I'd also like to know what deal Patch offered him.'

Benson chuckled. 'Maybe later you can get to ask him. Oh, one other thing.'

I looked at him. 'Good, bad or indifferent?'

He smiled. 'One of those. Can't categorize it. It's just that Urundi's chopper doesn't seem to be here. More to the point, I don't think it's *been* here!'

'How the hell can you tell that?'

He tapped his nose. 'Us pilots know stuff.'

I laid a heavy sigh on him.

He shrugged. 'I looked especially, when I over-flew the junction. Short of where I put down over near Tengalla, there's only one spot that would suit as a landing pad. If the chopper was in operation there'd be signs around that area. Re-fuelling drums. Flattened grass. *Signs.* You know, stuff like that.'

I said, 'Okay, fine. What d'you think that means?'

He shot me a quick glance. 'I only fly helicopters. You, for your sins, are the man who figures out the whys and the wherefores of it all.' He added a heavy, 'Well, you are now!'

I saluted him with a forefinger. 'Touché!' But, still more or less in reaction mode, I had not given that fact the consideration it deserved.

He smiled. 'I don't even know which side of my bread I'm supposed to butter. So I'd be useless on matters of high import!'

'Okay,' I said, 'Let's try an easy one. What's the general feeling in Echo-Section?'

He said, 'Now there I can help. Santana keeps managing to pull morale out of the slump. They're okay now. But I guess you don't want to give them too much thinking time. I suppose that goes for everyone.'

I said, 'What about you?'

Benson looked over at me and smiled. 'Don't worry about me. You'll get plenty of warning if the call of the south gets too strong.'

I said, 'Thanks.'

He nodded. 'Don't mention it.'

I said, 'Can you switch me over to channel three?'

Benson pushed a few buttons then gave me the thumbs up. Into the mike, I said, 'All sections report.'

Santana said, 'Charlie here. All secure. No activity that I can see. Not any place. Mortars are ready to go again.'

Wood's voice: 'Mortar crews in. No activity.'

Then Jamie: 'Echo! Where's our bloody transport!'

I said, 'Sight-seeing. You okay down there?'

He said, 'Are we pulling out?'

I said, 'Well, I'm not.'

He said, 'Fair enough. Just so long as I know.'

'Sweeney,' Graham's voice came in. 'Well, you just left here, so I don't guess you'll need anything from me. But I still want my ice cream!'

Benson gave me a sideways look. I placed a palm over the mouthpiece. 'You had to be there.'

Then Curly came in. 'Dove here. We're okay. Well, *now* we are! No more casualties. Listen, skipper . . . '

Skipper?

' . . . I think you ought to know. From where I am right now I can see smack dab into the junction. They've got a bloody great gun down there, on the back of a truck!'

I said, 'That bloody great gun is an Oerlikon, and I know about it. See any movement?'

Curly said, 'Not a lot. Certainly can't see no hundreds of blacks. I thought Patch was supposed to have received an intake.'

So did I. I said, 'Keep your eyes skinned. We're pulling it together.'

Benson said, 'Now *there's* a thing.'

I nodded. 'Right. So where are they?'

By way of a reply Benson heaved over on his stick and the aircraft described a half circle that did that thing with my stomach again. He said, 'I've got a hunch.'

Into the mike, I said, 'All sections. Hold your positions. Set up your pieces and dig in. Report any activity.' On an impulse, I added, 'Oh, and, Colonel, just in case you're listening, I think you've made a big mistake. I never did like you much, but now you've got me mad at you! Out!'

Benson smiled over at me. He clucked his tongue. 'Sticks and stones.'

I said, 'If only that was all it took.'

Benson pressed a button that took us off the air. He curled us around the northern end of Tengalla and dipped the helicopter's nose at the trees. The rail line flashed up. Then he hauled back on his stick, adjusted his revs, and zoomed off. If the aircraft had had seventy foot legs on its wheels we would have been running on the rails. Ahead, the rolling countryside stretched to infinity, disappearing finally into the mid-morning haze.

Some fifteen minutes later we saw the smoke well before we saw the train. Benson said, 'It's nice to be right . . . for a change!'

As we zipped over I saw this angular sea of black faces staring up at us. Two flat-tops and a carriage. The whole thing, engine and all, was alive with men. Then it was lost behind us.

Benson hauled us back into the sky. 'So we really did catch Patch with his pants half off!'

I said, 'Right. But it's more luck than good judgement. How far out are we?'

'For us? Or for them?'

'The train.'

'An hour. Maybe more. Can't be making more than thirty, forty miles an hour.'

'Can we stop that damned thing?'

Benson swung us around until we were headed back along the line. He said, 'I refer the honourable gentleman to the remark I made earlier, regarding the difference between a pilot and a commander.' He laughed. 'I guess Curly's at last realized his limitations. How does it feel to be a commander-in-chief?'

I said, 'Commander-in-chief of what?'

Benson shot me a glance. 'It's all down to you now, chum. All of it! You do realize that, don't you?'

I said, 'One thing at a time. Right now all I want to do is stop that train. You wouldn't have a few bombs aboard, would you?'

Benson shook his head. 'I have grenades. Two boxes of them. But I can't put you down anywhere close enough.' He waved a hand at the terrain. There was not a break in the trees anywhere along the line. In some places the line was hidden beneath the dual overhang of the trees.

I said, 'Well, if Patch gets that lot we could be in deep shit!'

Benson pursed his lips. 'Presupposing we're not in deep shit already . . . '

The radio clicked. 'Dove! Dove! They've got that gun down off the flat-top now. Shall we try and take it out?'

I had already thought about that. 'Negative! All sections! Do not expose your positions!'

I put my mind back on the train.

More than simply stop it, I needed, really, to destroy it. Two boxes of grenades was not going to do that. No one, not even Bhamas, are going to sit still to have a helicopter fly over them, dropping random grenades on their heads. The combined effect of a hundred automatic weapons, even poorly handled weapons, would rip us to bits.

Then I had an idea.

'Get us ahead of them, Benson. Quick as you like.'

'What are you going to do?'

'I'm going to stop the bloody thing. What else!'

The sea of faces stared up at us as Benson piled on the speed and took us forward to overtake the train. No guns fired. But that was not surprising. They did not have a clue who we were, or whose side we were on. We were a military helicopter in military livery, and that would have been enough to cloud their issue.

It also meant that there were no radios down there. Certainly none in the hands of anyone who knew what they were doing. This told its own story. There was something that Patch had not covered. Or that he had not had time to cover. Or that he was too busy to cover. Or, more importantly, that he had not even thought of!

'The grenades back in the belly?'

He said, 'Yep. Problem is I'll have to stay fairly high. I don't much care for grenades going off right under my wheels. We could end up down there ourselves.'

'Okay. Get us far enough ahead for me to do my thing, then hold her steady.'

Back in the cargo space I broke open one of the boxes then slid back the door. The rotor's downdraft burst in like a hurricane and the noise was deafening. And the way the floor was sagging and rising underfoot told me that Benson was having problems with the warm air currents that would be rising off the trees.

I grabbed a grenade and pulled the pin. Then I leant out the door, aimed and let the grenade fall. The retaining pin pinged off in flight.

The grenade exploded well before it hit the rails, and the aircraft gave a vicious lurch that all but ditched me out the door. I heard Benson yelling. I went back to the flightdeck.

Benson was shaking his head and fighting to control his aircraft. He yelled, 'No go! I can't hold her. One more like that and it's goodnight nurse!'

I said, 'You got a hoist back there. Right?'

He nodded. 'Yeah. But it needs a third person back there to operate it.'

'How about a rope? Do you have a rope?'

'Yes. In the locker. About a hundred feet of it.'

I said. 'Okay. Just hold here as you are. When I'm down there you zap off. But not too damned far.'

He shot me a glance. 'Well, whatever you're going to do, do it bloody quickly. That train can't be far behind!'

I went back into the hold. The rope, I tied to the hoist mechanism. Then I tied the unopened box of grenades to the other end of the rope and eased it out into space. It was not easy. The box was so heavy I had to use both hands on it. Several times I thought I was a goner as the open door swayed over to suck me out. But the box of grenades reached the ground.

Then, hand under hand, I started down myself. That wasn't easy either. The down-draft kept wanting to blow me away. But I made it.

Benson had his nose pressed to his side window. I waved up at him. He showed me the fingers of his right hand twice. I guessed that was his estimate of how long I had before the train reached us. I waved back at him and the helicopter roared away out of sight beyond the tree canopy.

The relative silence was blissful.

I did not waste time.

I tunnelled into the stones under one of the rusting rails, throwing them over my shoulder like a mad thing. Out of the corner of my eye I caught a glimpse of the helicopter, reappearing way down along the track.

Benson obviously wanted to watch, but from a safe distance. I ripped the lid from the box of grenades and settled it into the hole. I could not hear the approaching train. I could not see it, either. The track to my left was straight for about a hundred yards before a gentle curve took it out of my line of vision.

I took a grenade, pulled the pin, dropped it into the open box, and ran like hell.

I was still running when the makeshift bomb went off like a thunderclap of doom. The shockwave lifted me clean off my feet and threw me to the dirt, all arms and legs. But I don't think I felt a damned thing. I did not bother to look back. I dragged myself to my feet and charged on towards Benson and his machine, some fifty yards ahead now. The rope snaked towards me.

That climb up that damned rope, against the force of the downdraft, is a thing I'll remember for a long time. It tortured every muscle in my body and very nearly beat me. The rope was not thick enough to offer any real grip, and my hands were drenched with sweat and covered with lichen. I used the mountaineers' foot grip which helped slightly. But none of it was easy.

But I made it in the end.

I was laying there flat out on the floor of the hold for several minutes, completely winded, and for all I cared the world could have taken a running jump at itself. But I came back slowly, heaved myself to my feet and picked my way forward to the flight deck.

Benson had a rueful look on his face as I collapsed into the copilot's seat and slipped on the headphones. 'Impressive stuff! The rail ended up at right angles,' he said. 'But they saw it in time to stop. The train isn't going anywhere, but those kaffirs are.'

I was too winded to speak. So I just nodded.

He said, 'Still, it's bought you some hours. Three or four, I guess.' He smiled over at me. 'The ICSRC will be sending you their bill, y'know!'

I found my voice at last.

'Great! Just as long as I'm around to send them a terse reply!'

16

Me, With Some Help From Patch

I was not feeling chipper.

That Oerlikon was going to be the big bad wolf. We had nothing to touch it.

I had another worry, too — a more personal one. It had jumped up and grabbed me as we were headed back in to Tengo. I gave it a little thought, but came to the conclusion that I was much more comfortable with the Oerlikon worry.

Our HMGs were good. Pretty near the best in their class. But they did not fire exploding shells. The Oerlikon did.

And with HMGs your target had to be in line of sight.

And if the Oerlikon was the target, it would be operating on the same criteria.

Put a Heavy Machine Gun up against an Oerlikon in a line-of-sight contest, and a contest there would not be. The HMG might take out the Oerlikon operator, if the bullets penetrated one of the very few holes in the operator's protective shield, but the Oerlikon could blast the HMG into scrap, and it would

283

not necessarily require a direct hit to achieve this.

Mortars were the best bet.

Mortars can be hidden in holes. Deep holes.

Then again, the Oerlikon was on wheels. It could simply be moved out of harm's way.

Benson said, 'Just in case you're looking for something else to think about, I have a fairly pertinent concern.'

I dragged my mind back. 'What's that?'

'Fuel . . . or, rather, a probable future lack of the stuff.'

Of course! I said, 'How much flying time do you have left?'

He tapped one of his dials and pursed his lips like a garage mechanic. 'An hour, maybe two. Tops! After that I'm running on fumes.'

I gave it some thought. But there are only so many things a man can consider at any one time. I said, 'Okay, remind me about it when you've only got thirty minutes more in the air, and I'll do something about it.'

'Like what?'

I don't know why, but a touch of totally unreasonable irritation leapt into my throat. 'Like I don't have a clue! I'll deal with it, okay!'

Benson held a mollifying gloved hand in the air. 'Fine . . . I just thought you'd better know the score.'

We lapsed into a prickly silence.

I knew where my flash of anger had come from. I was angry at myself, certainly not Benson. Nor anyone else. Not even Chang.

That other worry had slunk back into my mind.

I tossed it out again. Maybe I'd forget about it in time.

A night attack might adjust the balance sheet. But, come nightfall, there was going to be an additional hundred or so men in there.

And our element of surprise had jumped off the roof the moment Chang had taken his own walk. Which thought led me right back — again! — to that other worry.

This was no good. I had to sort myself out before I could sort anything else out. It was this mechanical voice inside my head that kept yelling 'Why?'

Why drag B-Company down with you?

Do you need a crutch?

B-Company doesn't want Patch, *you* do!

As far as B-Company was concerned the game, in purely mercenary terms, had been over. *Was* over!

The name of our game was lucrative deals.

A mercenary soldier engages in business deals.

Mercenary soldiers do not fight for pleasure, or for revenge or for an ideal. Not a

285

true mercenary. One like Chang.

Nothing personal, old chap, but — *bang!*

A gentleman farmer farms because there's money in it. He rarely gets his hands dirty.

Did this make Chang a gentleman mercenary?

So, what was I?

I sure as hell was no gentleman.

I probably wasn't even a mercenary soldier any more.

Patch had been my reason. Still was. But Patch was mine, not B-Company's.

Was I too scared to hack it on my own? Did I have to have a small army to hide behind? Was that why I had opened that first abortive action so blindly?

I had this sick feeling in the pit of my stomach. A man is not really a man if he can't hold a perfectly fit body upright without a crutch.

And yet, despite this realization, I still could not bring myself to consider letting B-Company off the hook. Perhaps this was why I had allowed myself to take command in the first place.

Why?

Had I subconsciously taken myself back to Iraq? To Grenada? Was I deluding myself along different lines? Did I think that B-Company was fighting for itself? Had

B-Company become an ideal without my even noticing it?

Without B-Company itself even noticing it?

Let's do it for B-Company!

Shit, that was ridiculous!

Let's do it for money . . . and a lot of it!

And yet . . .

Pride?

Were we proud of what we had become . . . what we had never set out to become?

Did we see ourselves as some kind of a Thin Red Line? Or was it just me seeing it that way?

Was Santana proud of B-Company?

Was Jamie?

Curly? Wood? Sweeney Graham? Pett? And the rest?

How about Benson?

It is impossible to know what is going on in a man's mind. Any deductions must be based on pure guesswork, aided to some degree by expression and actions. Everyone's actions, so far, had persuaded me that they were happy with the way things were. It was as if my taking over had been preordained in some way; that I was the natural successor. Not Curly. Not Jamie. Maybe I had been that all along, but had been too blind to notice it.

I glanced over at Benson as he played with his controls. His expression seemed blank, yet he must have known, and damned well, that our position as it stood was as good as hopeless.

Then I remembered Graham's expression, when Chang's voice had come over the loud speaker. Disbelief at first, moving to something like disgust and then, finally, to a teeth-gritted resolve that seemed to say, '*You bastard! I'm going to tear you apart for this!*'

But for what?

Chang had offered everyone the choice. And, in retrospect, it had been a pretty damned reasonable choice.

'This man is *no longer* the enemy . . . '

People had been saying that for eons. The Hun is no longer the enemy! The Zulu is no longer the enemy! The Gook is no longer the enemy! The Black Man is no longer the enemy! The White Man . . .

Make a new deal. Sign a paper. And that was that!

An exchange of signatures wiped all legal mercenaries clean.

I dragged my mind back off that treadmill. I had grappled with it too many times.

My question remained.

Could I ask, could I expect, B-Company to follow me into an impossible situation, when I personally was looking no further ahead than Patch's dead and mangled body?

288

Or could I persuade myself that everyone else's reasons for doing so were as valid, in personal terms, as my own?

If B-Company wanted to go ahead, for its own reason, then, fine. But I was not going to employ tricks to hold up their resolve, to keep the impetus going. They would have to do that on their own terms.

Into the intercom, I said, 'Tell me something, Pilot. Why are you doing this? Why stick around now, the way things are?'

Benson eased his stick and held the aircraft at a hover above the trees east of Hill-19. He kept his eyes directly ahead for a moment, and I had the feeling that he had been searching his own thoughts, the way I had been searching mine.

Then he sighed gently and shrugged. He turned to me with a blank smile pulling at his mouth. He said, 'D'you know, Marty, I don't have a clue!'

I said, 'I thought not. Keep us right here, and put me on channel three.'

He hesitated momentarily, then his expression slid into one of resignation. He leant forward and flicked a switch.

'All sections! All sections! Stand by for a message. Report my signal.'

One by one they reported that they were receiving.

I said, 'I have a statement in two parts, then I have a question. The statement is . . . right at this moment Patch has upwards of a hundred irregulars coming in. They're on foot at the moment, but they'll be in Tengo in about four hours.

'That's part one . . .

'Part two is that, for those of you who don't already know, Patch has an Oerlikon with him at this moment. And the Oerlikon is well on the top side of anything we can bring to bear . . . bar nothing! They're obviously well dug in, and we're scattered to hell and back.

'The question is for *everyone*, not just you section leaders. Make damned sure you get a majority vote! What are we going to do about it?'

For several seconds nothing came over the air but hiss and static.

I knew damned well that I had very probably de-winded a lot of sails. But this was the way I wanted it.

Let's start from scratch.

If I ended up on my own, then that would be my tough luck. But that was the way I was seeing things.

However, the voice that eventually came over the air, was not one I recognized; not as belonging to anyone in B-Company. It was an

American voice, and full of sickly-smooth honey.

'That's the way, old buddy. Glad to hear you've woken up at last. Listen to him, B-Company. The man sayeth sooth . . . '

It was Patch's voice of course. And it went on,

'I don't normally hand out second chances. And I've *never* been known to go for three! But everyone's allowed an exception . . . this is mine! Listen very carefully. This is your third, and very last chance to walk in. Do it now and you'll live to make more money. Hesitate, and you're a bunch of dead men!'

I did not cut in. I let him say his piece.

'You're not idiots, B-Company . . . your commanding officer assures me of that. So don't *act* like bloody idiots! Wake up and smell the bloody roses! What is it with you? You get a good offer and you blow it. For what? I'll tell you for what. For nothing! You're being led by a fool who's only just realized he's a fool! So listen to him. He's just given you the best advice he's ever given! Don't act like a bunch of amateur arseholes!'

He was overdoing it.

If he'd shut up after his first couple of sentences he might have had takers. Probably would have. But he was going over the top. I couldn't think of a single man in B-Company who'd sit still for that kind of talk.

Benson glanced over at me, eyebrows raised. He pulled a face, but said nothing.

Patch went on, 'That's it, B-company. Come on in now and I'll let you walk in. Leave it and you won't walk anywhere any more! We'll rip you to bits and we won't even have to try hard!'

I flicked over to transmit.

I said, 'Thank you for those few kind words, Patch. Okay, B-company, this is my last call, too. Let's have it . . . '

I might have known that Santana would be the first to respond.

'This is Charlie-Section. Patch? You still there? We got a message for you and your flashy Oerlikon.'

He left his mike on transmit.

Pteeewwww

Crump!

'Did you get it . . . old buddy!'

'Echo-section here.' This was Jamie. 'Patch? There's a man here who'd like a word.'

'Hey, Patch! Remember Hill-701? Up near Goomi village? 'Bout three months back? One of 'em got away. Remember? That was me! And you can stuff your third chance up your arse!'

Then Jamie came back on the air. 'Let's get moving, for Christ's sake! It's cold up here on this damned mountain! And a commander bloody well commands; he doesn't keep offering bloody options!'

The airwaves clicked. Jamie had the needle and I couldn't fault him for it.

'Dove-Section here. I'll go along with that, skipper. But are you going to do something positive, or do I have to take over?'

I said, 'Perish the thought, Curly. You were enough of a handful as 2i/c. What about you, Baker?'

Graham came in. 'I think you'd better get back here!' There was a new, dubious tone to his voice.

I said, 'What's the problem?'

'No problem.' Pause. 'Just get back here quick!'

There *was* a problem. I said, 'Roger. Coming in.'

Benson swung us around Hill-19, hugging the treetops, keeping well below sight of the junction and the Oerlikon. Patch was saying something over the radio. I switched to transmit.

'Sod off, Patch! You've had your answer! Everyone else, stand by.'

I switched the radio off.

Benson was looking at me strangely. I said, 'What?'

He laid a smirk on me. 'Can I take it that

you have now purged your conscience to your entire satisfaction?'

'Is that was I was doing?' He was correct, of course.

He nodded. 'You know bloody well!'

I said, 'I'll never be satisfied with the state of my conscience. But, broadly speaking, I guess I *have* sorted myself out, yes.'

17

Star Sapphire Again — With Flaw

Tengo Valley was a sun trap.

You could see the heat rising from the rocks as translucent flames rising into a sky that was purged of all colour.

Graham had rigged up a makeshift awning of ground sheets suspended between a couple of bushes. The piquets were out keeping tabs on the junction, but the rest of Baker-Section were scattered around in whatever shade was available. I don't have a clue how, or from where, but Graham had also conjured up coffee. There was probably someone out there with self-heating cans of the stuff. We carried with us three days worth of K-rations in our packs, but that was all. Subsistence only. Coffee and the like was well over and above. He handed a tin cup to the girl.

The girl said, 'I was very frightened when I heard Patch talking with Chang over the radio last night. I did not hear it all, because I was just taking some coffee in. But I heard Chang saying that he would turn B-Company over to Patch if he would agree to certain conditions. I think he was talking about money, but I can't be sure. I don't think I have ever been more frightened in my life!'

She certainly looked as if she had had the stuffing knocked out of her. She did not look the same girl we'd talked to at the delta. Though, if my memory serves, and except for a scarf she had tied around her head, she was wearing the same clothes.

I sat myself down on an ammo box. 'Well, you can relax now. You're out of it.'

But she did not relax. She was a bundle of raw nerves. And her eyes, wide and staring, kept flitting around as if she were trying to keep a specific fly in sight. She went on, 'I knew that if Chang was turning traitor he would be bound to tell Patch about me and my brother. I tried to find him, my brother, to warn him, but he was not in any of the huts. And then, when Chang arrived, I thought I would die. I was again in the room when one of the men brought him in. I can't tell you how frightened I was.'

She took a slurp at the coffee.

Benson stood just outside the awning. He was a picture of concern. It's odd the effect a pretty girl has on an otherwise perfectly sane man. I'm a candidate for sex myself, but give me the no-complications kind every time. Start meddling with the helpless sort and you're immediately in trouble.

Picking up her thread, the girl went on, 'But Chang just glanced at me and said nothing.' She fumbled with the mug with trembling fingers. The mug took a nosedive. She was beside herself with apologies.

Graham darted off to get her a refill.

I did not know why, or even if I was imagining it, but the girl somehow couldn't bring herself to meet my eye. She kept looking down at her hands.

I said, 'So your brother's still in there. Why didn't he come out with you?'

She said, 'He insisted that I come alone. He said that if Chang had not already betrayed us, then he was not going to do so. He said it was a chance we had to take.'

Graham came back with the refill.

She looked up at him. 'Thank you,' she said, the fly back in front of her eyes again. She went on, 'He said he was going to try to find a chance to ruin the big gun.' For a few seconds the trembles seemed to leave her. 'You see, we had already ruined the helicopter. That's good, isn't it?'

Benson breathed, 'Good girl.'

I said, 'How'd you manage that?'

This time she looked straight at me. And she smiled. 'My brother told me how to do it.'

Benson spluttered, 'You did it? Yourself?'

She nodded, the smile brave and proud now. 'Oh, yes. It was not hard. All I had to do was put a kilo of sugar in the petrol tank. I didn't know how that would do it, but it did. Then, just after the helicopter had taken off, its engine just seemed to stop working. It crashed back down and just . . . just blew up.'

The smile left her face then. 'I — I was sorry about the pilot. Of all Patch's men he was, well, the best.'

I said, 'Yeah, well, helicopter pilots are a breed . . . ' I looked at Benson.

Benson gave a chuckle. 'I said I knew him, I didn't say we were bosom buddies.'

Graham, only barely short of Benson's obvious state of mind, said, 'But how did you get away from Patch?'

The shakes came back in earnest.

'That was quite easy, too. You see, there is no running water in any of the buildings, so I have to go to the spring to get water. The spring is just below the hill. And they only have one guard over there. My brother kept him talking, and I slipped into the trees. It was very easy.' Then she frowned. 'That part was easy, but the trees were very thick and overgrown, and I had to make my way along the edge. That was hard.'

Graham put in, 'Villiers found her down

there opposite the signal box. Bloody good going, for a girl!'

And it was. I said, 'But there'll be all kinds of problems for your brother when Patch finds you gone.'

Here she really faltered.

'Well, I . . . My brother . . . we think, well, *he* thinks, that he will be able to get away himself, when he has done something with the big gun.' She looked pleadingly at Benson, not me. 'That big gun is very dangerous to you, my brother says. He says it will kill you all if you attack the junction.'

Graham pursed his lips and glanced at me. 'Hell, sir, if he can take out that Oerlikon before those blacks show up we could stand a chance in a frontal!'

We could indeed.

It was all very promising.

But what the hell was it with Chang?

Why would he not say anything to Patch about the girl and her brother?

Chang, for what must have been to him very sound reasons, had switched sides, had offered B-Company to Patch on a plate. And, with B-Company, Patch would have the whole shooting match. Mtomo would be finished. Why queer it for —

Mtomo!

It was his name, and his face, flitting

through my mind, that turned my thoughts in a new direction.

Mtomo was panting to take Patch alive.

Chang and Mtomo had obviously discussed my own wishes as far as Patch was concerned. And Chang would have agreed to put a bullet in my back to stop me. Mtomo had very probably offered . . .

Something slotted into place then. I was not entirely sure what it was, but I figured I had the bones of it. On impulse, I said, 'Graham! Search her!'

He and Benson looked staggered.

Benson peered at me as if I'd gone crazy.

The girl looked panic-stricken, and her shakes had kids. I knew I'd hit it right.

A couple of the guys, who had been sheltering from the sun under a nearby bush, looked over our way. They'd been discussing the obvious merits of the girl's figure, the way men do, with occasional leers in her direction. They, too, looked at me strangely.

I said, 'That's an order, Graham! Just do it. Search her!'

He spluttered, 'Eh! Why?'

I was very patient, and I kept my eyes on the girl. She was looking for somewhere to run.

I said, 'Just do what you're bloody well told! Search her. Now!'

I slipped my Webley from its holster and thumbed back the hammer. I guess Graham thought I was using it to bolster my order, because he moved quite briskly.

And he was only just in time.

The girl leapt to her feet, her eyes suddenly ablaze. I thought about shooting her. I had the chance with time to spare. But I didn't want to shoot her, because I had an inkling of what she was supposed to have done and, more to the point, why she was supposed to have done it.

And she tried.

Even then she tried, her eyes screaming frustrated anger. And no one was more surprised than Graham. Her shot sang out under his outstretched arms and ricocheted off a rock, leaping into the air on the tail of a new note. But Graham was on her then. And he was now all business.

The girl was screaming, 'No! No! No!'

And she fought like a wild cat.

Able-Section crowded in around the lean-to.

I stayed where I was. I would have moved, I could have moved. But I didn't.

Graham knocked the gun from her grip, but he wasn't making so much as a dent in her struggles to get free and at me. I motioned one of the men to help him.

Benson was stood there like a fish out of water, just staring at the spectacle.

Together, Graham and the other guy, one of my Askaris, got her spread-eagled on the dirt. She was crying, cursing, spitting and hissing. It went on that way for several minutes. But they had her pinned.

Suddenly, the struggling stopped.

She lay there on her back. Graham on her arms, the black on her legs. All three were sweating buckets, panting and wheezing. And she broke her heart in a way I had not witnessed before, and hope never to see again. I leant forward and picked up her gun. It was a Detective Special. Small, compact, and ugly looking.

I said, 'Okay. Leave her.'

Benson woke up at last. He grabbed the black by his ammo belt and yanked him bodily away from the girl, despite that the poor sod was climbing wearily to his feet in any case.

The girl was drenched in sweat. And her blouse was half off her, exposing one half of her brassiere. The brassiere was sweat-soaked into nothing at all, and her nipple stood out darkly, effectively exposed. Able-Section crowded around, leering.

That tableau opened my eyes to many things. Stories of rape and pillage are commonplace in Africa; unremarkable. And at that moment it was as if I could have been on the extreme edge of such an event. I was staggered at how one thing had turned into something else completely in a few short seconds, if only in my own mind. A crowd of randy men; a single, utterly helpless slip of a girl lying on the ground with her legs more or less open. This must be how it is, how it happens out there. Up until that moment I had never given it much thought. I was embarrassed for the girl but, more importantly, I was sickened by the whole thing.

I said, 'Okay, you lot! Break it up. Benson! For Christ's sake cover her up!'

The girl made no move to stop him as he eased the blouse back into decency between an almost embarrassed thumb and forefinger and nudged her legs together with his knee. She just lay there breaking her heart.

The men hadn't moved.

I said, 'Anyone within ten yards of this lean-to by the time I've counted to twenty, draws the van when we go in. And I'm talking a two hundred yard lead here!'

The men disappeared.

Graham, still panting heavily, looked at me. Benson, looking as if he'd just lost everything he owned, turned and looked at me. I had a feeling that they had both experienced a

303

similar epiphany. Then Graham saw the girl's gun in my hand. I think that unlocked his mindset.

'Christ, sir, that was close. How did you know she had it?'

I said, 'I didn't know. Anyone got any booze?'

Benson was ahead of me. He nodded. 'I have some brandy in the cockpit.'

I said, 'Get it.'

The girl had ended up half out in the direct sunlight. I had Graham adjust the lean-to so that her head was in the shade. We could have dragged her in, of course. But I was utterly unwilling to lay as much as a finger on her. Strange, that.

Benson came back with a hip flask. He also had with him what looked like a fold-away picnic chair, which he flicked open and placed beside the girl. I looked at him. He shrugged.

'Us pilots have time on our hands. Might as well sit around in some degree of comfort.'

I said, 'I didn't say a word.'

He said, 'You didn't have to.'

He fussed around her for a bit and eventually got her up and into the seat. He placed the flask to her lips. Submissively, she took a sip. Then she sat there, still sobbing gently, but more in control of herself. She looked ghastly, her eyes red and swollen. And somewhere along the way she'd picked up a cut to her cheek. Benson dabbed at it with his handkerchief. That was something about Benson. He always carried a spotless handkerchief with him, neatly folded in his breast pocket. He fell short of actually having it poking its pointed corner out, but it was always there nonetheless. As far as I knew he was the only guy who bothered with such niceties. Even Chang would simply sniff hard.

He put the flask to her lips and fed her another slug.

She was looking at me now. Eyeball to eyeball.

But there was no anger to be seen there. No hate.

Just this great sadness.

Then she said, 'I *have* to kill you. Don't you see?'

I thought I did. I said, 'Sure. They've got your brother, right?'

Her mouth opened as she searched for words. Then she seemed to slump.

I said, 'So what was the plan? Shoot me . . . then what?'

It was a long time coming. But eventually she said, 'I was to shoot you, yes. Then . . . then . . . '

She was slipping again.

305

To Benson, I said, 'Give her another slug.'

But the girl waved his hand away, pulling herself together. 'They'll kill Paul.'

'Paul's your brother, right? He's Star Sapphire.'

She nodded. She mumbled something about God, but I didn't catch it.

I said, 'I can't help you if I don't know the score.' But I was not sure what I could do even if I did know the score.

She shook her head tiredly. 'No one can help me now.'

Graham, standing just inside the lean-to, said, 'Shit!' But I don't know why he said that.

I said, 'You'd be surprised. So, after you'd put a bullet into me, what?'

She sat there for an age, saying nothing, doing nothing.

Then her hand came up slowly and reached inside her blouse — under her bra, I assumed — and came out with a sweat-soaked piece of folded paper. It would have been over her right breast because it certainly hadn't been over her left.

Benson took the paper from her and passed it over to me without so much as glancing at it.

That piece of paper was warmer than the ambient temperature and I confess to a few lewd — if uninvited — thoughts of my own.

306

18

A Commander Commands

The note read:

> 'Your position is now totally hopeless.
> Most of all it is unnecessary. In a short
> time Joshua Mtomo must concede defeat
> and relinquish the eastern territories to
> Robert Urundi. To continue your
> present course, especially without leader-
> ship, is foolhardy in the extreme, and can
> only result in your defeat by superior
> forces now, or your execution by firing
> squad later.
>
> I remind you that you are contracted
> to me, personally. As your commanding
> officer I commend you for your fighting
> spirit. You have shown yourselves to be a
> credit to my example.
>
> You now owe allegiance to no one but
> yourselves. And to me, your command-
> ing officer.
>
> Come in peacefully now, B-Company.
> Your new contracts, the rewards of
> which far exceed those of your current

undertakings, are ready to receive your signature.'

It was signed: Ping Yi Chang. Officer Commanding, B-Company.

Benson said, 'You'd think the bastard was English the way he uses the bloody language!'

Graham, who'd stepped over to read the note over my shoulder, said, 'I hope to Christ you're not going to give us another choice, sir. That was my last brain cell.'

I realized that only part of that was a joke. I was reminded of just how indecisive I had been. I looked at him. He had dark shadows beneath his level grey eyes. He was being asked to do far more than his fair share. But he seemed alert and ready for anything, like a predator ready to pounce. Silently, I thanked him for putting up with me. I had taken too much for granted. I said, 'No more choices.' Then, to the girl. 'Do you know where they are holding your brother?'

She shook her head wordlessly. She was all cried out. For her, the apocalypse might have been just around the corner, if it hadn't already come and gone.

Benson said, 'I'll tell you something about that note, Marty.'

'What's that?'

'For an outfit with such supposedly

superior forces they're keeping a bloody low profile. If Patch was half as sure of his ground as that note says he is, then why isn't he here walking all over us?'

I nodded. It was true. Obviously we had caught Patch very far from being ready for a push on the compound. Just as obviously we had caught him unprepared for a solid defensive action, let alone any kind of an *offensive* one. Time was the factor, of course. Chang's deal with him could hardly have been more last-minute. Chang had probably arrived there about the time me and Graham were taking that outpost. The pair of them would have had minutes, just, to pull something together.

To the girl, I said, 'What about the helicopter? Was all that a lie too?'

She shook her head. 'No,' she said, oozing lethargy. 'We — I — did that. Back at the base, shortly after I met you on the beach.'

I said, 'About your brother — '

She cut in, 'My brother is dead. And I have killed him.' Her face was stony, set, resigned. 'I should have shot you the moment I saw you.'

Bizarrely, I felt vaguely guilty that I had not allowed her to do just that. It was not a huge part of my thinking, for sure, but it was there, lurking in the background. But it wouldn't have solved a damned thing in any case. Not in the long run. I said, 'Do you honestly believe Patch would let either of you walk away? Whatever the outcome of this bloody business?'

I was wrong about the tears. She did have some left in her. Not many, certainly. But enough. They came tumbling down her face while she sat there like a lifeless rag doll.

Wetly, the tears trickling into the corners of her mouth, she said, 'But I had to believe that, don't you see! I had to believe that he would keep his word. There . . . there was nothing else to believe.' Her shoulders slumped and her head went with them.

Benson mothered her as only Benson knew how. This was obviously his *Jekyll* side.

Graham stepped out from under the lean-to. 'Let's just plough on in there, sir. Sod the Oerlikon! If we get in close enough, and fast enough, it isn't going to do them a lot of good.'

I looked at him. He had a point. But I was not about to go off half-cocked. Not again! I stood up, stepped around Benson and the girl, out into the blazing sun. Most of the section had moved well away from the lean-to and seemed to be studiously ignoring what was happening. Some had rigged up their own groundsheets for shade; others were digging into tins of K-rations. A couple were playing cards.

Over the valley to the east I could just see the summit of Tengalla. It appeared to be sitting on a bed of steam. A single column of dirty smoke reached into the sky. That would be the signal box. It seemed such a small gain for the lives we had already lost. I wondered what was going through the minds of everyone out there, including Chang and Patch and the rest. We all seemed to be in a lull, waiting for something to happen.

Patch would be waiting for the arrival of his reinforcements.

Chang, thinking — or *hoping* — I was dead by now, would be waiting for a reaction to his note.

Baker, Charlie, Dove and Echo sections would be waiting for leadership. I was reminded of Jamie's words.

'*A commander commands!*'

And it all slotted into place in my head.

The start had not been back at the sidings, as Wood had joked. *This* was the real beginning! And this was the real beginning because the reins, by some kind of disjointed default, were now completely in my hands. Chang's actions had determined that, not mine. Not even my bit of business with Nessie and Benst had affected the real issue.

Except that, perhaps, had I somehow received a bullet from Chang, it would have been for a wildly different reason to the one whose seed I had implanted back at the compound. Either way, it might have been possible that B-Company and Patch's outfit would be bosom buddies right now. But things had not fallen that way, and they were not bosom buddies.

And I knew exactly what had to be done. I also had an idea of how we might take a good stab at achieving it.

To Graham, I said, 'Do we still have piquets out there?'

'We do, sir.'

'We' was a generalization, of course. *He* had piquets out. It had not been my idea, when it certainly should have been. That was yet another failing that would not happen again. I wondered whether or not I ought to make his current, unqualified, role of 2i/c more official. I discounted the notion straight away. The situation had gravitated through natural succession to where it was now. Explanations and directives might only clog up whatever cohesion we had going for us. And Graham seemed happy with the undeclared way things were. I certainly was.

'Right, we'll have them in quick as you like. What's our strength? This section, I mean.'

Graham reached into his breast pocket, took out a slip of paper and ran his eyes over it. 'Well, we ain't in bad shape.' He smiled at me. 'Depending on what your version of *good* shape might be!'

I wondered how his obvious qualities of leadership had not been picked up long ago. Pett's, too, for that matter. Then again, this was actually Nessie's section, and Nessie's mind had run along totally different lines. He would have been looking for corruptibility, not leadership. Graham went on, 'I left one HMG crew up on the ridge and brought the others in. That gives us a total of twenty-three reasonably fit and ready to go. Pascal's arm is shot to hell and back, but Benjy's fixed it up pretty good, for now. Four dead out on the pan.' He pulled an apologetic face. 'Pett's one of them. I didn't bring them in . . . but I'll fix that too, if you like.'

I shook my head. 'Time for that when it's all over.' Which constituted Pett's epitaph. It burned a bit that I didn't have a clue who Pascal and Benjy were. 'And I need a transistor radio.'

Graham looked blank. He slipped his piece of paper back into his pocket. 'A trannie?'

'Yep. Just your ordinary, common or garden steam radio.'

He pulled a dubious face. 'Well, *I* don't got one.'

Benson, from the shade of the lean-to, said, 'Someone has. I've heard it.'

I said, 'Where did you hear it, Pilot?'

Benson nodded over his shoulder. 'Back on the other side of the cut. One of the new boys, I think.'

Graham trotted off.

I lit up a cigarette and waited. I could have murdered a coffee. The girl was mumbling something about how much she hated Patch, and Benson was saying 'There, there.' A few minutes later Graham came running back, a pocket-sized commercial radio in his hand.

'Compliments of Les Crowther.' Which was yet another name, and another man, I did not have a clue about.

I tuned the radio to some African music station and handed it back to him. 'Take it, and your walkie-talkie, down the line. Get as close to the junction as you can, back in the trees. Tape the walkie-talkie on transmit, but make sure it's on low power, and lay them nose to nose.'

Graham said, 'Jamming?'

'Yep. We'll catch some of it, I guess. But Patch'll get most of it. Enough to rattle him, anyway. Take a half a dozen men in case you run into trouble. But before you do, get me

314

someone to keep tabs on . . . ' I nodded over my shoulder. ' . . . her'

Benson said, 'I'll do that, Marty.' Of course he would.

I said, 'No, you won't! I need you for something else.' I smiled at him. 'That's your fault for being the only pilot.'

Graham, either thinking back, or thinking ahead, obviously had someone in mind for that job, because he ignored the men closest to us and loped back out of the cut.

The guys close by were all looking at me now. Several had stood up and were sorting themselves out. They had either caught the change in me, or in the situation. I saw Ammas over by the verge of the cut. I called, 'Ammas, I need your crew! Get your shit together and close on me!'

He waved acknowledgement.

Graham came back with a man in tow. He said, 'This is Simons, sir. He's okay.'

Simons appeared older than most of Able-Section. He looked tall, but that was an illusion aided by the fact that he was thin and wiry. His face wore a hang-dog expression. I did not remember him as being one of the guys who had witnessed the debacle in the lean-to. I nodded back at the girl, who was easing herself up out of Benson's picnic chair.

'See this girl, soldier?' Wasted words, I

know, since he couldn't possibly have missed her.

He nodded. His eyes flashed over to her, hovered on her for a moment, then came back to me. 'Yes, sir.'

I said, 'You're going to watch her like a hawk!'

The girl stepped up to us, with Benson close behind her, holding out his hands as if she were about to fall over. It was actually painful to watch. If he was one of the fighting troops I'd be getting a little worried about now. *Smitten*, didn't appear to cover it. 'I'm alright now,' she said. 'Honestly I am! If you are going to attack I want to come with you.'

She looked like death warmed over.

I said, 'Sorry, kid. But I can't trust you. Not yet!'

She pulled herself away from Benson, trying to look big and strong. 'You needn't worry about me, I can handle a gun as good as any man!'

I smiled. 'That's what's worrying me.' To Simons, I said, 'If she gets closer to a spare weapon than six feet, belt her. And I do mean belt her!'

Simons nodded, but did not seem certain.

She said, 'I won't do anything . . . I promise.'

I said, 'You won't do anything and you

don't need to promise. When we get under way and it's too later to matter I'll maybe let you join in. Until then stay out of my way. You got that?'

She pouted her lips and looked hard done by. But I wasn't joking, and she realized it. So did Benson, who stood there looking down at his feet. I turned to Graham.

'Get your men and go do it. The quicker it's out there, the quicker we get this thing done! Get back here if there's time. But if not you go in from there. We'll be moving in left to right of you. Just slide in as you can. And if the jamming thing doesn't work, we're going in anyway. Okay?'

He nodded. 'Okay. Break a leg!' And he was gone.

Ammas was hovering in the background with two men and a small pile of equipment.

To Benson, I said, 'Pilot, take these three guys and put them down on the Tengalla side of 19. There's a good view of the railway line there.'

I did not wait for a reaction from Benson. He had to be snapped out of his trance. I was not blaming him, and I was not judging him. Someone once said that infatuation makes coincidental fools of us all. And in my younger days I had been there and done that! You're big and strong and fearless one

317

minute, a screwed-up kitten the next.

To Ammas and his crew, I said, 'You guys are going to cover the gap and the junction. When the Bhamas finally show up — and they will show up, eventually — keep them away from Patch . . . ' I added, 'for as long as you can.'

To Benson, I said, 'Drop them off, then I want you to pick up Wood and as many of Baker-Section as you can get on board. Those you can't bring, tell Wood to have them join up with one of the other sections somehow. On the way, drop in on Santana, Curly and Jamie. In whatever order you like. Bring them all up to date and tell them I'll be on the radio with more instructions shortly.' I added a friendly, 'don't ask me to repeat any of that because I've forgotten it already.' I looked at him. 'Can you do it?'

He smiled. 'Sure.'

I nodded. 'Fine . . . and keep well out of reach of that bloody Oerlikon. Okay?'

He looked me straight in the eyes. I had the impression that he would have liked to give the girl a final glance. But to his credit he didn't. He nodded. 'I'm already gone.'

And off they went.

I motioned the girl back under the lean-to, and waved Simons after her. 'Get in there out of the sun. And, Simons, you don't move out of there until you get the word from me. And she's under your gun every second!' I recognized the look on his face. 'You don't have the first clue what this is all about, do you, soldier?'

He sniffed. 'No, I don't, sir.'

I said, 'Well, that doesn't matter much. All that matters is that I've told you what to do, and you're going to do it. If you want to have long conversations with her, that's cool.' A little softening of the situation was called for.

To the girl, I said, 'What's your name?'

She sucked in a breath. 'Elise.'

'Fine.' To Simons, I said, 'And yours is?'

Simons looked vaguely uncomfortable. 'Harry, sir.'

'Okay, Harry, meet Elise. Elise, meet Harry. The pair of you get acquainted.'

And I left them to it.

* * *

The radio came to life. The music was not loud, even on full gain. But I guessed that down at the junction it would be loud enough.

I pressed the transmit button. 'Charlie-Section. Do you read?'

To receive.

Nothing but far away music. I tried again.

'Charlie! Charlie! Come in!'

Nothing. This was good news.

To transmit again. 'Echo! You there?'

Jamie's voice came in, as if he was talking under water, the words ebbing and flowing with the Martian type music. 'Echo here! What's happening with the radio? You're strength three, but garbled! Are you getting this?'

I said, 'I'm getting you. But I don't think Patch is. See if you can contact Charlie from there.'

I heard him calling for Santana. I did not hear a reply. Then Jamie came back. 'I got him. Did you copy?'

'Nope. Now try Dove.'

Same again. It seemed to be working.

I said, 'Okay, Jamie. You're my relay station. Stay where you are for the moment. When we kick it off I need you to slide your section over to the rock face at the base of 806. But not where *we* came down. Pick your own spot, with good cover. You should be able to see us moving from there. Have Dove hold fire at first, to give us time to get in close. Same goes for Santana. When we're drawing all the fire, give Dove and Charlie the word to open up. Then, everyone not on the heavy pieces, goes in. No stopping, Jamie. Tell them that. When we're off, we're off. Did you get all that?'

'I got it!'

I added, 'You can tell your men that Patch is not as well off as I thought he was. And he's certainly not as well of as *he* thinks he is. But that's only if we get in there fast. And that's what we're going to do. How're your wounded holding up?'

'I don't have any. But I know that Santana does. Maybe Curly has some, too. Shall I check?'

'Do that. Not that I can do too much to ease their load. But, just in case Patch is hearing your transmissions clearly, the radio traffic will keep him interested for a bit. And all we need is a little time to stack this thing up. And it's coming. Out!'

Wood was hovering at my shoulder. I was glad to have him where he should be at last. He said, 'So we go . . . ' Pure statement.

I nodded. 'We go . . . like, now!'

The sun was past its zenith but not far enough to have lost any of its severity. The air was still and scalding hot. The whole valley shimmered and bounced in the heat haze. I made the mistake of checking my watch. It was approaching 14.30. I realized that I had been on my feet for the best part of two full days. And with that realization, came the tiredness, pricking at my eyes and turning my

321

limbs into lead weights. So far it had obviously been mind over matter. I wished I had not bothered checking the time. Any kind of rest was still a million miles away. Discounting, that was, the eternal kind.

19

The Divine Madness

Able-Section, plus the few Baker-Section men Benson had brought in, were strung out in a long line right across the valley. The sun was directly overhead now, and scalding hot. All colour seemed washed out of the world. Shadows were starkly defined, heat-shimmering black holes. Cussedly, there was no breeze now to make life a little easier. Breathing was like sucking steam from a boiling kettle. I could not hear the helicopter. Either Benson had set down somewhere, or was on the far side of Tengalla, out of earshot. The silence seemed absolute, deafening.

I glanced back over my shoulder. The wounded man — I tried to remember his name, but couldn't — lay on a groundsheet under the makeshift lean-to. In the harsh shadow his blood-soaked bandage looked black, not red. The Able-Section medic — what the hell was *his* name! — stood over him. *Benjy,* that was it! And the man with his arm shattered beyond hope was called Pascal. Weirdly, remembering their names seemed to slide some long-misaligned cog into place.

The girl was standing by the lean-to with Sweeney Graham's man, Simons, at her side, his weapon loosely aimed at her hip. She would not stay there. I knew that. And Simons wouldn't belt her. I knew that too. And it no longer mattered.

All along the lines either side of me the men were looking at me. Waiting. I sucked in a breath, let it out slowly, then stepped forward. And the line came with me.

At first we moved at a walk.

Not even a brisk walk. Just a walk.

The only sound now was the occasional clatter of boot on rock.

From somewhere over on Tengalla a monkey screeched. The sound echoed around the valley like a soul in torment. Maud Peroni, to my right, hissed, 'Shut your fucking mouth!'

Someone out on his flank called an admonishing, tongue-in-cheek, 'Language, Maud!'

I smiled, and was suddenly, and desperately, proud of these men. And I knew that whatever happened here today I would take that pride to my grave. They had rallied to me when others, with good justification, would have split. I wondered whether I deserved that loyalty. I didn't think so. But I didn't hold that thought longer than a heartbeat. None of it actually mattered any more. There was only the here and the now. And the junction somewhere up ahead beyond the scrub. Invisible, beckoning. Inevitable.

I lengthened my stride and the ragged line came with me.

Then I caught a momentary glimpse of the burnt-out signal box, still way off.

A covey of birds lifted lazily out of the bushes ahead and rose silently into the sky. I was reminded of the delta, and those flamingos. And I experienced a fleeting, burnt-in-the-brain image of the surf line, blue and beautiful, super-imposed over the washed-out scene ahead.

A monkey screeched again. The echo of its call came back at me from 806. I wondered if it was the same monkey. Maud made another remark but I didn't catch it. Someone else, to my left, said, 'Bags I Patch!'

Ginger Wood — I think it was Wood — said, 'Get in the fucking queue!'

Villiers was over to my left. He nodded at me, smiling. He had a tooth missing. I nodded back at him. It was strange that I was remembering names now. Men who I'd only seen momentarily, and men whose names I had only heard others use. They were right there, faces, names. Like a mental dictionary revealed for the first time. An epiphany of some kind. The only thing missing was history of some kind. A story, a reason. And, in Villier's case, a first name.

Another of those men, Les Crowther, was over beyond Maud. He was puffing contentedly at a cigarette as if we were out on a Sunday stroll. Except that you do not go on Sunday strolls dressed in battle dress and festooned with belts of bullets and grenades.

Well, we did!

I heard the girl's voice saying something, but couldn't make it out. I did not look back.

The line walked on.

And on.

In almost total silence.

And the signal box drew closer.

Away to the right I could see the rock face. I looked up at the twin peaks of 806. Not a sign of movement.

Then the spell broke, as it had to eventually.

It was another damned grenade trap. At least, I assumed it was a grenade trap as opposed to a thrown grenade, because there was no preceding gunfire. And the use of grenades in a head-on action will mostly, in my experience anyway, be preceded by at least *some* small arms fire. But the explosion, whatever its origin, did not come from our end of the valley, it came from way off, near Hill-19.

Tripped or thrown. It turned the key in the lock.

Maud started to run first. He just said, 'Shit!' and off he went.

I went with him.

Then the entire line was running.

Not a flat-out dash, just a run.

Then all the demons in hell were let loose.

And the run became a flat-out dash.

It was as if someone had shouted, 'Action!' and the effects boys had thrown every switch on their board. The air became suddenly alive with bees and wasps, and humming birds and crackers.

Then the first mortar shell landed. And it wasn't one of ours. It landed way back behind the lean-to, exploding with a detonation that became continuous thunder. Then another one came down. Ahead this time. And a great cloud of lethal metal, rocks and dirt cascaded into the air. And the sky was criss-crossed with red, yellow and white tracer rounds, weaving fantastic patterns in the sky.

The din was indescribable, deafening, everywhere. Great claps of metal-edged thunder, the echoes scarcely less ear-shattering than the original explosions. From absolute silence, to this. Brain-numbing.

Peroni, some way ahead of me now, seemed to run straight through the debris of an explosion. He came out the other side, still on his feet, still running. Maud must have been very fit. I was running at my best, yet he was still pulling away from me.

I leapt over great boulders and blasted my own path through tight-knit stands of bushes, the branches and the thorns trying, and failing, to stop my charge.

I think my last totally conscious tactical act was to glance up at 806. But the sweat, running freely down my face and into my eyes, blurred any sight of Jamie's section. Or maybe I was looking in the wrong place. But from that moment on I was simply a victim of adrenalin-charged events.

I pulled my arm over my face to get rid of the cascading sweat.

From somewhere up ahead a curving line of red tracer walked a path through the bushes. Leaves, branches and dirt filled the already cluttered air.

The ground was suddenly a trampoline underfoot.

I hit the dirt hard, totally enveloped in a choking mist of dust.

The Divine Madness.

The Zulus called it that.

They would spend hours invoking it before

a battle. Working themselves into a frenzy of unleashed fury, from which only time, and a bloodbath, would release them.

They believed that once the Divine Madness caught hold of a man he was unstoppable, impregnable, indestructible. Fear was no part of a man in the grip of that soul-sucking lunacy.

There would be no restraint either.

Murder was the antidote.

Murder, blood and yet more blood.

The Zulus were savages.

And I was headed that way.

I fell, rolled, gained my feet again, my ears singing from the crash of the explosion. What did it for me, I think, was that I could see nothing to shoot back at. So far I had not fired a shot. That made me angry.

I just took off.

I had a vague impression of more tracer coming at me. Then it was gone, leaving more clouds of dust and smoke.

I could taste bile in my mouth, and the dirt grated between my grinding teeth.

Then I could see the buildings of the junction. They seemed a hundred miles away, still.

I went flying headlong into a crater. My body jarred but I felt nothing. The ammo belts I had strung around my shoulders fell about, getting in the way, and that made me angrier. Then I was running again.

More rocks. More bushes.

Another crater.

Another wall of red dust reared up in front of me and the world went suddenly silent again. Absolute, perfect silence. But I was still running. Another rock loomed ahead of me. I pumped some more power into my legs and the rock simply disappeared beneath me. I sailed over another crater as if it wasn't there at all. The tracer rounds were still there, and the mushrooms of dirt were still appearing. But there was no sound. None.

More bushes.

A line of boulders.

Then there was a strange hissing sound, like a burst steam pipe.

I misjudged the height of one boulder, turned a half-circle in mid-air, and landed heavily, all arms and legs. I cursed everything and everyone. But I felt nothing. The world was cotton wool and I had wings. Angry wings. I needed something to shoot at! Any damned thing!

The anger seemed to be boiling up inside my head, expanding my consciousness until it was my whole body. Then I was running again.

I could now hear my own breathing. But

not through my ears. I was hearing it from some place deep inside me. Suck . . . blow . . . suck . . . blow.

And there was the thump, thump, thump as my feet hit the ground. More a feeling than a sound.

Then, with a loud, almost physical POP! the noise came back.

Pteeewwww!

CRUMP!

An anvil CRACK!

TrrrrrTrrrrrTrrrrr!

Yelling. Screaming. Mayhem!

But nothing was going to stop me. Not mortar shells. Not machine guns. Not grenades. I had eyes for nothing but those buildings up ahead. Nothing was going to stop me reaching them and, at last, firing my weapon into a human target.

The madness was on me.

I forgot about Patch.

About Chang.

About everyone.

The fight did not matter.

B-Company did not matter.

All that mattered was that I got to fire my gun, and at another human being. I needed to see blood fly and bodies disintegrate.

The Divine Madness has a great many so-called atrocities to answer for. You start eating peanuts, you can't stop eating them until there are no more left to eat. A stupid parallel, for sure, but in the end it comes down to an elementary question of degree. When the Madness is directed towards killing, another man becomes the peanut. To be eaten until there are no more left to eat.

It's as simple and as uncomplicated as that.

It's a miracle brought about to help a fighting man do what he has to do. And you cannot kill a man *just a little bit.*

And the madness, The Divine Madness, was on me.

The buildings of the junction were suddenly right there in front of me. Two hundred yards. No more. A mere two hundred yards and I could do what I was there to do. I could pull my trigger and let death fly.

My clothes were a sodden mess and my flesh was caked with dripping mud. My feet slopped in my boots. None of it mattered.

A hundred yards.

I was aware of Villiers, to my left, running into a line of red tracer and catapulting backwards out of my line of vision.

Seventy.

The tracer came at me then, floating almost lazily left to right directly in my path. I felt the bullets zipping past me, either side. I laughed aloud.

Fifty.

I felt the elation washing over me in great waves.

Then I saw my first target.

A figure was running from the open door of the nearest hut. His gun was aimed at me and it was spitting flame.

You can't hurt me, you bastard!

I yelled something as I yanked back on my trigger. My gun kicked in my hands for the first time. The hammering recoil felt wonderful. I was laughing. Joyous. Because I had made it through to fire the gun at last. The man went over in a tangle of arms and legs and dust.

How do you like *them* apples!

I ran on, searching frantically for another target. C'mere you bastards, I need you!

There was still the open door. And there were flames spitting from a window alongside it. I tugged a grenade from my belt, bit out the split-pin and let the retaining arm fly off. I tossed the bomb in the open door as I charged past, leaping over the body of the man I had brought down.

Then there were buildings all around me. And bangs and crashes and yells.

And more running men.

Without stopping or even slowing down I squeezed my trigger and pulled the gun around in a loose arc in their direction. The figures tumbled and fell, chests and faces exploding.

Pandemonium was everywhere.

My trigger was no longer firing rounds.

I wrenched off the spent magazine and rammed home a fresh one, my hands absolutely in control. I doubt I was even breathing heavily any more. But it wasn't me in charge of my limbs and body; it was the Madness.

Someone charged past me, firing from the hip.

Then someone else.

It took a supreme effort on my part to hold off spraying their backs. But I managed that. So there was a deeper, more settled instinct at work on my system.

What happened after that is nothing but a blur of explosions and noise. No real memories. And it is pointless to even begin to describe it. Except to say that without The Madness — and it was, it seemed, rampant throughout B-Company that day — the attack would probably have failed.

Patch's command did not possess that madness. How could they? The Divine Madness is bred by knowledge of an impending, open, frontal attack. A near suicide mission — an *actual* suicide mission — where there is absolutely no way back. No retreat, whatever happens. And it feeds upon itself. Until you pass the point where you give a damn about anything. Defence, where you sit, almost relaxed, behind what you assume is perfect cover is something else entirely. That breeds nothing but dangerously false courage which, put to the test, can easily falter. And for Patch's men it must have done just that. It faltered.

But I can remember little of it.

I do not, for example, remember seeing Benson pulling his steed all over the sky, drawing fire from the Oerlikon, as the HMG crew sprayed hell out of the junction through the open-belly door.

Nor did I see Jamie and three of his section blown to hell just after they had taken the strongest position, the old administration block.

I did not see Ginger Wood and his stalwarts close a machine gun nest, two brens and a Maxim, and tear the gunners apart almost with their bare hands.

I wish I had seen Pearce dive full-length into the window of what used to be the old ticket office with a live grenade in his hand. Nine of Patch's men had been in that hut; two with HMGs, the rest with brens and a

335

bazooka. I do not, to this day, know why Pearce had judged it necessary to go in with the grenade instead of simply throwing it. Of course, there would not have been anything *simple* about it. I just did not know. But that's what he had done. I can only assume that he had been fatally wounded, and had stopped caring. The Madness would have taken care of the rest.

I did not see Anders, White and two others walk slap bang into an Oerlikon shell fired from point blank range.

And I did not see Dove-Section drawing all the fire in the world as they raced in over open ground to close with the Oerlikon. I can only guess that a couple of them did make it, because Curly's body was found atop the breech mechanism. A grenade, probably dropped into the operator's lap, put paid to that monster.

I would not have wanted to see a group of Able-Section men, of which Maud was one, torn apart by a bevy of well thrown and well timed grenades, over by the flat-tops.

I wish I had been involved, with Wood and Les Crowther, as they took on a section of Patch's Askaris with nothing but bayonets. They could not have had time to reload. But I wish I had been with them to even things up a bit.

I would have considered it a pleasure to have seen Smarmy Patterson and Ying blast their way into one of the huts and cut Chang almost to pieces with their bayonets. Neither of them made it out of that hut.

But, hell, seeing it would have been a pleasure.

And I certainly would not have minded being the one to come face to face, at last, with Patch.

What I cannot get my head around is why no one, either then or later, actually dealt him the fatal blow.

When, later, I eventually did find him he had two bullet wounds, neither in any way fatal. Plus a bayonet wound in his stomach. That one could well have proved fatal. In the end.

There is a lot I would have liked to have seen for myself, and some I would not.

But I had my hands full, living my own Armageddon.

But the end had to come. Everything comes to an end. Eventually.

It was like the down slope of a very bad trip, and I've slithered down a few of those in my time. Reality didn't want to stay still long enough for me to get a grip on it. I found myself standing alongside the burnt-out loud-speaker truck. I waited a spell. And it seemed to stay there. Behind me, the truck on the other flat-top was burning furiously, as were the two huts on the far side of the rail line. Smoke billowed everywhere and I seemed to be surrounded by dead and dying men.

My legs seemed to lose strength and I sank to my knees and sucked in a great, shuddering, rasping breath.

The noise of the explosions, the cries and the screams, still echoed hollowly. But the sounds were only in my head.

There were no more explosions, cries or screams. Just the crackling flames and the groans of nearby wounded. The world came back slowly from the brink of God knows where. And it came back in disjointed, flashing, nightmare images, settling only very slowly.

Then someone was beside me.

I felt a lighted cigarette being placed between my lips. A voice I recognized said,

'I suppose you know you're hit!'

I sucked hard on the cigarette and drew the smoke down into tortured lungs.

Then I began to feel the gnawing pain in my gut.

I looked down. I was covered in a layer of wet dirt, but some of it was a darker colour. I let my weapon fall to the ground and probed with my fingertips. It was a shrapnel wound, not a bullet. And it wasn't deep. I could feel the jagged metal shard right there underneath the skin. I do not even remember catching it. The voice said,

'You'll live, skipper.'

I hoped he was right. I looked up.

Sweeney Graham.

I said, 'How's it going, Sweeney?'

He eased himself down beside me. He was covered, head to foot, with dirt, sweat and blood. One side of his face was black with what appeared to be a powder burn, and that shoulder of his combat jacket was hanging down in a blood-soaked flap. He said, 'Hell, I'm fine!'

I said, 'Great,' and took another deep drag on the cigarette.

20

The Reckoning

Either everyone lives, or everyone dies. That was the formula. Neither was true here.

I had vague misgivings about who was and who was not still with us, simply because Graham's was the only really familiar face there. There were plenty of men wandering about but I could see none of Able or Baker sections anywhere. Come to that I didn't see any of Dove or Echo either.

So a reckoning was due. I knew it was going to be bad, but I did not know just how bad. So we, me and Graham, went looking amongst the carnage.

We found the girl in one of the first huts we entered, miraculously unhurt except for a bruise that seemed to cover half her face. She was giving what succour she could to, I guessed it was her brother, Paul. Star Sapphire. He did not look like a spy. He looked like a teenager. The rope that had obviously bound him lay cut through on the floor beside him. He had a single bullet wound in his chest but appeared to be still alive. The girl didn't even hear us at the door so we left her to it. I think any kind of practical help was beyond any of us in any case.

We stood there for a moment and looked around the killing field.

There were a lot of dead men scattered about. And there were a lot of wounded men scattered about. And there were a lot of guys wandering about doing what guys did at the end of a battle. There was no way of telling if they were our men, or Patch's. And that was another thing that didn't seem to matter any more, to anyone! It was all over now, and we were what we were.

I was glad to see Benson trudging wearily towards us through the chaotic scene. I don't know why, but for some reason I had expected Benson to be a casualty. But this was not a time for platitudes and congratulations and back-patting. It was time for the count, and nothing but the count.

Benson, everything else left thankfully unspoken, said, 'I called Mtomo. He wants me to go down and pick him up.' He looked at Graham and a small smile picked at his mouth. They exchanged nods. That was all. But it was enough. More than enough. Benson was doing what I was doing; making the tally. Each in his own way. Everything else could wait. I wondered if I was going to be exchanging nods with guys I'd got along with.

I said, 'Where is he?'

Benson glanced in the door of the hut we had just left. He seemed embarrassed by what he saw. He said, 'He hoofed it back home, apparently. So . . . Ngomo lake.'

I said, 'What's wrong with his own goddam helicopter?' But it was a rhetorical response and Benson knew that. He simply spread his hands.

Graham grunted. 'You're not going to catch Mtomo out and about on his own today . . . not today!'

To Benson, I said, 'How's your fuel?'

He shrugged. 'Enough for the compound. Just! I could stop by and top up. What d'you reckon?'

I thought about it. 'Okay. Go get him.'

Sweeney muttered, 'So long as the git doesn't want another fucking parade!'

Benson said, 'I could take some of the wounded down to the mission hospital, if you like.'

I must have pulled an uncertain face. He went on:

'Mtomo will be spreading word of the new order. So there's bound to be a few fair-weather friends there now. At the very least there'll be confusion!'

Which was probable enough. 'Okay, go for it. As many as you can get aboard. But just take guys who look like they can be saved.'

He gave me an old fashioned look. 'Now how the blazes would I know that, Marty? I'm no triage medic.'

I looked at Sweeney, who simply shrugged and shook his head. 'I wouldn't have the first clue, boss. Have we got any medics left?' He snapped his fingers. 'There's Benjy!'

Of course! I told Benson where Benjy and Pascal were. 'Go get them. Grab a couple of these guys to help you.' I nodded out at the milling men. 'Whoever the hell they are. Make your own executive decisions. Okay, Pilot?'

Benson sighed a deep sigh, nodded, mumbled something I didn't catch, then turned on his heel and went off on his impossible mission. Well, his *next* impossible mission.

Then I saw Santana and some of his blacks and my count went up several notches. Ammas was there too. Apart from the dirt and the grime they looked healthy enough. About that time I began to wonder about Curly and the others. They were conspicuous by their absence. Which did not bode well.

'In there!' Santana shouted, indicating one of the ruined buildings.

I called back, 'What the fuck's in there, Pancho?'

His face broke into a broad grin. 'What d'you think?'

He gave an instruction to his men and they wandered off. Santana trotted over. 'Go look,' he said, still smiling.

We went.

It was Patch.

The room must have taken a grenade, because it was a mess of splintered wood and smoking embers, dead men and bits of dead men. The acrid stench of spent cordite was still heavy in the air. Patch was sitting against a door jamb, fully conscious, but apparently unable to move either arms or legs. The three of us stood there looking down at him. And he sat there looking up at us.

Santana, his voice hushed as if there was a spell he was unwilling to break, hissed, 'Just in case there's a prize, or something, thems my bullets in him.'

I found that I didn't have a single gram of hate in me. Nor did I feel any desire to slit his guts. I would have ended his misery if it had looked as if he was in misery. I would certainly have gone that far. But he did not look to be in misery. He was just sitting there quietly. So, despite everything, he was not going to die by my hand.

I said, 'So, Patch. You caught a couple, huh?'

I could feel the lethargy, the reaction, beginning to seep into my system like the effects of a drug.

Patch didn't look like anything. His skin was pasty-white and his thin, black moustache stood out oddly from his face. His chest was blood-soaked and he sat in a slowly expanding pool of it.

He nodded loosely and his right hand rose from the floor a couple of inches, then flopped back. 'I guess so, old buddy.' He added, 'You gonna do me a favour?' His voice betrayed some pain, but that was all.

I said, 'What's that?'

He nodded at the gun in my hand. 'Give me one of them, then bugger off and leave me alone.'

I knew exactly what he was asking, and I thought about it. But there didn't seem any point. Humane killing was one thing. This was something entirely different. This was Patch. The difference may well have seemed moot to some. But it was the way my tired brain saw things. I said, 'We may get a medic down here soon. If we do I'll send him over. If not, I won't. But if you're going to die, then die. But do it at your own speed.'

We left him there, as he was.

Some time later I heard the helicopter lifting off.

We found Harry Simons's body near the old ticket office. He must have bought it shortly after I passed that way. Which meant that the girl would have braved that storm of fire too. And it was doubtful that she had the Madness to ease her passage. Then again she would have had her own kind of madness giving her wings.

I was not looking for Chang's body, not specifically. In fact I had forgotten all about him. But we found him, what there was left of him. Santana walked over and spat into what used to be his face.

At the mangled remains, he said, 'Clean boots? I'll give you clean fucking boots!'

I couldn't even imagine what lay at the roots of that remark. And I didn't try. Besides, it seemed utterly in keeping with the insanity that surrounded us. And my brain was getting woollier by the second.

Graham grabbed a couple of men and went back up the valley searching for wounded. He found a couple and dragged them back. Munro was one of them. He also brought the coffee makings back with him and we all had a mug, sitting on the ground like a boy scout jamboree. Despite the coffee I found myself too shattered to move. Every time I blinked my eyes they wanted to stay shut. And soon they made their own decisions. I did not want to, and I was not aware of it happening, but I fell asleep.

Tengo Valley echoed to the occasional pistol shot as the fatally wounded were sent on their way.

I do not know how long I was out of it, but one of the shots must have dragged me out of my stupor.

Later, Santana put a detail together and began to gather the dead.

I dragged Curly over and lay him with Maud, Ginger Wood and the rest.

Some time after that the Bhamas from the train began to dribble in. Cautiously at first, then they just stood there looking. When I looked again they were gone and there was just a pile of guns.

Santana said, 'Bhamas! Jeeeesus, Henry!'

A goodly percentage of Patch's command seemed to have melted into the jungle, probably when they saw which way the table was turning. But some had stayed. Seventeen or so. Two whites were amongst them. They came to where the survivors of B-company were sitting, drinking coffee and trying to forget. And they sat down too.

Then, just as it was turning dusk, the

helicopter came back. Benson put down between the ruined Oerlikon and the burned-out trucks, raising a storm of red dust. Out from that red cloud stepped two guys in white coats, a nurse in uniform. And Joshua Mtomo.

It was the first time I had seen Mtomo wearing a uniform.

A uniform with brigadier-general's badges of rank, no less. And a dress hat with gold braid all over it. The man even carried a swagger stick. I felt nauseated. It was as if the uniform, for its own sake, made it all okay. Justified everything. Legalized it. *Civilized* it. I could just about stomach the old Mtomo; the one whose money was the pretension to power. But this new one . . .

To what fresh heights would this new one aspire?

The medical contingent wandered among the bodies, and the piles of bodies and the scattered wounded as if in a daze. Mtomo came over to me and started raving on, all smiles. I just looked at him, and wondered. Then he went off somewhere.

About that time Sweeney Graham and a few others came over. Their arms were filled with money belts, and I do mean filled.

Graham said, 'What?'

I said, 'What, what?'

He said, 'This loot.'

I thought about it. 'Divvi it up.'

'Patch's men too?'

I said, 'Hell . . . why not?'

Then Mtomo appeared. He had Patch slung over his shoulder. Patch was either dead or unconscious. I felt my hackles rise. I said, 'Where the fuck are you taking him?'

He said, 'Back, of course!'

I said, 'Put him down, Mtomo. Besides, you're getting blood all over your nice uniform.'

He looked at me as if I'd just crawled out from under a rock. 'I'm taking him back. We arranged it.'

I said, '*You* arranged it, Mtomo. If you remember correctly. I didn't!'

He ignored that and turned for the chopper.

I called, 'One chance, *General*! Put that mercenary soldier down, or stop a bullet!'

Mtomo did not put him down. He continued on to the helicopter.

So I lifted my weapon and shot him in the back.

The girl had appeared.

I said, 'How would you like to be prime minister of the eastern provinces?'

She just looked at me.

Santana said, 'Jesus, Marty, there's only

one thing worse than bent politicians, and that's women ones!'

Sweeney Graham, proving that reincarnation is a possibility, said, 'A-friggin'-men to that!'

We do hope that you have enjoyed reading this large print book.

Did you know that all of our titles are available for purchase?

We publish a wide range of high quality large print books including:
Romances, Mysteries, Classics
General Fiction
Non Fiction and Westerns

Special interest titles available in large print are:
The Little Oxford Dictionary
Music Book
Song Book
Hymn Book
Service Book

Also available from us courtesy of Oxford University Press:
Young Readers' Dictionary
(large print edition)
Young Readers' Thesaurus
(large print edition)

For further information or a free brochure, please contact us at:
Ulverscroft Large Print Books Ltd.,
The Green, Bradgate Road, Anstey,
Leicester, LE7 7FU, England.
Tel: (00 44) **0116 236 4325**
Fax: (00 44) **0116 234 0205**

COMING TO THE EDGE

Theresa Murphy

DCI Mattia is struggling with a case that involves politics, big business and a psychopathic killer. He's depressed: the combination of his current investigation into the murder of young girl singer, his rocky relationship with his girlfriend, and his infatuation with a sexy private detective are all having an effect. But as members of his team are attacked, it looks like he might be onto something. Will he succeed in clearing the murder victim's husband, whom he believes to be innocent, or will his police career end in ignominy and the loss of the woman he now knows he loves?

BACK-SLASH

Bill Kitson

A ruthless killer is on the rampage, one with a distinctive trademark. So what is the secret of the forester living a hermit-like existence in the remotest part of the Winfield Estate? Is he a callous murderer, now exacting revenge on those who wronged him? Or, does the truth lie elsewhere? With resources decimated by a flu epidemic, Mike Nash must use unorthodox tactics to expose a web of corruption and deceit spanning the years. All the evidence suggests an inevitable conclusion, but can Mike discover the truth before it is too late for everyone concerned — innocent or guilty?

THE SECRETS MAN

John Dean

When DCI John Blizzard visits a friend in hospital, he is intrigued when an elderly villain in the next bed reveals much about Hafton's criminal gangs. These revelations attract a series of sinister characters to the ward. Blizzard wonders if they are seeking to silence the old man, but fellow detectives believe that the pensioner is suffering from dementia. It's only when people start dying that his colleagues take the DCI seriously. Blizard faces a race against time to save lives, and must face a part of his past he's tried to forget — and with the one man he fears.